SURVIVED BY HER LONGTIME COMPANION

BLUE FEATHER BOOKS, LTD.

To my Little Phyllis Valentine—
I love you.

ALSO WRITTEN BY CHRIS PAYNTER AND AVAILABLE
NOW FROM BLUE FEATHER BOOKS:

❖ PLAYING FOR FIRST
❖ COME BACK TO ME
❖ TWO FOR THE SHOW

COMING SOON:

❖ FROM THIRD TO HOME

SURVIVED BY HER LONGTIME COMPANION

A BLUE FEATHER BOOK

by

Chris Paynter

This is a work of fiction. All characters, locales and events are either products of the author's imagination or are used fictitiously.

SURVIVED BY HER LONGTIME COMPANION

Cover design by Ann Phillips

A Blue Feather Book
Published by Blue Feather Books, Ltd.

www.bluefeatherbooks.com

ISBN: 978-1-935627-88-3

First edition: January, 2012

Printed in the United States of America and in the United Kingdom.

Acknowledgements

As always, I start by thanking my publishers, the incomparable super heroines, Emily Reed and Jane Vollbrecht, of Blue Feather Books. Your encouragement and support have meant so much to me with each book I've written. I look forward to many, many more to come.

A huge thank-you to my editor, Nann Dunne, for your patience and, well, patience, in explaining all things grammatical. I also thank you for your suggestions and strong editorial guidance in making this a better book. Oh, and once again, I forgive you for being a Phillies fan. And to Ann Phillips: a big Hoosier shout-out for another fabulous cover!

Thank you, Cathy Rowlands, for reading the manuscript and helping me improve the story. I'll buy you a briefcase for your birthday (I know you'll get the joke). Thank you, too, to one of the biggest lesfic fans around and my friend from across the pond, Terry Baker, for answering questions about the British language and way of speaking. I hope I didn't annoy you too much with my, "I have one more question" e-mails.

Thank you to my parents, Nancy and Morris, my brother, David, my sister-in-law, Grace, and my niece, Cassie, for all your love and support throughout the years.

And to my best friend, my heartbeat, my soul mate, and my wife, Phyllis, thank you for… everything. It seems I can never find the adequate words to express what you mean to me. I always fall short in describing your generosity and kindness, but someone needs only to meet you once to understand what I'm saying. Just know if it weren't for you, none of this would be possible. I love you, sweetheart.

The last acknowledgement is a bit unusual. Thank you, Eleanor Burnett, wherever you are in the universe, for telling me your story. Although it was in my imagination, you made it so real each night when I sat at my computer to write your words. It was as if you were in the same room, whispering in my ear. I can only hope I did justice to the love that you and Daphne shared.

Chapter 1

"It looks like we're going to be here awhile at O'Hare," Bailey Hampton said over the phone. "The fog has us socked in. They don't think it'll lift for a couple of hours at the earliest."

Chelsea Parker's heart sank. She stared at the dining room table with its candles and fine china, set for a romantic night.

"Chelsea?"

"I heard you." She tried to keep her voice from giving away her disappointment at yet another spoiled evening.

"I'll call you as soon as we land. You won't need to pick me up since it'll be late. I'll catch a cab or limo."

"Sure."

"I'm sorry—"

"You can't control the weather, Bailey. I'll see you when you get home."

She hung up. She felt so hopeless. Their relationship had deteriorated to sitting and waiting for the other to return from an out-of-town trip.

Her position as a Professor at the University of Denver was part of the reason. Because of her expertise in her field of Gender and Women's Studies, she traveled out-of-state to lecture on lesbians and feminism in film at least twice a month. And Bailey was gone even more often. A highly sought-after researcher for biographers, she frequently traveled to another city—sometimes even out of the country—to hunt down an elusive interview or pore over rare papers at a library for days, often weeks, on end.

We need to talk, Chelsea thought. It was a talk long overdue. While she endured each passing hour in the stillness of their home, dread settled over her like the suffocating walls of a tomb.

She heard the key slide into the lock and waited for the door to open.

Bailey, her face drawn with exhaustion, entered and dropped her baggage with a huff.

"Finally made it out of Chicago?" Chelsea asked.

Bailey jerked. "Jesus. I didn't see you there. You shouldn't have waited up."

"Considering I haven't seen you for the past two weeks, I didn't think you'd mind."

"I didn't say I minded. Don't go putting words in my mouth."

And this is how we speak to each other now. "I wasn't putting... I'm sorry. I know you're tired. Can we talk?"

Bailey rolled her shoulders, and her neck popped with the move. "Can't this wait until morning?"

"No, I don't think it can. I've been holding off long enough on this conversation. I think you have, too."

Apprehension flickered in Bailey's eyes as she sat down beside Chelsea on the couch.

Chelsea took her hand. "Are you happy with us?"

"What kind of question is that?" Bailey said in a defensive tone.

"It's a legitimate question that deserves an honest answer." Chelsea waited, but Bailey remained silent. Realizing she would have to be the one to address the distance between them, Chelsea took a deep breath. "I think you know what I'm going to say. We should have had this talk months ago."

"Please, Chels. Don't." Bailey's voice trembled.

"I have to. Your job keeps you away weeks at a time—"

"It's not just me."

"I realize that. My job takes me away at least twice a month. It's been like this for going on two years, and I don't think I can take it any longer. The only words we seem to say to each other anymore are, 'When does your flight get in?' or 'When do you think you'll be home?' I need more, Bailey. I think you do, too."

"What are you saying? That we just give up?"

"What else do you suggest? Because right now, it's as if we're roommates who happen to share a house, not partners who share a home. This is more like a rest stop. A jumping off point from one destination to the next." Chelsea's voice got firmer. "What's left for us to hang onto? It's not enough. For either one of us."

"What about our nine-year relationship? Don't you think it's worth fighting for?"

"When? Tell me. When will we fight for it? We're never together."

"Damn it, Chelsea." Bailey stood up and started pacing.

"If you can remember the last time we shared a romantic dinner," Chelsea said and motioned toward the dining room table, "then I'll tell you we can keep trying."

Bailey stopped in her tracks and turned to the table. Her face fell.

With eyes stinging with tears, Chelsea walked over to her. "I have a chance at a professorship on tenure track at Indiana University. I'm going for it."

Bailey started to cry. She slapped at her tears with the palms of her hands as if angry. Her voice sounded angry, too. "How long have you been thinking about this?"

"A friend of mine from grad school called a couple of weeks ago. She's on faculty at IU. She thought I might be interested in the opening since I went to school there."

Bailey's expression changed, and her fingers curled into fists. "Is she more than a friend?"

Chelsea took a step back as if Bailey's words had physically struck her. "I would hope you'd at least give me some credit. I'd never do that to you."

Bailey grimaced and stared down at her feet. It appeared all the fight had left her. "I know," she whispered. "I think it would be easier to take if one of us had cheated on the other. This is like a slow, painful death from a disease. One without a cure." She finally raised her head. "When do you think you'll leave?"

"I might be able to get on there next semester."

"But all the way to Bloomington, Indiana? It's so far."

The sound of hurt in Bailey's voice and the pain in her light brown eyes almost brought Chelsea to her knees. *No. This is for the best.* "I think I need a fresh start, and I think the distance will do us good." She didn't add that it was where they'd met and she needed a familiar comfort to fall back on. Bailey's knowing look said she understood.

"I love you," Bailey said, her voice rough with emotion.

"I love you, too, but sometimes it isn't enough. We can't fix it, and I can't do this anymore. More talk won't help. I've got to go."

Chapter 2

Bailey welcomed the cool summer breeze that blew down from the Rockies and drifted across her porch. She pushed her feet against the tiled floor as she rocked her old metal glider, making it creak with each movement. She tried to draw comfort from the sound, but it only reminded her of what she'd lost.

Chelsea. Once upon a time, they sat on the porch and sipped wine. They smiled at each other over their glasses and basked in the love they shared.

But Chelsea left her, or more to the truth, they left each other. Neither realized her fate until the last dwindling hours of their relationship. If Bailey closed her eyes, she could picture Chelsea standing in the living room, tears streaming down her cheeks. And if Bailey listened, she could almost hear Chelsea telling her it was over.

When Chelsea boxed up hundreds of her books, packed up some furniture and her clothes, and drove out of Denver almost eleven months ago, she might as well have packed up Bailey's heart. It wasn't much use to her now except to keep her breathing.

Bailey blinked away tears.

"Damn it."

She swiped at them, angry with herself for replaying the same scene in her head like a movie stuck on rewind. She had tried to move on. Yet here she sat in the same spot as when Chelsea drove away in her loaded-down Outback and U-Haul trailer.

Her phone rang inside. She pushed herself up and entered the eighty-year-old house she and Chelsea had lovingly restored. They'd just forgotten to treat themselves with the same gentle care.

"Hello?"

"Bailey, glad I caught you at home."

"What's up, Joanne?" She hadn't heard from the award-winning biographer in a few weeks.

"Have you seen today's obituaries?"

"No, it's not something I normally read first in the paper." Bailey glanced at the *Denver Post* that lay unopened on her dining room table.

"I might have a job for you. I need a researcher for this biography I'm doing of Daphne DeMonet. And since you're my best, I thought I'd call you first."

"DeMonet? The old movie actress?"

"Yes. I started contacting people who knew her and worked with her, but I haven't had much luck. Which isn't surprising considering the woman was eighty-nine years old. There aren't many of her friends left."

"You're talking about her in the past tense." Bailey picked up the newspaper and extracted the obituary section.

"She died early Sunday morning," Joanne said. "Why don't you read the obit? What interested me is at the bottom."

Bailey scanned down to the last few lines. "You mean, 'DeMonet is survived by her longtime companion, Eleanor Burnett'?"

"I knew of this woman. She's one of the few remaining whom I can talk to, but she's refused to grant interviews. She's as private as DeMonet was."

Bailey thought she knew where this was leading.

"And you think because I'm a lesbian and Eleanor Burnett could possibly be a lesbian that she'd accept my request for an interview?" This grated on Bailey's nerves. Maybe her dark mood contributed to her annoyance.

"Please don't take it the wrong way, Bailey."

"How am I supposed to take it? You're using me."

"Ah, but I'd pay well to use you." Joanne laughed one of her deep, full-throated, raspy laughs that spoke of her years of smoking.

Bailey read the rest of the obituary. "There's not much to go on."

"Before DeMonet's death, I called Burnett three times and three times she refused my interview request. Always polite and proper, though."

"You think the old 'sisterhood of lesbians' thing will work, huh?" Bailey opened the refrigerator and grabbed a Coke.

"I do think you might have a better chance at this. It won't hurt. But there is, uh… a catch."

Bailey frowned and took a sip of her drink. "I don't like the sound of that."

"It's where Eleanor Burnett lives."

"Which is…"

"Bloomington," Joanne said.

"I hope you're about to say Bloomington, Illinois."

"Um, no."

"You can forget it. I'm not going to Bloomington, Indiana. I'm not going anywhere near Indiana."

"Look, I know Chelsea's teaching there now, but what are the chances of you two meeting up?"

"Joanne, have you ever been to Bloomington?"

"I gave a lecture there once at Indiana University on one of my biographies."

"And you think Chelsea and I won't run into each other? Be realistic."

"I'm prepared to triple what I normally pay you."

"You don't play fair. You know I'm struggling to make ends meet." Bailey still had a little reserve left in her savings account, but she'd worked on staying within her budget. Chelsea's job at the University of Denver had paid well. But when their relationship ended and Chelsea returned to Bloomington, her income left with her.

"Damn right I don't play fair where you're concerned. Like I told you, you're my best researcher. It's been, what? Almost a year? Don't you think you'd be okay if you saw her?"

"Said the woman still in a twenty-five-year marriage. What kind of question is that?"

"I repeat. Triple your usual fee."

Bailey carried the portable out to the porch and sat down on the stoop. She took a deep breath and inhaled the smell of freshly mowed grass along with the faint hint of rain. As if on cue, a few drops hit the driveway and made pitter-patter noises as they struck her Jeep Wrangler. The overhang from the porch kept her dry.

Joanne's words rang in her ears as if a thunderclap had rumbled overhead.

"Damn it, Joanne, you're asking for the impossible." Bailey gritted her teeth.

"It's not like you hate each other. Am I right? Didn't you remain friends?"

"Friends with broken hearts that haven't healed."

"But not because one of you cheated on the other. You told me once that never happened."

Bailey rubbed her hand over her face. "No," she said quietly. "We didn't cheat on each other. We drifted apart, each of us caught up in our own work until we'd only pass each other coming and going. Chelsea was the first to talk about it and tell me how unfulfilled she felt."

Christ, Bailey thought, I'm confessing more to Joanne than I did to my therapist.

"There. You're still on friendly enough terms that, if you did see her, you wouldn't rip each other's throats out, unlike some of my straight friends. Good God. And these people have kids together."

"You forget I have an obligation to the university. I do research for the professors there."

"Are you busy now?"

Bailey could have lied, but she told Joanne the truth. "No. I'm winding down on a three-month project with Professor Stanfield for one of her history books."

"So..."

Bailey downed the last of her Coke.

"Are you there?" Joanne asked.

"Yes, I'm here." Bailey tried to picture the worst-case scenario, which would be an encounter with Chelsea. How would Chelsea react? Hell, how would Bailey react when she saw the woman she swore she'd spend the rest of her life with?

"And?"

Bailey sighed. "When do you need me to leave?"

"As soon as you finish that project and can pack up your Jeep. I expect you to be successful in your quest to get this interview. You'll probably be in Bloomington several weeks. While you're working there, I plan on hunting down more leads. I still have some of DeMonet's old acting colleagues to contact."

They talked for another twenty minutes. Joanne offered Bailey the information she had on Eleanor Burnett.

"Hang on. I need something to write on." Bailey stepped back inside and searched for a tablet and pen. "Okay, go ahead."

"She lives about five miles outside of town," Joanne said. "I checked it on the map. I guess it's good you own a Jeep. Who knows how rough those country roads are?"

"She won't hang up on me, right? Or shoot me on sight if I knock on her door?"

"No, she won't hang up on you. I told you. She was very polite, but firm, in refusing the interview. As for the shooting on sight—that I can't help you with." Joanne let loose with another loud laugh.

"I'm glad you find this amusing."

"Hey, remember your salary on this one, and you'll be singing a happy tune all the way to Bloomington."

"Which sure as hell won't be 'Back Home Again in Indiana.'"

"Give me a call when you're set to go. When do you think that'll be?" Joanne asked.

"It's Monday. Probably by the end of next week."

They ended the call with Bailey's promise to keep Joanne posted.

Bailey felt exhausted. It was only nine, but a hot shower and an early night sounded good. She toweled off after the shower and wiped away the steam from the mirror.

"God, I look old." She ran her fingers along the deep shadows above her cheeks. "These didn't use to be here."

The shower had darkened her short, sandy blonde hair. On more than one occasion, women had told her she was handsome. She ignored the compliments until Chelsea whispered those words on their second date. Bailey had believed her.

She threw on a baggy Hanover College T-shirt and a pair of boxers. She almost switched off the bedroom light but hesitated when she saw the framed photo of Chelsea and her. The oak frame contrasted against the cherrywood of the dresser. Bailey picked up the photo and traced the outline of Chelsea's face. Chelsea was beautiful, with bright green eyes and auburn hair to her shoulders. Bailey's best friend, Tara Fowler, had snapped the shot two years ago at Tara's barbecue. Bailey, with a wide grin, sat behind Chelsea on the picnic table with her arms draped around Chelsea's neck. Chelsea was staring off at something past Tara's shoulder. Seeing Chelsea's distant expression in the photo should have been a clue to Bailey to just how far gone their relationship was.

Why hadn't they talked about it? Instead, they retreated into their books, their research, and their work as they sealed themselves off from their feelings.

Bailey set the photo down. She didn't know why she kept it, except as a reminder of the beginning of the end. She slipped under the covers and closed her eyes. What she saw in her mind wasn't Chelsea's sad, distant expression, but rather the full-dimpled smile of the woman she'd promised her heart to.

Chapter 3

Bailey drank her coffee while attempting to shake off a poor night's sleep. A sharp rap on the screen door startled her. She padded to the living room.

Her friend, Tara, stood at the door with her nose pressed against the screen. She held up two paper bags.

"I bring you tidings of great joy," Tara said. "Your favorite bagel and my favorite muffin."

"Come on in. I just made some coffee."

Tara followed her into the dining room. "In between jobs? I don't see as much shit on the table like when you're working on something."

"Are you calling what I do 'shit'?"

Tara grabbed a mug from the cabinet, filled it with coffee, and sat across from Bailey.

"No. What I said was your research papers spread out on the table looked like shit. Not what you do. I know how good you are."

"I like your hair," Bailey said.

Tara brushed her fingers across the top of her head. "Feels a little like a close-cut mowed lawn, but it's practical for the summer." Tara gestured at her. "What's with you? No sleep?"

"I tossed and turned all night. I think I checked the clock at least ten times."

"Bad dreams again?"

"I don't remember them."

Tara looked skeptical.

"Okay, maybe a little."

"Chelsea?"

"Yeah. She was in at least one." Bailey rose to go to the refrigerator.

"I'm sorry, Bailey. I really am."

"Me, too."

"So, what do you have lined up next?"

"You're not going to believe this. After I tell you, you'll understand the bad dreams." Bailey took out the tub of cream cheese.

"First of all, who are you working with? That would give me a little clue."

"Joanne Addison." Bailey brought the cream cheese to the table and slathered her bagel.

"Cool. She always pays you well, and I like that she acknowledges your assistance in each book you worked on. What's with the glum expression? Isn't she paying you as much?"

"That's not an issue at all. She's paying me triple what she normally does."

"Can't complain there. So what's the problem?" Tara took a bite of her muffin.

"I'll give you one word. Bloomington."

"Wait. Bloomington as in Indiana? Bloomington as in, that's where Chelsea's working? What's there that you can't research here?"

"Eleanor Burnett, surviving longtime companion of the old movie actress, Daphne DeMonet."

"Joanne wants you to interview her, I take it," Tara said.

"Of course, since I'm a lesbian and since we're all so chummy—if I invade her privacy, Burnett will open right up and chat about their closeted relationship."

"I guess you told her no."

"I need the money too damn much."

"Yeah, but there's a chance you'll run into Chelsea. You know that, right?"

"I know," Bailey said in a hushed tone. "But I didn't have anything lined up after this project, and it's harder to make ends meet since Chelsea left."

Tara sat back in her chair. "I wish I could hate her. It'd make this all so much easier. She was and still is my friend. If she'd done something mean or stepped out on you, I'd have no problem banishing her in my mind to the gates of hell. But you two just…"

Bailey thought how Tara's words echoed her own when Chelsea said it was over. "We gave up. Now she's a professor there instead of here. And apparently doing well."

Tara gave her a sad smile. "You're still keeping up on her."

"Not too much. About once a month since she left, I check the university's website to see how she's doing, if she's speaking anywhere, stuff like that."

They sipped their coffee in silence until Tara finished hers off with a flourish and set the mug down on the table with a loud thud. "I'm going with you."

"What do you mean?"

"To Bloomington. I'm going with you. I can turn over the running of the softball and baseball batting-cage facility to my very able assistant manager." Tara said the words with a little sneer.

"Don't tell me you're already sleeping with her."

"Okay, I won't. What I will tell you is she's freaking awesome in bed."

"Have I met her?" Bailey asked.

"Remember? At the spring bash at my house?"

"Do you mean the blonde who couldn't keep her hands off of you?"

"No, that was Laura. This was the cute brunette who showed up later, Natasha."

"I can't keep up with you." Bailey took their empty mugs to the dishwasher. "You're my best friend, but this is something I need to do on my own. I'll be there for a few weeks, more than a month for sure." She turned to Tara. "Oh, don't give me that little pout. The answer's still no. I appreciate it, but no. We'll stay in touch with that fancy cell phone you love so much."

"All right," Tara said. "I guess I won't argue."

"You can do me a favor, though, and keep an eye on the house while I'm gone."

"You still have that wonderful king-size bed, right?" Tara's expression turned mischievous.

Bailey pointed at her. "Don't even think about it."

Tara laughed. She headed toward the front door with Bailey trailing behind.

"When do you leave?" Tara asked as she stepped out onto the porch.

"Probably by the end of next week. I've got to get my stuff together."

Tara surprised Bailey with a hug.

"You'll be okay." Tara slapped her on the back. "It'll be good for you to get lost in your research. And if you see Chelsea, it'll be okay, too."

"I guess."

"Well, I know." Tara walked to her car. "Call me before you leave. Maybe we can get a drink."

"Nah. I don't want to horn in on your time with, what was her name again? Nanette?"

"Cute, Bailey. Her name's Natasha. She won't mind me having a drink with my best friend."

"I'll think about it."

"At least call me so I know when you're on your way."

"That I promise to do."

Tara backed out of the drive, and Bailey returned to her current project. She'd buckle down this week and finish it, so she could pack her clothes and gather what she needed for the trip to Bloomington.

* * *

Chelsea peered at her reflection in the mirror and frowned at the dark circles shadowing her eyes. She ran her fingers through her long hair. "Bailey would like this."

They'd had mock fights about the length of Chelsea's hair but never any insistence on Bailey's part that Chelsea let it grow out. After arriving in Bloomington, she'd only had it trimmed a few times.

Her alarm rang in the bedroom. She walked in and flipped it off. Since her split with Bailey, she hadn't been able to sleep much past five-thirty. Prior to their breakup, the knowledge they'd be together soon had always made it more bearable to wake up alone.

That time had passed.

Her vision blurred. Chelsea tried to shake it off and ignore the empty ache in her chest. She grabbed her briefcase on the way out the door and drove to the university.

When she entered her office, she flung her briefcase on a nearby chair and powered up her computer. She walked to the window overlooking the trees and greenery below and watched the summer students who had an early start on the day.

"Love the new outfit," a deep voice said from behind.

Chelsea turned. Rebecca Simmons, another gender studies faculty member, stood in her doorway.

Chelsea glanced down at her khaki pants and short-sleeved cotton blouse. "I hope you're kidding, because I just threw this together. They were my only clean clothes." She rifled through her briefcase for her notes.

Rebecca still hovered in the doorway. She'd asked Chelsea out a month after Chelsea settled into her position at the school. It wasn't that Chelsea didn't find her attractive. She still wasn't sure about her heart and had only had one date since she'd moved to Bloomington. It had ended badly.

"Come in. Did you have something you wanted to discuss?" Chelsea lifted her briefcase from the chair to make room.

"What are you working on?" Rebecca sat down and crossed her legs.

Chelsea hesitated. She was usually secretive with her new projects until they were well in motion, like an artist not wanting to unveil their unfinished painting or a writer not wanting anyone to read their fledgling novel. It wasn't as if she thought Rebecca would steal her interview subject. Well, possible interview subject. Chelsea hoped to reach the woman later by phone.

"Have you heard of Daphne DeMonet?" Chelsea asked.

"Sure. She died early last week, didn't she?" Rebecca picked up a paperweight on the edge of Chelsea's desk and shifted it from hand to hand. Chelsea resisted the urge to grab it from her. It was a replica of the Louvre. She and Bailey had visited Paris and the museum early in their relationship.

"She passed early last Sunday morning."

"So what about DeMonet? Something for your class that focuses on women in film?"

"No. It's more than that. There'd always been rumors DeMonet was a lesbian and had a longtime lover."

"I noticed the obituary listed Elsie Barnett as her surviving longtime companion." Rebecca kept tossing the paperweight. "I love the code words, don't you?"

"Her name is Eleanor Burnett." The paperweight flew in the air one time too many. Chelsea snatched it away before it fell into Rebecca's other hand.

"Sorry," Rebecca said. "I do that sometimes. It drives my friends crazy. Special souvenir?"

"Something I don't want broken." Chelsea set the paperweight carefully back onto her desk.

"You acquired it with Bailey?"

Chelsea didn't answer.

"Hear from her lately?"

Chelsea opened a file on the computer without meeting Rebecca's gaze. "No."

Rebecca brushed her fingertips along Chelsea's forearm. Chelsea pulled away.

"Still not ready to move on?"

"I need to get back to my notes. Do you mind, Rebecca?"

Rebecca stood up. "I know you don't want to talk about it, but if you ever do want to move on…"

"Thanks." Chelsea remained focused on the computer screen and hoped Rebecca would get the hint.

Rebecca lingered a little longer and then left, closing the door behind her.

Chelsea rubbed her arm where Rebecca had touched her. "I've moved on," she whispered.

* * *

Bailey splashed water on her face in the hotel bathroom. She'd driven straight through from Kansas City, and her aching bones told her she'd pushed herself to the limit. *Face it. You're not in your twenties anymore.*

She checked her watch and hoped 9:10 on a Saturday night wasn't too late to call Eleanor Burnett. She pulled out her cell phone, propped herself up on the bed, and punched in the number.

A strong voice with a faint British accent answered on the third ring.

"May I speak to Eleanor Burnett, please?"

"This is she."

"Hi, Ms. Burnett. My name's Bailey Hampton. I'm a researcher for the biographer, Joanne Addison. I was hoping to arrange a meeting with you."

"To talk about my relationship with Daphne DeMonet, correct? I seem to recall several phone calls from Ms. Addison while Daphne was still alive."

"Yes, ma'am. That's why I'm calling." Bailey waited for the refusal.

"This is interesting. I received a phone call from another woman earlier this week. I told her it had to be a face-to-face interview, expecting to hear she was in New York or Los Angeles, only to discover she's in Bloomington. I decided to grant an interview to show you people there wasn't anything that extraordinary in our relationship."

"I'm also in Bloomington, Ms. Burnett. I drove in from Denver, and I'm staying at a hotel in town."

"My, my. Aren't we the optimistic one?"

"Well…"

"All right, Ms. Hampton. Why don't you arrive at my home at the same time as the other interviewer? This way, we can kill two birds with one stone. Do you need directions to my house?"

"I'm sure they'd be better than the ones I printed from the Internet."

"Where are you staying?"

Bailey told her. She scribbled the directions Eleanor Burnett gave her in her notebook.

"Is Monday afternoon at four convenient for you?" Burnett asked. "I have my tea then and wouldn't mind sharing it with you both."

"That's fine, ma'am."

"Let's establish right now that you can quit calling me 'ma'am' or 'Ms. Burnett.' Makes me feel old. I'm eighty-one, and I'm not quite ready to kick the bucket. It's Eleanor."

"Then I insist you call me Bailey."

"There. Was that so hard, Bailey?"

"No, Eleanor, it wasn't. I'll be at your house Monday at four."

Bailey shut her phone and tapped it against her chin. Who could be her competition for the interview?

Chapter 4

Bailey pulled onto the graveled shoulder to allow an impatient truck driver to pass. She'd driven up and down the state road five times and still hadn't spotted the turn into Eleanor's place. She read the directions again and tried to ignore Chelsea's voice in her head, admonishing her for not having a GPS system that displayed and voiced directions as you drove. Chelsea had one installed in her car as soon as they became the fashion; Bailey had stubbornly refused.

She glanced at her surroundings and spotted an old mailbox perched between two tall oak trees. She pulled back onto the road, inched forward, and squinted at the numbers on the rusted metal.

"Ah ha! Didn't need a damn GPS to find the place anyway, Chels."

She turned into the gravel driveway. Oak trees that, judging from their size, had to be at least three hundred years old, created a canopy of branches over the long, winding drive.

"Jesus. How far back does this go?"

The lush lawn on either side of her Jeep reflected meticulous care. Bailey heard the low rumble of an engine and caught a glimpse of a dark-haired, shirtless young man on a riding lawnmower. She faced ahead in time to see a chubby squirrel dart in the path of her Jeep.

"Shit!" Bailey slammed on her brakes. Gravel flew up from her tires. A cloud of dust filled the inside of her Jeep, and Bailey coughed. The squirrel ran up the nearest tree and chattered at her from the branch above, probably scolding her for the near miss. She allowed a moment for her pounding heart to slow before continuing to her destination.

Another fifty yards rolled by. The trees ended abruptly and parted to reveal a stunning Spanish-style home aglow from the sunlight bouncing off the white stucco. The modern appearance of the home was an anomaly compared to the old farmhouses Bailey had passed along the state road.

She eased the Jeep to a stop in the circular paved drive in front of the home. A small pond nestled inside the circle. Bailey got out of the Jeep and paused to watch multicolored koi swim in lazy rings in the water. She grabbed her tape recorder and notebook from the back of the Jeep and walked through the arched entry. Flowers of multitudinous hues adorned the walkway. Chelsea would know what those are, Bailey thought, as she drew nearer to the huge wooden door. She wondered if she'd even make a noise when she knocked, but then she spotted the doorbell and rang it. It played a vaguely familiar tune. From an old movie—an old Daphne DeMonet movie if Bailey's memory served her well. *A Sheltered Heart?* In between packing, she'd watched some of DeMonet's films for her research.

At length, the door opened. Bailey almost gasped at the sight of the gray-haired beauty before her. The woman stood about Bailey's height, five-six, maybe an inch taller. She'd styled her hair in a short cut, feathered away from her face. She wore blue jeans and a light blue, short-sleeved cotton blouse. Her flawless skin held only slight wrinkles, nothing belying her age. Her thin nose angled to a point, drawing Bailey's gaze to her sensuous lips. The blue of the blouse brought out the woman's startling blue eyes that appeared amused at Bailey's reaction.

My God, this woman must have been gorgeous when she was young, Bailey thought. Hell, why am I qualifying it? She's still gorgeous. Bailey found her voice.

"Eleanor Burnett?"

"You must be Bailey. I don't think you're the other woman with whom I spoke. I remember voices and inflections. Your voice is much huskier."

"Yes, I'm Bailey Hampton. As I told you over the phone, I'm here on behalf of Joanne Addison, the biographer."

Eleanor stepped aside to allow her to enter.

"Let's go to the back where we can enjoy my gardens while we talk. You do realize that it's tea time."

"Yes, ma'am."

"What did I say about formalities, Bailey?"

"I apologize, Eleanor."

"Better. Pretty soon, my name will flow freely off your tongue." Eleanor laughed, a light laugh that reminded Bailey of champagne glasses clinking together. "Now, when I say tea time, I don't mean iced tea. I hope you're aware of that."

Bailey followed Eleanor through the home. They passed by

simple, yet elegant, furniture in the spacious living room. When they neared the fireplace, Bailey stopped dead in her tracks.

A large oil painting of Eleanor and Daphne DeMonet hung above the mantel. They both looked to be middle-aged, with Daphne's hair slightly grayer than Eleanor's. But what struck Bailey was that they were nude. The artist had posed the women in a way that allowed the viewer's imagination to take flight.

Eleanor sat in front of Daphne with her knees cradled to her chest, her arms wrapped around them, and her breasts pushed against her thighs. A slight smile creased her lips, and a faint blush tinged her cheeks. Daphne sat behind Eleanor, her long legs straddling Eleanor's body. Her arms draped around Eleanor's neck, with her fingers tantalizingly close to Eleanor's cleavage. Her salt-and-pepper hair brushed her shoulders. She sported a wicked grin, her dark brown eyes staring down at Bailey as if she knew a secret no one else would discover.

Bailey was unable to move. Eleanor's voice behind her nudged her from her trance.

"A gay artist friend of ours in Hollywood painted it for us. I never would have posed like that for someone straight. It was Daph's idea, of course."

Bailey turned to Eleanor who stared at the painting with a wistful expression.

"She suffered her first stroke right after Douglas finished it, although we didn't know it was a stroke at the time."

Bailey looked up at the painting again. "How old were you?"

"I was forty-five when we had this done. She was fifty-three, just shy of her fifty-fourth birthday."

"Eight-year age difference," Bailey said, almost to herself. "So young to suffer a stroke."

"It might have been an eight-year age difference when we first met, but I eventually caught up with her." Eleanor winked. "Let's continue. Niles will bring the tea out to us on the patio."

They walked to the back of the home. The patio's speckled tile stretched out for several feet, ending at the foot of a large fountain. A flower garden flourished to the left. The lawn continued on for several yards to a privacy fence separating Eleanor's property from her neighbors'.

"Come. Sit."

Bailey settled into a cushioned wooden chair across from Eleanor. The sliding glass door opened behind them, and a well-dressed, elderly gentleman brought out a silver tray. On it, a teapot, sugar bowl, creamer, and three cups and saucers sat next to a plate of cookies. Obviously, the third cup was for the other interviewer who would join them. Bailey wondered about her.

As if sensing her thoughts, Eleanor said, "The other woman should arrive shortly. She phoned to say she was delayed at school."

"School?" Bailey thanked Niles after he poured the tea. He stepped back inside.

"Cream?" Eleanor pointed at the creamer.

"Please." Bailey held up her cup for Eleanor.

"One lump or two?" Eleanor asked, motioning toward the sugar bowl.

"None, thank you."

Eleanor dropped two sugar cubes into her cup. "I believe the young woman said she was a professor at Indiana University."

Bailey almost spit out her first mouthful of tea.

"Beautiful voice. She sounds very much like she might have been a singer at some point in her life."

The doorbell rang before Bailey's runaway thoughts had a chance to careen off the track.

"That should be her, I think," Eleanor said. "Excuse me for a moment, won't you?"

"No, no, no," Bailey said under her breath after Eleanor left. "This can't be possible. It has to be someone else."

Voices drifted in through the slightly opened sliding glass doors.

"We're drinking our tea out here. I hope that's okay with you, Professor…"

"Parker. But you can call me Chelsea. I noticed a Jeep out front with Colorado plates…"

Blood rushed to Bailey's head when Chelsea appeared behind Eleanor. Bailey stood up abruptly, as if that would somehow help her state of mind. But it only made her more lightheaded.

The expression on Chelsea's face was a mixture of surprise and sadness. Then, as if someone had flicked a switch, an impenetrable veil lowered over her eyes.

"Bailey." Chelsea shifted in place.

"Chelsea." Bailey wanted to tell her she was still beautiful. She wanted to embrace her and smell the shampoo Chelsea had used that morning as she had so many days of their time together. She wanted to feel Chelsea's body against hers. But she didn't move.

Eleanor looked back and forth between the two women. "You

know each other?"

Chelsea nodded and noticed Bailey doing the same.

"Let's sit down, and you can tell me how." Eleanor motioned them to the chairs.

Chelsea scooted her chair closer to Eleanor's before sitting down.

"Tea, Chelsea?" Eleanor asked.

"No, thank you." Her heart pounded in her ears. She hadn't prepared for this. How could she have? She didn't think Bailey had, either, if her bouncing knee was any indication.

"Don't tell me you don't like tea, especially an afternoon tea."

"I'm... ah... sorry," Chelsea stammered.

"When we spoke earlier, I mentioned sharing tea while we chatted. You didn't disagree." Eleanor's voice held a note of challenge. The sun creeping through the lattice above the patio bathed her gray hair in a bright light, giving her an imposing appearance.

"I have to admit I wanted the interview, which is why I agreed." Chelsea hoped she hadn't offended her.

"Well, in ancient England, we might have taken you to the center of town and had you hanged and quartered for that offense." Eleanor shuddered. "We won't stoop to that barbaric act. Instead, I'll ask you, what do you drink?"

"Water is fine." Chelsea gripped her briefcase against her chest as if it could protect her from her swirling emotions.

Eleanor picked up a small porcelain bell and rang it. Bailey flinched at the sound.

"Madam?" Niles appeared at the sliding glass door.

"Ice water for Professor Parker, please."

After he left, Eleanor took a sip of her tea and stared at them over the rim of her cup. "So. Who's going to tell me first?"

Chelsea shot a quick glance over at Bailey whose bouncing knee had hit a frenzied rate.

"Bailey and I... we... well, we..."

Eleanor finished her sentence. "You were lovers."

"Yes," Chelsea answered.

"How long?" Eleanor asked.

"How long..." Chelsea grew more uncomfortable with the questions. Who was interviewing whom here?

"How long were you together?"

Chelsea was about to answer, but Bailey interrupted.

"Nine years, three months, and thirteen days."

Chelsea swallowed the lump in her throat in an attempt to stave off her tears.

Niles brought out a bottle of water and a glass of ice. After he left, an awkward silence shrouded the table.

"Interesting," Eleanor said. "Very interesting. And how long apart?"

Chelsea answered this time. "Eleven months."

"How did you meet?" Eleanor shifted back in her chair and crossed one ankle over her knee. With the move, the heel of her sandal drooped down from her toes.

"We met in Bloomington at a coffee shop. There wasn't an empty table. Bailey sat alone with her laptop, so I walked over and asked if I could sit with her."

"Of course you answered yes," Eleanor said, addressing Bailey. "How could you not? Professor Chelsea Parker is quite beautiful."

Bailey smiled. "Yes, she is, as she was then."

The lump in Chelsea's throat made another appearance. She opened her water bottle, poured it into the glass, and took a long drink.

"I take it you were both in school at Indiana University?"

"I was in grad school," Bailey said. "I received my undergrad degree from Hanover, a college located a little farther south."

"I've heard of it." Eleanor turned back to Chelsea. "And you?"

"I was working on my dissertation."

"Ah, that's right. Of course you would have earned a Ph.D. I should call you Doctor Parker."

"Chelsea's fine."

"All right. Here's the big question. Why did you separate?"

Bailey tapped the side of her cup with her index finger.

When it was clear Bailey wasn't about to respond, Chelsea answered. "We got too busy with our work and grew apart."

Eleanor's sharp laugh echoed in the backyard.

"That's it? You were busy and grew apart?"

"Well…" Chelsea tried to think of something else to say but was at a loss.

Eleanor waved her hand in the air. "Don't try to justify it with any more words. I get the picture."

"I'm sorry. I didn't mean to upset you." Chelsea wondered whether she'd lost the interview before it had even begun.

"Upset me?" Again, Eleanor laughed, but there was no humor in it. "I'm not upset. I'm angry. There's a difference."

"What did I say wrong? I didn't mean anything by my words."

Chelsea gave Bailey a pleading look.

Bailey leaned toward Eleanor. "We were both at fault."

"You most certainly were. How could you let a nine-year—what did you say? Nine-year, three-months and—"

"Thirteen days," Chelsea said.

"Right. If you both can remember the exact time you were together, how could you now be apart? It makes no sense. None."

Eleanor rose to her feet and stomped off toward the garden.

Chelsea watched her leave and then whirled toward Bailey. "What is this? Why are you here?"

"Hi, Bailey. How've you been? I've been fine, Chelsea, how about you?" Bailey rolled her eyes. "Why do you think? For the same reason you are."

"Let me guess. Joanne Addison thought because you're gay, Eleanor Burnett would talk to you."

"Yeah. That's pretty much it."

"And you came anyway, knowing I'm here teaching?" Chelsea's voice continued to rise.

"Why are you mad? It's not like you have the right to an exclusive." Bailey stood and shoved her chair back. It teetered and then settled on all four legs.

Chelsea rose to her feet to avoid Bailey towering over her. "I still can't believe you're here."

Bailey looked like she was about to say something more. Instead, she marched toward the direction Eleanor had taken.

"Wait!" Chelsea hurried to catch up with Bailey's long strides. "I'm not done."

"I don't have to listen to this anymore, remember?" Bailey's jaw was tight.

Chelsea stumbled and began to fall forward, but Bailey caught her under the elbow. When she did, Chelsea fell into her arms. They stared at each other, both breathing heavy. Bailey's gaze dropped to Chelsea's lips. Then she blinked, pulled away, and continued toward Eleanor who stood in the distance.

I almost kissed her, Bailey thought. I can't believe I almost kissed her. What is wrong with me?

She caught up with Eleanor who was weeding the daffodils.

"Ms. Burnett…" Bailey started to say.

Eleanor raised her head and glared at Bailey.

"I'm sorry. Eleanor. Please don't let our former relationship keep you from talking to me."

"To us," Chelsea chimed in as she moved beside Bailey.

Eleanor straightened and brushed the dirt from her hands. "Tomorrow morning. Seven o'clock sharp."

Bailey and Chelsea spoke at the same time.

"I'm sorry?"

"Excuse me?"

"Seven o'clock in the morning. You Yanks are capable of arising that early, aren't you?"

"Yes," they answered together.

"I see some habits are hard to break. I bet you still finish each other's sentences, too. Return tomorrow at seven and we'll talk. I'm tired. It's time for my afternoon nap. You can find your way to the front by following that path." Eleanor gestured at a dirt path lined with stones and strode back to the house.

"That was interesting," Bailey said, but Chelsea was already walking down the path. "Hey, wait, Chels. I still don't know why you're so angry."

Bailey caught up with her as Chelsea reached the Outback. She was about to open the door, but Bailey pressed her palm against it and waited for Chelsea to face her.

"Talk to me." Bailey reached out to touch Chelsea's shoulder but let her hand drop to her side.

Chelsea spun around, her face wet with tears. She wiped at them in jerking motions.

She's that angry, Bailey thought. No. Wait. She's hurt.

"I can't believe you came out here thinking there was no chance we could meet. Are you that desperate for a job?"

Bailey bristled. "Now, hold on. My job is as important to me as yours is to you. Or have you conveniently forgotten that and twisted history?"

"What do you mean, 'twisted history'?"

"Seems like the only one you're thinking about is you. Just like when…"

"Just like when, what, Bailey? When I was the brave one and actually acknowledged we couldn't go on the way we were? Is that what you were going to say?"

"I didn't say it."

"You didn't have to. I know how you think, and right now the only one you're thinking about is you." Chelsea poked her in the chest with her index finger. "You could have told Joanne no."

"Well, I didn't. So grow up and accept it that we're both here to do our jobs."

Chelsea opened her mouth to say something but stopped.

"What?" Bailey asked.

"It's too damn soon." Chelsea reached behind her, opened the door, and got inside, not looking up as she started the engine and drove around the circular drive to the gravel road.

"It's not like I planned it!" Bailey shouted at the dust left behind by the Outback. She tramped to her Jeep. She buckled her seatbelt and was about to pull away when she noticed a curtain in the front of the house move aside before dropping back into place.

"Crazy old broad," Bailey muttered as she drove back to the main road. "Thanks a lot, Joanne."

* * *

After she arrived at her hotel room, Bailey called Denver.

"Pick up the damn phone." She flopped onto her bed with her cell phone pressed to her ear.

"I hope you have good news from the Eleanor Burnett front." Joanne sounded chipper, which annoyed Bailey even more.

"Here's some news for you. Remember how you said the chance of Chelsea and me meeting up was slim to none?"

"Uh-huh." Joanne's tone mellowed noticeably.

"Remember how I told you that you were full of shit?" Bailey's voice rose.

"Yeah…"

"Guess what? I was right."

"Oh, crap. Where did you see her? At a store? A restaurant?"

Bailey snorted. "Try again."

"Don't make me play twenty questions."

"You know the reason I'm in Bloomington?"

"Yes." Joanne drew the word out.

"Guess who also gets a quote, unquote, exclusive interview?"

"You're shitting me."

"I wish."

"Well, that's just not going to work."

Bailey heard the all-too-familiar clicking sound of a lighter and the exhalation of smoke. It was times like these where she seriously considered taking up the bad habit.

"I'm sorry. Do you think I have some control over this?"

"What do you mean?" Joanne asked.

"Eleanor Burnett is one formidable old woman."

"You mean to tell me you couldn't convince her that one

person writing a biography on Daphne DeMonet was enough?"

"Trust me. You only need to meet her to know the answer to that one. This is all beside the point. I'm not sure I can stay here and do the interview."

"Come on, Bailey. You can't sit in the same room with Chelsea and do your job?"

Anger flowed through Bailey's veins. "Did you hear what you just asked me?"

"Jesus. Calm down. At least tell me how it was meeting Eleanor Burnett."

Bailey pictured Eleanor sitting out on the patio. "She's beautiful and strong-willed. I can see what attracted Daphne DeMonet."

"You sound smitten."

Bailey couldn't help but smile. "I can imagine what she was like in her twenties when they first met."

"Were you able to get in any questions today?"

"No. She's asked us to come back at seven in the morning. I'm not sure what she has in mind."

Joanne sighed. "This is very hard for me to say, but if you think you're incapable of being around Chelsea, then give me the word. I'll send out Lois on the next plane."

Bailey cringed as she thought about the abrasive researcher who was often her rival for projects. And how she and Eleanor would mix like oil and water.

"Lois Charleton? Ugh."

"You don't have much say in this if you're out of the picture."

Bailey noticed the smug tone. "You're doing this to irritate me, aren't you? And to goad me into staying."

Another inhalation and puffing out of smoke. Bailey had no trouble picturing Joanne's self-satisfied grin, knowing she was getting exactly what she wanted.

"Sometimes, I really don't like you, Joanne Addison."

"And your answer is…"

"Fine. I'll stay. But if it gets uncomfortable, you'll be getting another phone call from me."

"I have no doubt that your professionalism will win out."

"You don't need to lay it on that thick. I said I'd do it."

"Good. Keep in touch."

Bailey snapped the phone shut and stared at the far wall for five minutes. She grabbed the TV remote and flipped to the channel that played classic programs. She tried to get lost in an episode of

Gunsmoke. Chelsea used to tease her about her affinity for the old program. Thinking of Chelsea immediately brought up the memory of their argument outside Eleanor's house.

Bailey turned off the TV and grabbed her keys. Sitting around the hotel room and lamenting about their failed relationship wasn't exactly how she wanted to spend the rest of the afternoon. She'd have a beer and get a bite to eat. And then try to convince herself that seeing Chelsea again hadn't seriously messed with her mind.

Chapter 5

The next morning, on the drive to Eleanor's home, Chelsea made a vow to be professional and accept that Bailey wasn't going away. Her cool demeanor evaporated when she saw Bailey's Jeep already parked in the circular drive. When they were together, Bailey hadn't made it a habit to be early for anything. What had changed?

Chelsea got out of the car and was about to step up to the door when she heard laughter and music from the backyard. She walked down the path to the patio and stopped in shock at the sight before her.

Bailey and Eleanor were dancing. To an Elvis tune? And when did Bailey learn how to dance like that?

The two women moved like they'd danced together for years. Chelsea's gaze dropped to Bailey's backside where the jeans hugged her tight. *God, what am I doing staring at her ass?*

"Ms. Hampton, but you do dance quite beautifully," Eleanor said, affecting a southern accent.

"Why, Ms. Burnett, are you flirting with me?"

Eleanor giggled.

Chelsea's fascination with Bailey's dancing ability vanished quickly. She remembered they were there to get an interview. And who knew if Eleanor would continue to grant them both access? She'd already proven to be difficult.

Chelsea cleared her throat before approaching.

Eleanor spotted her over Bailey's shoulder. "I do believe Doctor Parker has joined us. I'm afraid this dancing lesson has come to an end."

Bailey stopped and waited a half beat before turning toward Chelsea. A slight blush rose up her neck. "Hey, Chels."

"Bailey." Chelsea barely acknowledged her. "Eleanor, I was hoping we'd get started today."

Eleanor walked to the portable CD player and punched the Off button.

"Why don't you both sit down? I assume you want coffee. I know how you Yanks love your coffee in the morning."

"I'll have coffee, Eleanor, but Chelsea doesn't have a cup until—"

"Coffee's fine," Chelsea said and glared at Bailey before sitting down.

Eleanor left for the house. "Niles isn't up yet," she said over her shoulder. "Never rises before eight. I'll be right back with your coffee and my tea."

After she left them, Bailey swiveled toward Chelsea. "You'll have to get over this shit. I'm not going away. We're capable of being civil to one another, aren't we?"

Chelsea was about to fire off a retort but stopped. She took a calming breath. "You're right. I'm sorry. It was a shock seeing you yesterday, and I'm still trying to adjust to it."

The sliding glass door opened. Bailey got to her feet to help Eleanor.

"Let me carry that." Bailey took the tray from her and set it on the table.

"I hope you two have ironed out your differences," Eleanor said.

Bailey questioned Chelsea with an upraised eyebrow as she handed her the mug of coffee and sat down between the two women.

"We're fine." Chelsea held the mug in her hand but refrained from drinking. She *didn't* like coffee this early, but she didn't want to give Bailey the satisfaction of knowing her so well.

"Ah, 'fine.' I remember hearing that word over the years with Daph. I often called it the other four-letter 'f' word. Are you really fine, Chelsea, or are you humoring an old woman to get an interview?"

Chelsea set down her mug. "No, Bailey and I are good. Aren't we?"

Bailey raised her mug toward Chelsea. "Sure, Chels. If you say we're okay, we're okay."

Chelsea didn't miss her smirk. She resisted the urge to glare at Bailey again. Instead, she retrieved her notebook and tape recorder from her briefcase.

Eleanor's voice stopped her. "You won't need those."

"I'm sorry?" Chelsea looked up.

Eleanor continued to stir her tea. "The notebook and that

contraption you have there"—she pointed at the tape recorder—
"you won't need them."

"I'm confused."

Bailey, who had her finger poised over the buttons of her tape
recorder, also appeared perplexed.

"I've agreed to the interview, but on one condition and one
condition only." Eleanor stood up. "If you'll excuse me a moment,
I'll bring that condition to you."

Chelsea waited until Eleanor had entered the home before she
spoke. "I wonder what she has in mind."

"I wouldn't put anything past her." Bailey stared out at the
gardens with her brow furrowed.

Chelsea observed her in this unguarded moment. She looked
tired and older than her thirty-one years. The sun captured the
blonde highlights of her hair. Bailey ran her long fingers through
her tresses. Yesterday afternoon's harsh words momentarily
forgotten, Chelsea felt a sudden stirring inside as she recalled what
those fingers could do to her body. She raised her eyes, and her
breath caught when she locked gazes with Bailey.

The sound of the door sliding open behind them broke the
spell. Eleanor approached the table cradling a well-worn leather
book to her chest. She sat down and held the book in her lap,
rubbing the leather as she spoke.

"This book, like the others to follow, is precious to me. I've
never let anyone else read them, not even Daphne. But that's
changing today. This is the first of my diaries. I started it when I
arrived in Hollywood at the age of twenty." Eleanor smiled at their
reaction. "Don't act so surprised. I didn't have the best home life in
the world. My mother died when I was twelve, and my father did
the best to raise my two younger brothers and me, but…"

She shook her head. "When he remarried three years later, we
were afterthoughts. His new wife sent us off to boarding school as
soon as she had the chance. I'd sit in class, watch the rain as it
pelted the window, and dream of another life far away from
Banbury and Oxfordshire. As far as I could go. When I graduated, I
used the money I'd saved working part-time in a bakery and
traveled to the States in the summer of 1950."

Chelsea silently chastised herself for not taking down notes
once Eleanor had started talking. She thought Eleanor would at least
grant her this concession, since it was a prelude to the diaries. But
Eleanor's words had captivated her to the point she'd forgotten
about the interview.

"When the steamship pulled into the harbor, and I saw the green lady staring out at the distance…" Eleanor's voice caught. "My heart stopped. My God, what a wonder. Has either of you seen her?"

"No, I haven't," Bailey said. "I've wanted to, though, and hope to before I die."

"I saw the Statue of Liberty a couple of months ago. I went to New York to a conference, and a friend and I took the tour." Chelsea felt Bailey staring at her, but she remained facing Eleanor.

"Everyone needs to go at least once in their lives." Eleanor again brushed her fingertips against the diary. "From there, I started on my cross-country bus adventure. That was an eye-opening experience, one I'll never forget. I arrived in Los Angeles shortly before my twenty-first birthday. It was hot and steamy. I remember how my dress clung to my sweaty legs as I searched for a decent hotel." She laughed. "I was so naïve. With what I could afford, I ended up staying for a week in a flea-ridden hovel until I found a one-bedroom apartment in West Hollywood. I worked at a diner a few miles from the opening gates to Taylor-Goodwin-Mays Studios. I'd take a bus to the studio sometimes on my lunch breaks and linger outside with another ten or so women who shared the same dream."

"You were an extra in two of Daphne's movies," Bailey said.

Eleanor smiled. "Very good, Bailey. I attended readings around my work schedule. I learned very fast that a lot of the casting agents were scum who expected their clients to sleep with them to get even a sniff at a reading. But then I met Hal Marker. What a gentleman, a rare breed in Hollywood. He hooked me up for a reading with Frank Teller, the director for Daphne's *The Brave Few*, which is how I earned my walk-on in the nightclub scene. I was the cocktail waitress. My only line was—"

"On the rocks or straight up?" Bailey said.

"Now, I truly am impressed."

"I enjoyed watching Ms. DeMonet's movies. And when I found out I was coming to interview you, I researched where you fit in with her film history."

"That's a nice way of putting it. Fitting in."

Chelsea wasn't too pleased with the chummy exchanges between Eleanor and Bailey. She felt like an outsider. "You said we could interview you on one condition, and I—"

"You are such an impatient young woman, Doctor Parker. Has she always been like this?" Eleanor asked Bailey.

Bailey smiled as she looked at Chelsea. "She had her moments. She's curious and sometimes wants things to move faster to get the information she needs. She was hell around her birthday, always trying to guess what her gift could be."

Chelsea's cheeks burned. "Don't talk about me like I'm not here, Bailey. I'm not invisible."

"No, you're definitely not that," Eleanor said. "You're beautiful, as I said yesterday. And you..." She turned to Bailey. "You're one handsome woman."

Bailey ducked her head.

"Oh, we're shy? Somehow I find that difficult to believe." Eleanor grew quiet as she gazed at them. "This is my condition." She held up the diary. "I want the two of you to read this book out loud. Here, at first. Once I'm confident that you'll continue to read together on your own, I'll permit you to take the other diaries with you. But you have to gain my trust, and it will take several readings here."

"I don't mean to be impolite," Chelsea said, "but how does this constitute an interview?"

"Because after each reading, I'll allow you to ask me any questions you like and I'll answer them to the best of my ability. These diaries are my life. At least it's when my life began. They give you as much insight as if you sat there and asked me questions point blank without any reference." She offered the journal to Bailey. "Do we have an agreement?"

"I can't answer for Chelsea," Bailey said as she took the diary from Eleanor. "But I'd be honored to read your words."

Chelsea shifted in her seat.

"Doctor Parker?" Eleanor asked.

"It's Chelsea."

"It's Doctor Parker when I anticipate you're about to be difficult."

Bailey started to laugh, but coughed into her hand when Chelsea glowered at her.

"Fine," Chelsea said.

"There's that word again. You remind me of Daphne in so many ways. You wouldn't by chance be of Irish descent?"

"On my mother's side."

"There you have it."

"DeMonet doesn't sound Irish to me," Bailey said.

"It was her stage name. Her given name was O'Shea, but the studio heads didn't like it and tried for something fancy that went with her first name. There was another reason, too, but we'll touch on that later."

Chelsea shifted in her seat again, causing the cushion to squeak.

"Back to our impatient Doctor Parker. You've agreed. Why don't we begin? Who wants to read first?"

Bailey handed Chelsea the diary. "Why don't you read, Chelsea? You're the one with the good voice. Eleanor's already commented on how she can tell you sing."

"I've marked where you can start," Eleanor said. "I've already given you the background leading up to where you'll begin."

Chelsea thumbed the marker and opened the diary. "You have beautiful handwriting, Eleanor."

"Those years in boarding school weren't all lost." Eleanor motioned at the book. "Now, read."

Chelsea cleared her throat. "Monday, 21 August 1950. It's my twenty-first birthday, although there'll be no celebration. There hasn't been much celebrating since arriving in the States…"

Chapter 6

Nothing at home compared to the heat here. On days like this, my dream seemed so far away, even though it was a few short miles from the diner where I worked. I tried not to think about managing thirty dollars at the most in tips a week and eating like a bird to make ends meet.

I entered Joe's Diner and grabbed my apron. "Hi, Rose."

"Heya, Eleanor. How's tricks?"

My tall, platinum blonde co-worker said the same thing to me every morning. Every morning, it struck me what a silly question it was.

"No dillydallying," Stella shouted from the kitchen.

"That woman needs to get laid," Rose said under her breath as she brushed past me.

The typical morning crowd came. Al and his wife Tonya asked for their usual—scrambled eggs, bacon, two glasses of orange juice. I only wished something would change. Anything to break up the monotony.

"Eleanor! Phone!"

Stella handed over the receiver and pointed at me with a thick finger. "Two minutes, tops. We're too busy to have you chatting."

"Hello?"

"Eleanor, it's Hal Marker. Good news. I've snagged a reading for you for tomorrow afternoon. They're in the middle of filming the picture but want to go another route with the casting of one of the extras. They're looking for a Brit, and you fit the bill. Can you get to TGM's lot by two?"

An immediate swarm of butterflies assaulted my stomach.

"I'll have to ask Stella, but I think so. I can take my lunch then."

"Got a good feeling about this one, kid. Get there a little early if you can."

I hung up the phone and stared at it as if in a trance.

"Eleanor! Back to work. Table six, remember?" Stella glared at me.

"Right. Sorry." I fetched the coffee pot, thankful now for the mundane to keep my mind occupied for the next several hours.

* * *

Tuesday, 22 August 1950. "Miss Eleanor Burnett?" The young man glanced up from his clipboard.

I rose from my chair and smoothed my skirt before following him into the studio.

"You stand there." He pointed at a white *X* on the floor.

A man with greying hair spoke from his director's chair. "Miss Burnett, I'm Frank Teller. Please try to relax and read the line on the script that Tom's handing you. You're the cocktail waitress. Janet will be reading with you."

I took the dog-eared script from Tom. A red-haired woman in a tight-fitting blouse and trousers popped her gum at me while gazing down at her own copy.

"Go ahead, Janet," Teller said.

One more gum pop prefaced her line. "Hey, sugar, I need a Scotch next time you swing by."

As I was about to deliver my line, a woman appeared in the back of the studio. She sauntered up to the empty chair beside Teller, sat down, and crossed her legs. Her skirt hiked up high on the side with the movement.

Oh my God. Daphne DeMonet. She placed a cigarette between her lips. Teller flicked a lighter and held it toward her. She cupped her hand around his and took a long drag. The smoke obscured her face. But those legs. You couldn't mistake them for anyone else's. I'd read once she'd insured them for a million dollars, and I thought it ludicrous. Until seeing them in the flesh…

"Miss Burnett?" Teller prompted. "This is where you speak your line."

"Oh. Forgive me. Can we try again?" I tore my gaze away from Miss DeMonet and attempted to concentrate.

"Again, Janet."

Janet repeated her line.

"On the rocks or straight up?" There. At least I didn't stumble.

Miss DeMonet leaned over and said something to Teller.

"That's fine, Miss Burnett. We'll call Marker if we're interested."

My heart sank. Other directors had dismissed me in the same manner so many times before. The only calls I received from Mr. Marker started with, "Sorry, Eleanor. They're looking for someone a little taller... a little plumper... a little older." It didn't matter what followed. The phone call always began with, "Sorry, Eleanor."

On the bus back to the diner, while sitting in the stifling, stagnant heat, I thought about Father's last letter. He'd sent money. I wish I could send it back to him to show him I could stand on my own two feet. But I needed the money. He told me to use it to come back home. I watched the palm trees flash by my window and made a vow. If Mr. Teller didn't offer me this part, I'd heed my father's advice.

* * *

Thursday, 24 August 1950. "Eleanor! Phone!" Stella handed me the receiver. "Second call this week. Try not to make this a habit, okay?"

"I'm sorry."

She grunted and pushed through the swinging door into the kitchen.

"Hello?"

"You got the part," Mr. Marker said, his voice bubbling with excitement.

Shocked, I sat down on a stool at the counter. "I did?"

"Yes, you did. You need a nice gown lickety-split. Do you have one? Or do you need me to advance you some money?"

I remembered the cash my father had sent me. "No, I have money, but why do I need a new gown? Won't I be costumed for the movie?"

"There's a party tomorrow night at DeMonet's house. She throws a shindig for every one of her movies. You're invited."

"Why would she invite me? I'm only an extra."

"I don't know. What I do know is you need to be there and look your best. Let me give you the address."

I pulled the pen down from behind my ear and scribbled the information on a napkin.

"It's at seven. You can be fashionably late at eight, but don't push it. I suggest taking a taxi."

My mind spun as I replaced the receiver. Where could I get a decent gown with the money Father had sent me?

Rose breezed by with a full tray.

"Rose, can you help me tonight?"

* * *

Friday, 25 August 1950. I arrived at the gated entrance to Miss DeMonet's Beverly Hills home at seven-thirty, gave my name to the attendant, and followed others garbed in elegant tuxes and party dresses down the winding path to her home. I glanced down at my attire and wondered again about my choice. Rose had helped me find a soft blue satin gown that fell to my knees.

"It brings out the blue in your eyes," she'd said.

But it also showed plenty of cleavage. I felt exposed and checked around before tugging the front a little higher.

The sprawling Spanish-style mansion was everything I expected it to be. The sun was descending in the western sky, and its dying golden rays suffused the white stucco in a soft orange light.

A doorman again stopped me to check off my name. After passing inspection, I moved from the foyer into the large living room overflowing with beautiful people. Searching where to stand to blend in, I spotted a small alcove by the hors d'oeuvres table and bar. It seemed safe enough.

I approached the bartender. "A glass of white wine please."

An excited murmur rippled through the crowd. I craned my neck to see Daphne DeMonet enter the room. Her smile lit on everyone she turned to while her gaze held them in place. A glowing aura surrounded her. I blinked, thinking it must be the lighting. A silver, jewel-encrusted barrette pushed her dark hair back on the side; the rest cascaded onto her bare shoulders. A slit in her white, sequined gown, rising almost to her hip, allowed a generous view of one tanned leg as she moved through the crowd.

My mouth felt suddenly dry. I took several sips of wine and tried to tear my eyes away from her, but I failed in the effort.

A group of four or five young, handsome men descended upon her and surrounded her, preventing her from walking farther. One handed her a drink, leaned in to kiss her cheek, and pressed his lips to her ear. She threw her head back as she laughed at something he must have said. My gaze was drawn down her long neck to her cleavage below.

I snapped my eyes up when I realised where I'd been looking and held back a gasp.

Daphne DeMonet was still laughing with the men surrounding her, but she was staring at me.

I took another long drink to finish off the rest of my wine and searched for a place to set down the glass. When I turned around, my heart leapt to my throat.

Daphne was walking slowly toward me and seemed to be sizing me up, like a lioness hunting a gazelle on the plains of Africa.

"Hello," she said in that famous, husky voice that was almost a growl. "I was in the studio when you read this week. Eleanor Burnett, right?"

I nodded, unable to find enough saliva to utter a word.

"I know you can speak. I heard you read your line," she said in a teasing tone.

I swallowed. "Ye-yes. I'm surprised you remember me, Miss DeMonet."

"Oh, I never forget names." She locked in on my eyes. "Or pretty faces."

Fire heated my cheeks.

"Why don't we go someplace a little quieter to chat?" Not awaiting my reply, she took my hand and led me through the throng. She allowed several actors to give her air kisses along the way. She manoeuvred me to the backyard to a cement bench ensconced within a beautiful flower garden. "Sit with me."

There wasn't much of a choice as she pulled me to her side.

"So, Ellie... may I call you Ellie?"

"Yes." I don't know why I agreed. No one had ever called me that. Mesmerised in her presence, it was as if a pixie had sprinkled magic dust upon my head and rendered me helpless to do anything but what she bid.

"I love your accent." She pressed her leg against mine. "I've been to England a time or two. Where are you from?"

"Banbury in Oxfordshire."

"A long way from home, hmm? I imagine it gets lonely." She placed her hand on my knee. It felt like a red-hot poker had seared through my dress.

"S-sometimes," I stuttered. My skin ablaze, my body reacted in ways it never had before. Only two young men had sat this intimately with me. I had felt nothing with them but a sense of dread as to what happened next. With her, I felt fear and something else unforeseen... longing.

Her gaze dropped to my mouth. She questioned me with one upraised eyebrow as she drew even nearer.

I took a breath before her lips pressed into mine. Her long, thin fingers entwined into my hair and pulled me closer.

"Daphne DeMonet is kissing me" ran through my mind until a second thought hit me like a hammered spike. A woman is kissing me. And I'm kissing her back. Oh my God.

I yanked my mouth away with a soft cry and jumped to my feet.

"Miss DeMonet, I… I…"

The dimming light from the setting sun captured the amusement on her face. "I think you can call me Daphne after a kiss like that."

Terrified and shaken, I fled from her and from the conflicting emotions raging inside of me.

"Wait! I'm sorry!"

I heard her gown rustling behind me as she rushed to catch up. Just as I made it to the back door, she grasped my wrist.

"I'm sorry. I thought you… well, I thought you…"

"You thought I what?" I asked with tears streaming down my cheeks.

Her cheeks grew flushed, and her dark eyes pleaded with mine for something I knew I wasn't able to give.

"I'm so sorry. Please don't think ill of me. I presumed something, and I took advantage of you."

I stared at her hand still holding my wrist in its tight grip. She let go.

"Please, you won't tell anyone, will you?" Gone was the sleek huntress, replaced by a frightened young woman concerned about her reputation… and most likely her career.

"No," I answered quietly. "No, I won't tell anyone. But you must know I'm not that way." A sudden thought came to mind. "The reason I got the part. It wasn't because of this, was it?"

She hesitated. Enough for me to know the answer.

Anger boiled inside of me. "You and Mr. Teller can find someone else for your Brit." I barged through the back door of the house and shoved past anyone in my path, not caring who it was nor what kind of dark looks I received.

Before I left, I couldn't help myself. There was such a pull to turn back to her as if I were the ocean tide and she the moon. Her admirers had surrounded her once again, all vying for her attention.

But Daphne DeMonet only had eyes for me.

Chapter 7

"I think you can stop there for now."

Eleanor's voice jarred Bailey from the compelling words Chelsea had finished reading. Bailey wanted to protest but thought better of it. She'd already discovered Eleanor Burnett wasn't one to pressure.

Chelsea shut the diary with a sigh.

"Was that a sigh of impatience, Doctor Parker?"

"It's Chels—"

"Chelsea. You must know I love to tease you. I'm sure you both have questions."

"I take it from what you'd written that you'd never been with anyone before Daphne," Bailey said.

"By 'been,' I'm assuming you mean in the biblical sense."

"Well, yeah…"

"I'd shared some furtive kisses with boys back home. Enough that I knew what a kiss was and what it felt like. Something had been missing, though, until her lips touched mine in the waning light of that day." Eleanor ran her fingers over her lips. "Incredible," she murmured.

"Was she really apologetic over what happened? Obviously, you still took the part. What changed your mind?" Chelsea asked.

Eleanor wagged a finger at her. "Ah, ah, ah. That's a story for another day. I'm tired and need to stop." She rose from her chair. "Why don't you both return tomorrow at the same time? That is if it's not too much of an inconvenience. I apologize, but I do tire easily these days."

Bailey glanced at Chelsea, who at first appeared miffed, but then she apparently schooled her expression to one of acceptance.

They stood up.

"That's fine, Eleanor. I can't speak for Bailey, but I can be back again at seven."

"Me, too," Bailey said.

"Why don't you and Chelsea get some lunch together?"

"Oh, no. I'm sure Bailey has to report to her biographer, and I need to get back to school."

Bailey tried to hide her disappointment.

"Nonsense. Ms. Hampton has time to call Ms. Addison later this afternoon or evening, correct, Bailey?"

"Joanne knows I'll be calling her periodically. There's no hurry." Bailey waited for Chelsea to pipe in to protest. She was afraid to look her way.

Eleanor turned to Chelsea. "And I'm sure with it being summer, you're not needed back at the university immediately."

"I guess not," Chelsea said.

"Good. You two enjoy lunch and catch up with what the other has been up to these past eleven months. It won't kill you to spend some quality time together. I'll see you in the morning."

After she left, Chelsea picked up her briefcase. "We don't have to share lunch if you have other plans."

Bailey grew angry. "Chelsea, if you can't stand to be alone with me, I get it." She stormed off to the front of the house.

"Bailey, wait."

Bailey slowed and Chelsea hurried to catch up.

"I'm sorry. If you want to go to lunch, there's a pub not far from campus. They have excellent burgers. You still like burgers, don't you?" Her mouth turned up in the cute way that Bailey remembered so well. Her anger melted away.

"Yeah, I still like burgers."

They walked toward their vehicles. "Do you want to follow me?"

"Sure. Lead the way."

As Chelsea was opening the car door, she dropped her keys. She bent over to pick them up.

Bailey hesitated getting into the Jeep and took a moment to admire the way her white Capri pants clung to her hips.

Chelsea straightened and caught Bailey staring. "Try to keep up."

* * *

At the Hoosier Hang Out, Bailey parked behind Chelsea's Outback.

"Still have the lead foot, huh?" Bailey held the door open for her.

"I wasn't speeding."

"Right." She followed Chelsea inside where they found a quiet booth in the back.

A solicitous waitress popped up at their table. Too solicitous, Bailey thought.

"Doctor Parker, it's good to see you," the waitress bubbled. "What can I get you?"

"Hi, Marci. I didn't know you worked here in the summer."

"It helps with spending money in the fall."

"I'll take a Heineken. Are you still drinking those, Bailey?"

"When I do drink, yeah. That's fine."

Marci acted as if she'd just noticed her. "Okay. Two Heinekens coming right up." She swished away with an exaggerated sway to her hips.

Bailey watched her retreat to the bar. "Well, well, well, Doctor Parker. Seems like you have a way with your students."

"Don't you start," Chelsea said. "I had to deal with her hangdog looks all last semester."

Bailey chuckled and held up her hands in defense. "Only kidding. Geesh, what happened to your sense of humor?"

"It left me about a year ago."

Bailey sank back in the booth. She could tell from Chelsea's expression she already regretted her words, but it still hurt to hear them.

"I'm sorry," Chelsea said. "God. What is the matter with me?"

"I don't know," Bailey mumbled. "Maybe this wasn't such a good idea."

Chelsea grabbed Bailey's hand. "Please forgive me. This is still a shock, you know?"

Bailey placed her other hand on top of Chelsea's. "Hey, it's not something I pictured happening, either, remember? But I think we can do this."

Chelsea stared at her, and the sounds in the bar became muffled to Bailey.

Chelsea slipped her hand from her grasp as Marci returned with their beers.

"Here you go." Marci thumped the glasses on the table, setting Bailey's down with a little more force than necessary. Beer sloshed over the lip of the glass and dribbled onto Bailey's hand.

"Sorry." Marci whipped out a towel from her back pocket.

"No need. I've got it." Bailey took her napkin and wiped her hand.

"Are you eating today?" Marci asked.

"Chelsea told me you have great burgers, so I guess that's what I'll have, medium well. And fries."

"The same," Chelsea said.

This time Marci stomped away.

"I think you broke her heart," Bailey said in a lowered voice.

Chelsea laughed. It was the first genuine laugh Bailey had heard from her in too long a time.

Bailey grinned. "Good to know I can still make you laugh."

"You always made me laugh, even when I was mad at you, remember?"

"Which seemed to piss you off even more." Bailey took a drag of her beer.

"Only because you knew me so well." Chelsea shook her head. "Sometimes I was mad at you over the silliest things, and you knew it and would say something off the wall."

Bailey was about to respond, but a voice stopped her.

"Chelsea, I thought that was you."

A tall, dark-haired woman approached their table.

"Rebecca, hi." Chelsea shifted in the bench.

Bailey waited for Chelsea to say more, but she'd suddenly found an interest in the wood grain of the table.

The woman thrust her hand at Bailey. "Hi. I'm Rebecca Simmons, a colleague of Chelsea's."

Bailey returned the handshake and noticed how tightly Rebecca squeezed her fingers. Chelsea still hadn't made a move to introduce Bailey, so Bailey did it for her.

"I'm Bailey Hampton."

Bailey didn't know someone's eyebrows could shoot up that high.

"Oh, *Bailey*."

Bailey glanced over at Chelsea who took several long gulps of her beer.

"That's my name. Has been since my mom and dad settled on it when I was born."

Rebecca gave her a faint smile and turned to Chelsea. "I'll talk to you back at school. I wanted to discuss next semester's syllabus with you."

"I'll see you there."

Rebecca looked at Bailey. "Nice meeting you. Do you plan to be in town long?"

"For a few weeks at least."

"Maybe we can all get together over dinner." Rebecca didn't wait for a response. She glanced at Chelsea, or rather the top of Chelsea's head, and left.

Marci brought their meals and asked if they needed seconds on the beer. Bailey noticed Chelsea had finished hers off.

"Sure." Bailey waited for Marci to leave the table. "I'm thinking that makes two women interested, although Marci doesn't count. Am I right?"

"Rebecca's asked me out a few times." Chelsea picked at her fries.

Bailey wanted to ask what Chelsea's answer had been, but it wasn't any of her business. Not anymore.

Strained conversation hung between them for the remainder of the meal. Bailey insisted on paying the bill and walked Chelsea to her car.

"See you in the morning?" Bailey asked, opening the door for her.

"Bright and early." Chelsea wouldn't look at her as she started her car and pulled away.

Deflated, Bailey walked to the Jeep.

Chelsea adjusted her rearview mirror to watch Bailey. She didn't miss the hanging of her head or the slumping of her shoulders. Guilt washed over her.

Why did I do that? Chelsea thought on the drive to the campus. Why didn't I tell her I never went out with Rebecca? *Because I'm protecting my heart.*

She parked in the "A" lot next to Memorial Hall. She stayed in her car and thought about the past as she pondered the present. A tapping on the driver's window startled her from her reverie.

Rebecca made a motion for her to roll down the window.

"You okay?" Rebecca asked.

"I'm fine." Chelsea rolled the other windows down a crack, grabbed her briefcase, and got out of the car. She walked quickly down the sidewalk toward the entrance.

"Do you have time to talk about my syllabus?" Rebecca jogged to keep up with her.

"A few minutes, yes." Chelsea took the stairs to the second floor almost on a sprint. They reached the top and entered Chelsea's office. "What is it?" she asked a little too sharply, the intrusion at lunch still fresh on her mind.

"Hey, if you don't have time..."

"No, I do now. Have a seat."

For the next fifteen minutes, Rebecca asked her what she'd focused on during the previous semester in the "Gender, Sexuality, and Popular Culture" course. Chelsea had taught a similar class her last semester in Denver before she jumped at the chance to put her life in Colorado with Bailey behind her and accepted the position at Indiana University. Two more years and she'd achieve full professorship in her department.

She gave Rebecca a few of her handouts.

"Thanks." Rebecca shuffled the papers into a stack but made no move to leave. "How was it for you seeing Bailey again? I had the feeling it wasn't planned."

"Definitely unexpected."

"What's she doing here?"

Chelsea almost didn't answer but didn't see the harm. "She's also interviewing Eleanor Burnett."

"Wow, what are the odds, huh?" Rebecca drummed her fingers on the desk. "Are you two…"

"No, we aren't." Chelsea wasn't sure how she felt about it when she spoke the words. An unexpected twinge of disappointment crept into her heart. She looked up to find Rebecca staring at her. "We aren't." She repeated the words more for herself than as an answer to the question.

"That's good. Because I'd like to take another stab. How about having dinner with me Friday night? No pressure, though. It'd be a simple dinner at Lorenzo's in town."

"No" was on Chelsea's lips, but the word came out, "Yes."

Rebecca seemed surprised. "Really?"

"How does seven-thirty sound? I'll meet you there."

"Fantastic. I'll make the reservations." Rebecca rose. "I'll get out of your hair. You probably have a lot to do."

After Rebecca left her office, Chelsea slumped back in her chair. "What am I doing?" She knew the answer. Bailey had reentered her life, and Chelsea needed to prove to herself that it was over between them.

The paperweight caught her eye. She picked it up and traced her fingers over the surface of the miniature model of the museum. An image of Bailey's infectious smile when they stood in front of the Mona Lisa ran through Chelsea's mind as if it were a photograph.

She set the paperweight back down, unable to grasp the emotion she was feeling. "It's a start." The start of what, she wasn't sure.

Chapter 8

"How was your lunch with Chelsea?" Eleanor, dressed in a lemon-colored linen pantsuit, handed Bailey a mug of coffee.

"Okay."

Eleanor sat down at the table and stirred her tea. "You arrived fifteen minutes early this morning for a reason."

Bailey stared at Eleanor's beautiful white hair and delicate features and momentarily forgot why she had come there so early. "You are a stunning woman." The words slipped out of Bailey's mouth before she had a chance to censor them.

Eleanor laughed. "Flattery will get you nowhere, Ms. Hampton. But it's still nice to hear at my age."

"You and Daphne were quite the couple, weren't you?"

"That we were. Although to prying minds, I was her close friend." She framed the words with quotation marks in the air. "Or her traveling companion. Or her secretary."

"You were never called her lover, were you?"

"You know the answer to that one. Back then, it was unheard of. Even today, how many out gay actors and actresses do you know about in Hollywood? It's rarely done."

"How difficult was that? And how difficult was it for you when she married in 1954?"

Eleanor grimaced as if in physical pain.

Bailey mentally kicked herself for bringing it up.

"It nearly killed me, my girl. But let's stop talking about me. Remember our agreement?"

Bailey nodded.

"I think you came early to talk about someone else, someone who still means a great deal to you."

At those words, Bailey choked up. Eleanor's thin fingers wrapped around her wrist.

"You still love her very much, don't you?" Eleanor asked softly.

"Yes, but it's too late."

"Don't be silly. It's never too late for love."

Bailey blew out a breath. "I don't think she feels the same way."

"Do you know what I think? I think the two of you gave up much, much too easily. Love isn't always simple. Sometimes you have to fight for it. I see so many young people walk away from relationships when it begins to get a little rough. There's something going on between you two. You have chemistry, and you only need to mix the ingredients properly to make the formula whole again." Eleanor looked past Bailey's shoulder. "Hello, Chelsea."

"Hello, Eleanor. Bailey." Chelsea approached the table and noticed Bailey wiping at her cheeks. *Was she crying?*

Bailey kept her face averted.

"While we've awaited your arrival, we've been having a lovely discussion. Bailey even tried to get me to open up to some questions. No worries. I almost fell under her spell. Tell me, was she always this persuasive when you were together?"

"She could be." Chelsea pulled out her chair and sank down in the soft cushion.

"Coffee?" Eleanor asked.

"No, thank you."

"I imagine you're ready to move forward this morning?"

"Speaking for myself, yes. I can hardly wait."

Bailey's reaction was a slight nod.

Eleanor pushed the diary toward Bailey. "Your turn, my dear."

"I think Chelsea sounded fine, and you said you loved her voice. Why don't we let her read again this morning?"

Chelsea was about to object but didn't get the chance.

"Begin, Chelsea," Eleanor said.

Bailey slid the diary across the table. Chelsea reached for it. Their fingers touched, and Bailey jerked her hand back and shifted farther away in her chair. Chelsea was about to say something, but Eleanor interrupted her.

"Please." Eleanor nodded at the diary.

Chelsea thumbed to the marker and opened the book.

"Monday, 28 August 1950. The delivery boy from the florist down the street appeared at the door, struggling to open it. He shifted the large bouquet of roses over to one hand as he pulled the handle and staggered inside…"

Chapter 9

Rose approached the young boy. "Let me guess. Our fair Eleanor has received yet more roses from a mysterious admirer. But the question is, will she react as she has the past two times?" She snatched up the card.

I tried to get it from her, but she held me at bay.

"Come on, Eleanor. Let me in on the secret."

"Give me the card." I made a leap for it, but she switched it to her other hand. "Damn it, Rose."

Rose's expression changed. "Oh my. Miss Goody Two Shoes used profanity. Here." She handed me the envelope.

I opened it, and the strong script leapt up from the card: "Please do forgive me, Ellie, and accept these with my sincerest apologies. You must know I'll never give up. Fondly, DD."

Rose peered over my shoulder. "Who's DD, and what did he do to you?"

I shoved the card back in the envelope and thrust it toward the boy.

"Please take them back."

He looked shocked. "Gosh, lady, I've never had anyone refuse flowers, let alone three times in a row. I'm not sure what to do."

"Do whatever you want with them. Donate them to Mount Sinai Hospital. I don't care." I walked away from him, not wanting to discuss it further. Daphne had sent flowers Saturday morning and yesterday morning, and I'd refused them both times. Curious as to how she knew where I worked, I surmised she must have contacted Mr. Marker. The gall she had, thinking she could buy me off that way.

Customers trickled into the diner. We'd already had our influx of the early morning crowd. These were the stragglers just before lunch, when workers bombarded us on their breaks.

Those moments with Daphne DeMonet passed through my mind, unbidden and intrusive, as the afternoon came and went. I tried to think of anything else other than the kiss we shared in the sanctuary of the garden.

Thankfully, five o'clock arrived. I untied my apron, grabbed my pocketbook from behind the counter, and began the walk to my apartment. At first, the presence of a car trailing behind me didn't register. But then I felt compelled to turn around as you do when you sense someone's watching you. The black Cadillac limousine inched next to the curb and pulled to a stop. The passenger-side back window rolled down.

"Ellie," an unmistakable voice called to me.

I kept walking.

The car edged up and kept pace with my hurried steps.

"Please, Ellie, don't make me get out of the car."

Daphne, wearing dark sunglasses and a scarf tied tight over her head, leaned out the window. "Please," she repeated.

I slowed down and approached the car.

She opened the door. "Come inside."

"Why should I?"

"Because I still need to talk to you."

I folded my arms over my chest. "I think you did quite enough talking Friday night."

"My behaviour was inappropriate. I'd like to ask you to reconsider the part."

"Didn't Mr. Marker call your studio and speak with Mr. Teller?" That hadn't been a fun conversation with Mr. Marker when I told him I'd decided not to take the part. He'd tried to find out what had happened between Thursday and Saturday morning when I'd phoned him at his office from a pay phone outside the diner.

"Yes, he did call. Frank let me know." Daphne held out her hand. "Please. Take a ride with me."

I debated one last time and moved to the opened door. She slid over to the other side to allow room.

"Perkins," she said, addressing the driver, "take us along the side streets for the next thirty minutes."

She'd dressed casually in brown trousers and a sleeveless, white cotton blouse. The multicoloured scarf did nothing to hide her beauty. She took off her sunglasses. I tried to calm the butterflies in my stomach and stared out the window to catch my breath.

Daphne touched my arm, and I jumped.

"I'm sorry. I didn't mean to startle you."

I mustered the courage to look at her but tried to focus on something else besides her eyes. My gaze dropped to her lips. The backyard and the garden appeared in my mind, and my legs no longer felt the cool leather of the backseat but rather the cool cement of the bench where we'd sat.

"Ellie? Did you hear me?"

My faced flushed with embarrassment. "What did you say? I'm sorry. It's not often I've ridden in a limousine." What a fumbled excuse.

"I said please don't allow my indiscretion to keep you from this opportunity. I promise it won't happen again."

"Why?" I cringed at my words. "I don't mean why won't it happen again, but why did you kiss me?"

She turned away. "I told you. It was a mistake on my part."

"That's not an answer, Daphne." I said her name for the first time without fear. It felt light on my tongue as I said it aloud, like cream soda fizz tickling my lips.

She shifted in the seat. "It may not be an answer, but I'm not sure you want to hear why I took the chance in kissing you."

The fluttering returned to my stomach. "Tell me."

She took a moment before speaking. "It was the way you looked at me at the party."

There it was. The feeling that had consumed me when I'd seen Daphne in her gown. I'd tried to tuck it away into a safe place in my mind, just as I'd tried to forget the sensuousness of the kiss. Both feelings had visited my dreams in the nights following the party.

"How… how did I look at you?" I asked, already knowing the answer but wanting to hear her say it.

"With desire." She rushed on with her words. "But it's my mistake, Ellie, and mine alone. I misread you. Can we get beyond this? And can you at least consider rejoining the picture? I'd hate what happened between us to keep you from pursuing your career."

My career wasn't even an issue at that moment. Knowing she'd read me perfectly was.

"I'll think about it."

Relief washed over her face. "That's all I ask. Thank you for listening. Where do you live? I'll have Perkins drive you home."

"You don't need to go out of your way." Embarrassment coursed through me as I pictured the run-down condition of my apartment building.

"It's no trouble at all. I insist."

Hearing the finality in her voice, I told Perkins my address. A few minutes later, we pulled up in front of the decrepit brick structure with its shutters hanging askew and the door in dire need of a heavy coat of paint.

Daphne showed no reaction to the state of my residence. She held out her hand.

"I hope to hear that Mr. Marker contacted Frank and that you're not dropping out."

I grasped her hand. The warmth of her touch rippled through my body like an electric current. When she let go, I had to bite my lip from gasping aloud with disappointment. I opened the door and stood outside the car.

"Take care, Ellie," she said from the open window.

"Yes. You, too." The sleek, black car drove down the street and disappeared around the corner. As I walked to the building entrance, there wasn't any doubt that I'd call Mr. Marker in the morning. I had no idea what I'd tell him other than I wanted back on the picture.

* * *

Thursday, 31 August 1950. "Quiet on the set!"

I moved behind the extras, who stood well out of camera range, and watched the scene before me. The set resembled an English pub. Daphne sat at a corner table with another actress whose name escaped me.

"Action!"

Gordon Scott, one of the hottest leading men in film, pushed through the door. Rugged, with thick dark hair, he was especially handsome in his Army uniform. He walked over to three similarly clad actors.

The scene ensued with Scott's friends daring him to talk to Daphne. Daphne and Gordon played off each other well and had for the three previous films they'd made. They were often linked together romantically in the trade papers. Thinking about that made my mind wander back to the party. Did she prefer both men and women? It was all so confusing to me.

Caught up in my musings, I missed Daphne's last line. Whatever it was must have been humorous because Gordon laughed. The laughter sounded so genuine, it made me want to join in.

"Cut!" Teller shouted. "That's a wrap until tomorrow, everyone. Nice work."

Daphne stood up and smoothed Gordon's lapels with her fingertips. They shared a muted conversation for several minutes. I noticed for the first time how tall Daphne was. I'd been so flustered at the party, I hadn't noticed anything but the heat of her touch. Gordon was probably six feet in height, which would make Daphne perhaps five-nine or five-ten.

As she talked, she moved her hands in graceful arcs with her fingers floating here and there like a ballerina's polished moves. Her high cheekbones and long lashes accentuated those dark eyes full of animation that never seemed to miss all that was around her.

I found myself smiling at the beauty of her grace.

She and Gordon broke off their conversation, and she went to Teller to speak with him. She motioned above at the lighting before she noticed me. Her face lit up as she waved me over.

"Ellie… I mean Eleanor, I'm so glad you reconsidered and are back with the picture. Frank, you remember Eleanor Burnett, don't you?"

He stood.

"Of course. Our wayward Brit." His smile took away any sting I may have felt from his words. "Marker and I spoke. We'll shoot your scene next week." One of the crew called him away.

"I really like that man," Daphne said. "He's always been fair with me, always respected my privacy. You have to be careful whom you can trust in this business. He's one I can rely on." She turned to me. "Have you eaten lunch?"

"No."

"Good. Why don't I have Perkins drive us to my house, and we can share a lunch out in the garden?"

"I don't want to impose."

"Don't be silly. I'm a rich and famous movie star. I can afford to have a friend over for lunch." She smiled. "You should see your expression. Yes, I'm rich, but I hope as we become better friends, you'll know when I'm pulling your leg. I'd want to have you over regardless of how much money I make. Oh, now I've made you blush. Come on, before I talk you out of lunch."

Unaware I'd agreed to go, I allowed her to lead me off the set to the lot where her limousine awaited. We stepped into the backseat.

"Watch this," she said, tapping on the dividing window. Perkins slid the glass aside. "Home, James." Daphne tossed her head back and laughed. Like at the party, the move drew my gaze down her neck to the hollow of her throat. "I love saying that because it's true. His name *is* James." She turned to me and her smile faded. "Eleanor, you shouldn't look at me that way."

"I'm sorry."

"Don't be sorry. It's just disconcerting to see that expression on your face."

"I wasn't aware I was looking at you any differently." I knew that was a lie as soon as the words left my mouth.

"Well, you were." Daphne gazed out the window and grew quiet.

Maybe this wasn't such a good idea. As the long minutes passed, the silence that fell between us bordered on uncomfortable. I debated about asking her to take me to my apartment, but we'd already reached her home.

Perkins opened the door before I had a chance to do so myself. I stepped out. Daphne moved around me toward the front door. Seeing the rigidity in her back, I hesitated following her.

She glanced over her shoulder. "Aren't you coming?"

I followed her inside. This time, I walked slowly through the foyer into the living room and took in the grandeur of her home. Her furniture was lush, but not garish, upholstered in mostly muted earth tones with an occasional splash of colour for contrast.

The artwork adorning the walls was modern, more modern than I would choose. Perhaps she'd purchased the most expensive prints. As we neared one painting, I viewed it more thoroughly and noticed "Picasso" scribbled in the bottom right-hand corner. Was this an original?

"Pablo gave that to me two years ago when we met on my vacation in the south of France. Charming man."

Her voice was close, close enough I could feel her breath against my ear. I gathered the courage to turn toward her. She'd fixed her gaze on the painting, her expression growing more intense. She lifted her hand and traced her fingers in the air above the painting as if her fingertips were an artist's brush. The move brought her even closer, her face inches from mine.

I was enthralled with the concentration with which she'd made the move and consumed with the desire to do the same thing with my fingertips but, instead, brush them against her skin. My eyes widened with the thought, and a fire began to burn low in my belly.

She looked at me then, and her mouth gaped open in surprise. She made no move toward me but also made no move to back away.

I had a choice to make. My heart pounded with the knowledge that the next few seconds would define who I was.

I watched in fascination as I lifted my hand to her face and touched her cheek ever so softly. I no longer had any control of my body and felt ethereal, seeing the scene unfold below me as if I were an angel floating above.

Her breath caught. It came to me then that perhaps she was just as scared and, dare I say, excited, as I.

I stared at her full lips and shifted my body so that we pressed together, our chests rising and falling as one. And I kissed her, at first tentative, but then more boldly when her mouth opened to allow me entrance if I chose to take the chance. When I dipped my tongue inside, her moan hummed against my lips, almost bringing me to my knees.

Daphne must have sensed this. She put one hand to the nape of my neck, the other to the small of my back, and pulled me tighter against her body.

My God. It was as if she were devouring me. But I didn't want the moment to end. I kissed her as I'd kissed no other. I kissed her as if I knew exactly what I was doing, as if I'd done this a million times before. The thought flew through my mind that I wanted to do this a million times more with her. Only her.

Daphne tore her mouth away and took a step back. "Eleanor."

"Ellie. You can call me Ellie, remember?" Now that we were apart, I only knew I wanted her mouth against mine again and inched toward her.

"No!" She pressed her hand against my chest but snatched it away as if she'd scalded it with the touch. "Please, don't."

"But I *want* to kiss you."

"Maybe I caused you to be confused. You're young. You probably aren't even sure—"

I placed my fingers to her lips. "Don't say it. Don't say I don't know what I want."

Daphne turned away. "Have you ever even been with a man?"

The question took me by surprise.

"Well, no, but that doesn't mean—"

She whirled around. "Oh, but it does mean exactly that. How do you know if what you're feeling isn't some sort of pent-up sexual frustration?"

I staggered backward as if she'd slapped me. Her eyes instantly filled with regret.

"I'm sorry," she said.

But I'd already started for the door.

"Wait, Ellie." She rushed to me and grabbed my arm. "You have to see this from my point of view. The other night, you told me you didn't feel this way about women, yet here you are, kissing me as if you'd kissed women before."

"Only you," I whispered. "You haven't thought to ask me how I feel. You've only told me how I should."

Daphne pressed the heel of her hand to her forehead. "You were so damn sure of yourself Friday night. How could I not react this way?"

"Ask me the question, Daphne."

"All right." She took a defiant stance. "How do you feel?"

I moved to her and ran my fingers through her thick, dark hair as I spoke. "When you kissed me Friday, you opened a part of me I'd locked away. For what, I never knew. It was frightening, yes. But I thought about you constantly, about how I felt when you pressed your hand against my knee. How I felt when our lips touched."

I searched her eyes that now brimmed with tears. "I began living that night in the garden. Up to that point, I'd only been breathing to survive." Speaking no longer became possible as she claimed me with a searing kiss. The fire down low in my belly dropped even lower between my legs.

Daphne ended the kiss and hugged me tight. "Ellie Burnett, you'll be the death of me."

Chapter 10

"Let's stop there," Eleanor said.

Bailey snapped her head up. "You've got to be kidding."

Chelsea was about to utter the same words but was glad Bailey beat her to it.

Eleanor laughed. "So now you're the impatient one."

"I noticed something in the diary," Chelsea said. "I love the way you spell certain words differently from ours like 'maneuver,' or 'color' with the 'u' added. It's much more poetic to read."

"I've lost a lot of my British way of speaking after living in the States all these years but not so much of the British way of writing, even today. Can't break all the old habits, nor would I want to." Eleanor glanced at her watch. "It's late morning. I need to take my medication and rest, but I have a wonderful idea. Let's not meet again until Friday evening when we'll break our pattern of early mornings. Join me for dinner."

"Sure," Bailey said, "but I can't believe you'll make us wait until then."

"Don't you know by now that the longer things are drawn out, the more you can savor the shared moments? What about you, Chelsea?"

Chelsea squirmed under Eleanor's intense gaze. "I'm sorry, but I won't be able to make it."

"Do you have a date?" Eleanor asked.

Chelsea almost blurted out, "It's none of your damn business." This woman was insufferable.

"Yes."

Bailey stiffened beside her.

"Bailey, it seems it's just you and me. And before you ask, Doctor Parker, we may discuss my relationship with Daphne and we may not. It depends on my mood." She rose from her chair. "I'll see you Friday night," she said to Bailey. "If you'd like to come Saturday afternoon, I'd be happy to talk with you, Chelsea."

Eleanor entered her home, and Chelsea turned to Bailey. She'd already left for the front of the house. Chelsea thought of hurrying to catch up to her before she drove away, but she didn't know what she'd say.

* * *

Chelsea approached the hostess at Lorenzo's. "My friend might already be here. Her last name is Simmons."

The hostess ran her finger down the list. "Yes, right this way." She led Chelsea to the back. After noticing that all of the tables were occupied, Chelsea was glad Rebecca had made reservations.

Rebecca stood when Chelsea and the hostess approached.

"You look lovely tonight, Chelsea." Rebecca pulled out her chair for her and sat back down.

Chelsea had debated for a half an hour on her wardrobe, switching from dressed up to casual and back to dressed up. She settled on a pair of black jeans with a mint green silk blouse tucked in and a soft leather woven belt to complete the ensemble. She tried to push from her mind that the belt had been a gift from Bailey. She'd chosen a pair of dangling earrings to match the color of the blouse, added more makeup than what she wore at school, and pushed her hair up off her neck with a gold barrette.

"You look nice, too, Rebecca." Rebecca was more dressed up than Chelsea had ever seen her at school with a white cotton shirt, black jacket, and black slacks.

They decided to share a bottle of wine. The waiter filled their glasses and took their order.

After he left the table, Rebecca spoke. "I hope this doesn't come out the wrong way, because trust me, I'm not complaining. But what made you agree to this date?"

Chelsea had to keep herself from flinching at the word "date" even though Eleanor had used that same word. She'd feigned a casual air she didn't feel when she'd answered yes to Eleanor's inquiry. She took a sip of wine while she pondered her response.

"I thought it would do me good to get out, and you've been so patient with me. I guess I thought, why not?"

Rebecca grinned and raised her glass. "Lucky me."

The waiter brought their entrées. As they ate, they discussed their preparations for the next year, with Chelsea offering further book suggestions for Rebecca's curriculum.

"How's your interview going with Eleanor Burnett?"

Chelsea hesitated before responding, afraid they were about to delve into a discussion about Bailey. "Very well."

Rebecca must have sensed it was a sensitive subject. They shifted the conversation back to school and the approaching semester until they finished their meals. Rebecca attempted to pay for the bill, but Chelsea insisted they go Dutch. They walked out to their cars, reaching Chelsea's first.

"I had a nice time, Rebecca."

"Would you like to follow me to my place and have one more glass of wine together?"

Chelsea hesitated.

"Or maybe a glass of water or soda," Rebecca said with a nervous laugh.

Chelsea thought of so many reasons why it wasn't a good idea, but she agreed.

*   *   *

She followed Rebecca into her small, brick, off-campus home. The living room was masculine with sports memorabilia hanging on the walls. Some framed photos caught Chelsea's attention. She walked over to them while Rebecca went to the kitchen to get soft drinks. In one photo, a very young Rebecca was pitching in a softball game, the ball a blur as it left her hand.

"My perfect game from college," Rebecca said, offering Chelsea a bottle of Sprite. "It's probably egotistical of me to have it hanging up—"

"No, no. It's not. You should be very proud." Chelsea twisted off the lid of the bottle.

They stood staring at each other until Rebecca said, "Let's sit down."

They sat on the couch and grew quiet. Chelsea wondered why she'd decided to come to Rebecca's home. Was it a test? A test for her heart? She turned to speak and found Rebecca inches from her face.

"I want to kiss you," Rebecca said. "But I want you to tell me it's okay."

Was it okay? How would she know unless she allowed it to happen? She nodded. They set their drinks down.

Rebecca touched her lips to Chelsea's. Chelsea's mind raced. Rebecca's mouth felt so different from Bailey's. Rebecca ran her tongue across Chelsea's lower lip. Chelsea opened her mouth, and they battled for dominance as Rebecca eased her back onto the couch and rubbed her thumb across Chelsea's nipple.

Chelsea moaned at the contact. It'd been so long since a woman had touched her like this. Rebecca undid the first two buttons of Chelsea's blouse and inched her hand inside, enclosing Chelsea's breast in her palm. She plucked Chelsea's nipple, and it grew even harder. Chelsea wasn't aware that Rebecca had unbuttoned her blouse more until Rebecca withdrew from the kiss and pressed her mouth against the pulse point of Chelsea's neck on her way down her chest. She pushed Chelsea's bra up to free her breast, captured her nipple between her lips, and nibbled at it lightly with her teeth. A gush of wetness soaked Chelsea's panties, and she arched up into Rebecca's embrace.

Bailey. God, Bailey, it's been so long. Chelsea tried to imagine it was Bailey's mouth on her, possessing her as she had all those times.

Rebecca unclasped her belt. The belt Bailey had bought her in Madrid. Chelsea grabbed Rebecca's hand and stilled it.

"Come on, Chelsea, I can tell how much you want this."

That sounded too much like a line from a teenager trying to score. Chelsea opened her eyes, jarred even more into reality with seeing the contrast between Rebecca's dark hair and Bailey's sandy blonde. *I can't do this.*

"Stop. Please stop."

Rebecca sat up. "Are you sure?"

Chelsea nodded. She reached down, tugged her bra back into place, and straightened her belt. She began buttoning her blouse.

"Wow," Rebecca said. "Okay. I read you wrong, I guess." She seemed miffed from her expression and the tightness of her tone.

Chelsea stood up abruptly. "I'm sorry I let it get that far." She walked to the door. Rebecca came up behind her and reached for the doorknob. In making the move, her arm brushed against Chelsea's overly sensitive nipple. Chelsea bit her lip to keep from gasping aloud.

"I understand," Rebecca said as she opened the door.

Chelsea stepped down the stairs.

"But if you ever get over her, I'm still interested."

Chelsea faltered in her gait before continuing to her car. She threw her purse on the passenger seat, slammed the door behind her, and slapped her palms against the steering wheel.

"Damn it, Bailey, this is all your fault."

* * *

"I'm afraid only five minutes have passed since you last checked, my dear."

Bailey thought she was being discreet, but Eleanor had caught her glancing at the clock. They were sitting at Eleanor's dining room table, playing another round of five hundred rummy.

"And if you don't pay better attention, you'll owe me another quarter." Eleanor picked up the discarded ten, laid down four of them, and tossed her last card into the pile.

"Crap." Bailey grabbed the pad of paper. She tallied the cards in her hand and subtracted from her total. "I think that put you over the top. Again."

Eleanor went to the refrigerator. "I used to drink these warm, but Daph got me in the habit of chilling them the American way." She reached inside and brought over two bottles of Landlord Strong Pale Ale. "Here. Twist these open for us," she said, handing Bailey the bottles. "I think this is much better for you than that silly Coke you're drinking."

Niles appeared at the entryway to the dining room. "If you don't need me, madam, I'll be off to bed." He glanced at the two bottles of beer, but his professional expression remained firmly in place.

"We're fine, Niles. I have it in hand."

After he left, Bailey twisted off both lids and held her bottle up to the light. "Why do I think this will knock me on my arse, as you British like to say?"

"I don't know. You seem like you're capable of handling yourself." Eleanor clinked her bottle against Bailey's. "Cheers."

"Cheers."

"Have you thought of phoning her later?"

"Who?" Bailey was beginning to love Eleanor even more as she watched her tilt back her bottle.

"Please don't insult my intelligence and pretend you don't know the person I'm talking about."

Bailey took a drag of her beer. "I don't think calling her would be too smart."

"It might be an even better idea than what you're thinking."

"Oh yeah? Why?"

Eleanor leaned her elbows on the table, her expression intense. "Because her heart wasn't in this date tonight."

Bailey wanted to believe what Eleanor was saying, but too

much insecurity had piled up brick by brick over the past eleven months. "And you can tell this by her declaration that, yes, she had a date."

"Let's say I do have a few more years of experience living with the same woman in a relationship than the two of you. Chelsea's struggling. Struggling to move on in her life, attempting to latch onto someone or something else, but I'm telling you that it won't happen."

"I suppose you're going to tell me how you know this."

Eleanor scowled at Bailey. "English ale brings out the smart-ass in you, doesn't it?"

"I'm sorry, Eleanor. I'm scared to put myself out there. It was so painful when we split up."

"Daphne was a lot like Chelsea. She sometimes was afraid of her own shadow, as if she couldn't believe we had the happiness we shared. That maybe we didn't deserve it. She pulled a lot of stupid stunts because of her fear."

"How did you overcome that?" Bailey asked.

"Initially, I confronted her about her indiscretions. She'd never been in anything close to a lasting relationship. She'd had numerous brief affairs. We got past those, and when I thought we had smooth sailing, she got married." The same look of pain flickered over Eleanor's face. "Although you and I could talk about this in more depth, I do want to be fair with Chelsea, even though I love to tease her so."

Bailey glanced at her watch. "It's 10:30. I should go." She finished off her beer. "This is excellent, by the way."

"I don't drink very often. Only special occasions, and this is one of them. There's a college pub in town that carries this ale. I have them drive a case out to me every six months or so."

They rose from the table.

"Can I give you a hug?" Bailey asked. She knew it wasn't the most professional thing to do in her line of work, but she felt she'd already crossed the line between professional and personal behavior.

Eleanor held out her arms. "It'll be all right. Please promise me you'll call her tonight."

"I don't know. It's late."

They withdrew from the embrace. Eleanor gripped Bailey's chin—a little forcibly. "Don't make me get ugly."

"No, we wouldn't want that to happen."

Eleanor walked her to the door and waved when Bailey drove away.

Bailey pulled to a stop at the end of the drive. She unclipped her cell phone from her belt and stared at the lit display as she debated about following through. She punched in Chelsea's number. She may have removed it from her speed dial, but she hadn't forgotten it.

"Hello? Bailey?"

Bailey sucked in her breath. "Chels, hey. Um… how are you?" She grimaced. *Lame, lame, lame.*

"I'm fine." There was a slight pause. "You're not checking up on me, are you?"

"No, no. Absolutely not. I… I …" She slapped her forehead with the palm of her hand. "This was a bad idea. I'm sorry I called." Bailey was about to hang up, but Chelsea's voice stopped her.

"Wait. It's okay."

"Yeah?"

"Yes. I'm glad you still care enough to see how I'm doing."

"Of course I still care. I've never stopped caring." Bailey chewed on her lower lip as she thought of telling Chelsea she'd never stopped loving her. There was silence, broken up with a few sniffles. "Chels? You're not crying, are you?"

"Maybe." Another loud sniff.

Bailey wanted to be there with her and hold her. She took a breath of courage. "Can I come over?" She awaited Chelsea's answer, every muscle taut with tension.

"I'm not sure that would be such a good idea."

Bailey slumped in her seat. "Sure, sure. I understand."

"It's very sweet of you, but I'm a mess right now and need some time to regroup."

Bailey stiffened. "Did she hurt you?"

"No, she didn't hurt me." Chelsea laughed softly. "Still the protector, huh?"

"I don't ever want to see you hurt."

"I'm fine, really. The date didn't end well, but I'm okay. How about I see you tomorrow afternoon at Eleanor's like we originally agreed?"

"As long as you're okay." Bailey listened for any change in Chelsea's voice to tell her Chelsea wasn't being honest.

"Don't worry. I'll see you tomorrow."

"Sure."

"Good night, Bailey."

"Chels?"

"Yes?"

"Never mind. Good night."

Bailey shut her phone and pulled onto the state road. Maybe Eleanor really did know what she was talking about.

Chelsea set the phone on the end table. She lifted her legs onto the couch and brought her glass of wine with her. She rolled the glass back and forth between her fingers.

Bailey called. A slight smile tugged at her lips. Bailey called, and Chelsea liked it. She took a sip of wine. The warmth of the liquid slid down her throat as she allowed the thought to sink into her consciousness.

Chapter 11

Chelsea pulled into Eleanor's roundabout. Bailey's Jeep wasn't there yet. She thought she'd feel smug satisfaction but instead felt disappointment. She tried sorting through that as she approached the door. It swung open before she had a chance to ring the bell.

"Come inside, Chelsea." Eleanor seemed refreshed today. "It's a bit too hot out there this afternoon. Why don't we sit in the living room?"

Chelsea followed her and stood in front of the plush couch to which Eleanor had gestured.

"I'll get us some refreshments. I gave Niles the afternoon off," Eleanor said and left Chelsea alone.

Chelsea studied the room, her gaze finally landing on the almost life-size portrait above the mantel. It was an exquisite painting. She smiled at Daphne's cocky grin and Eleanor's obvious shyness. She tried to picture Bailey and her posing the same way.

"Fascinating painting, isn't it?"

She turned around. Bailey stood there, her hair still wet from a shower. She focused on the painting before locking gazes with Chelsea.

Chelsea felt transported back in time to the café where they'd first met. Bailey was the young grad student who took her breath away that afternoon just as she did now.

"I see you've made it," Eleanor said from behind them. "I left the door open, hoping you'd get the hint to walk in." She entered the living room carrying a tray that Bailey took from her and set on the coffee table. "Sit next to Chelsea and grab a soda. I'll sit over here."

Chelsea reached for a Sprite from the tray at the same time as Bailey.

"You can have that one," Bailey said, taking the bottle of Coke.

Eleanor sat down in her wingback chair. "You've told me how you met," she said as she folded her hands in her lap. "But I'd like to hear more about the two of you and your relationship. What was it like the first time you made love?"

Chelsea sputtered on her mouthful of Sprite. Fizz shot up her nose and a round of coughing ensued.

Bailey pounded her back lightly. "You okay?"

When Chelsea finally caught her breath, she said, "Yeah. Sure. I'm okay after that totally personal question."

"Please," Eleanor said. "If I'm about to divulge intimate details of my first time making love with *anyone*, you can surely tell me about your first encounter with Bailey. Because I bet it wasn't your first time. Am I right?"

Heat rushed to Chelsea's cheeks. "That would be correct." Bailey had continued making smoothing motions on her back. Her hand fell away, and Chelsea felt the loss of the touch. "I had dated someone in undergrad, but it didn't last."

"And you?" Eleanor asked Bailey.

"I'd had fumbled exchanges in high school and college, but nothing serious. That changed when I met Chelsea."

"And?"

"I can't believe we're talking about this." Chelsea set her bottle down and held her head in her hands.

"My dear, if I show you mine, you should at least have the courtesy to show me yours."

"That's one way of putting it," Chelsea muttered. "We'd gone out, what, for three weeks?" she asked Bailey.

"Give or take."

"One night, Bailey came over to watch a movie at my place and—"

"What movie?" Eleanor asked with interest.

"*The Ghost and Mrs. Muir*," Chelsea and Bailey answered at the same time. They grinned at each other.

"Very romantic. Gene Tierney was so beautiful. She reminded me of my Daphne."

"I love that movie. And when I found out that Bailey did, too, well, I felt an even stronger attraction to her." Chelsea chanced a quick look to find Bailey smiling. "She had the DVD. We both watched and cried when Rex Harrison leaned over Gene Tierney, said goodbye, and faded into nothing."

"When it ended, I told Chelsea why I loved the movie and what it meant to me and—"

"I kissed her. We'd kissed before, but this was different. The kiss lingered and became more passionate. Then, Bailey led us down the hallway and suddenly stopped." Chelsea laughed. "She asked, 'Uh, where's your bedroom?' It was priceless. It was there, standing in the hall, seeing her embarrassment that I fell in love with her."

"You never told me that," Bailey said.

"You never asked. When I led you to the bedroom and you were so tender and giving while we made love... There was no going back for me."

Bailey took hold of her hand and brought it to her lips, but then, as though she realized the intimacy of her action, she pulled back. "Sorry." She let go and inched away to leave a space between them.

Chelsea's heart ached. The distance was maybe an inch, but it felt like a chasm—an insurmountable chasm.

"Thank you both for sharing," Eleanor said. She took down the diary from the mantel and handed it to Bailey. "This time, no excuses. You're reading. You'll notice I've marked a passage several months later."

Bailey opened the diary. "Tell me we didn't skip over the good parts."

"Are you one of those who flip through romance novels for only the sex scenes?" Eleanor asked with a bemused expression.

"N-no."

Chelsea snorted.

"I don't!"

"Whatever you say, Bailey."

"Hey, don't patronize me."

Eleanor interrupted their bickering. "Girls, do you want to argue, or do you want to hear what happens next?"

Bailey sat up straighter and cleared her throat.

"Friday, 3 November 1950. Tonight's the big movie premiere of *The Brave Few*. I'd never attended one and would have loved to sit next to Daphne at the cinema. But the studio had already arranged everything. Gordon Scott would accompany her as always..."

Chapter 12

Daphne had explained how things worked. How the studio needed her to maintain appearances. Showing up with me on her arm wasn't an option. I was, however, still there, seated a row behind her. She'd smile at something Gordon said and then turn her head to grace me with a look only the two of us shared.

Our intimacy had progressed since August when I quit fighting my feelings toward her. Mostly, the intimacy had manifested itself as heavy petting. A touch here. A caress there. The destination loomed before me, but Daphne was allowing me to choose when we'd arrive.

The Brave Few moved frame by frame until it reached the pub scene where I made my entrance. I mouthed my line along with my larger-than-life image on the screen.

Daphne's on-screen character answered my question about her choice of "on the rocks or straight up" with, "Whatever you want to bring me. You look like a woman who knows exactly what someone needs."

I sank a little farther down into my seat and glanced at the people around me. Couldn't they see the want in my eyes as I stood beside Daphne? Didn't they catch the quick quirk of her lips as she spoke her lines? How she leaned toward me with each passing second of our screen time?

Instead, the capacity crowd focused on the humour and erupted with raucous laughter. Daphne laughed with them and turned to wink at me.

The remainder of the film flew by. When "The End" appeared on the screen, the houselights came up and everyone stood. They turned toward Daphne and Gordon and applauded for several long minutes.

I moved along my row with the others filing out into the aisle. Frank and Gordon had already engaged Daphne in conversation as they inched their way out of the cinema. Hanging back, I allowed myself the pleasure of enjoying the smooth tan shoulders that peeked from her gown. The shoulders where I'd placed my lips in the fading hours of the previous evening. We'd stopped then, as we'd stopped so many other times.

The night air was cool, so I lifted my shawl up a little higher to take away the chill. Daphne did the same. Flashbulbs pulsed around her and Gordon, but neither blinked. Gordon kissed Daphne's cheek, which set off shrieks from the young women pressed against the velvet rope in front of the cinema.

I tried to shake off the image. Tried to convince myself it was all part of the business. But my stomach clenched when she kissed him back on the mouth. In a rush, I pushed past the cinema patrons, extras, and bit actors, the screaming fans who held out their pens and autograph books to anyone who seemed like someone. Apparently, I didn't pass inspection, because no one stopped me as I approached the curb to hail a cab. I ignored the movement of the crowd behind me as they followed Daphne and Gordon to their limousine. A cab rolled to a stop, but before I got into the backseat, their limousine cruised to a stop behind the cab. Perkins honked the horn.

I waved the taxi on and walked back to the limousine. The back door opened. Daphne gave me a "come hither" look, but this time, it wouldn't work.

"Get in," Daphne said.

I hesitated, still a little miffed over the second kiss.

"Come on, Ellie. I know why you're angry. Please get in, and we'll talk on the way home." She slid closer to Gordon and patted the seat.

I glared at Gordon. "I don't think you need me."

"Oh, come on, sugar. Don't be sore at Daphne. It's all part of the act." Gordon flashed one of his megawatt smiles that melted the hearts of thousands of women and moved mine enough to get inside. Perkins pulled away as soon as I shut the door behind me.

"So…" Daphne said.

Trying to ignore her intoxicating perfume, I did my best to maintain my dour expression. "So."

We drove in silence until Gordon tapped on the dividing window. Perkins powered the glass open.

"The next turn, Perkins, my good man."

I looked to where Gordon pointed. What could possibly be down that darkened alley? We stopped outside a nondescript door with one dim light bulb hanging overhead. Two men exited the building. I gaped as they moved off into the shadows, groping at each other, oblivious to our presence.

"Darling, this is where I bid you a fond goodnight." He kissed Daphne on the cheek again and stepped out of the car. He walked around the back and motioned for me to roll down my window. I fumbled with the unfamiliar switch before powering it down. Leaning inside, he startled me with a kiss on my cheek. "You take good care of my Daphne." Gordon slapped the roof of the car and waved as he entered the club.

I sat there, mute, unable to comprehend what I'd witnessed. Perkins backed out of the alley and started the drive to Daphne's mansion.

Daphne turned to me. "There's something you should know about Gordon."

"Before that happened, I would've sworn he was madly in love with you."

"No. He is, however, madly in love with Quinn Tucker."

"Quinn Tucker? The movie star?"

"Yes," Daphne said. "Quinn Tucker the movie star who makes a living playing in rough and rowdy westerns."

"But what about the club? Why would he go there?"

"He and Quinn have an agreement. It's an open relationship. They still love each other, but it doesn't mean they can't enjoy other men."

This line of talk made me uncomfortable. Is that what she did? Kept one at home while dabbling with others? "I had no idea about Gordon."

"You're not supposed to have any idea, Ellie. That's the point. Within the industry, we know who's homosexual and who isn't, and we do our best to protect one another. Gordon and I don't do anything to dispel the rumours that link us together romantically."

"I hate you have to live this way." I was still too scared to include myself in the equation.

Daphne gazed out the window, the headlights of the passing cars reflected on her face. "You'll need to get used to it because it won't change anytime soon. In fact, I can't see it ever changing. Let's face it. How would the typical moviegoer react if they knew that when I'm up on the screen kissing Gordon or another lead actor, I'm not enjoying it and that I'd rather be kissing a woman?" Her voice held a sadness that I hadn't heard from her before. "It's the price I pay for being who I am and doing the work I do. But that doesn't make it any easier on you or make this any fairer."

"No, it doesn't," I said softly.

Perkins pulled up to the gate at the mansion. Dorian, the guard, swung the gate aside for us to pass through.

"I won't need you until Monday morning," Daphne told Perkins as she got out of the car.

He touched his fingers to the bill of his hat. "Ma'am. Have an enjoyable weekend."

"You too, James."

As always, the lights were already on when we entered the home. Something about Daphne not liking to come home to a dark house. She let her shawl slide off her shoulders and tossed it on the chair.

"Here. Let me take yours." She stood behind me, placed her hands on my shoulders, and with a sensuous touch, slid the shawl down to the floor. She bent over and kissed my neck. I shuddered at the contact. Walking around me, she tilted up my chin with her finger and brushed her lips against mine. "Why don't we take that opened bottle of wine from the ice box with us into the bedroom?"

My stomach quivered. "Okay."

"You get the wine and glasses, and I'll meet you upstairs."

Somehow, my shaky legs carried me into the kitchen, which was miraculous considering the distance I had to traverse from the foyer. I reached inside the ice box and lifted out the bottle, grabbed two wine glasses, and flipped off my heels before attempting the winding staircase. My bare feet sank into the plush carpet as I walked down the long hallway for only the second time. Daphne had showed me the upstairs when we first began seeing one another, but she'd never made a move to carry our ardour up to her bedroom. Until tonight.

I cradled the wine bottle against my body and took a deep breath before opening the door.

Bent over, she was lighting a candle to join the other lit candles placed throughout the room. She turned around, and I almost dropped the bottle of wine. She'd changed into a lavender floor-length nightgown with a neckline revealing the swell of her breasts. Her long, dark hair hung loose on her bare shoulders. She moved toward me slowly. My gaze dropped to the way the gown clung to her lithe frame and to the hardened nipples pressing against the material.

"Let me have these." Daphne took the bottle and glasses and set them on the dresser. After popping the cork, she filled both glasses halfway. She handed me a glass and clinked it lightly with her own. "To us." The light from the candles danced across her face as she drained her wine.

At first, I took a small sip, but under the scrutiny of her heated stare, I finished the rest off in one big gulp.

"I know this might be a little frightening, Ellie." She set her glass on the dresser, took mine, and placed it next to hers. She brushed her thumb along my cheek. "But I think it's time, don't you?"

I swallowed hard as Daphne leaned in and placed her lips on mine. Willingly, I allowed her to lead me wherever this night would end. Our kiss deepened. When I felt like I couldn't stand on my wobbly legs any longer, she broke away, clasped my hand, and moved us to the side of the bed.

"We'll take this as slow as you need to." She reached behind my back and unzipped my dress. "We'll go at your pace," she whispered as she slid the dress to the floor. "You only need tell me if you're uncomfortable." She pulled down the straps of my bra and kissed the skin above my breasts. "Are you uncomfortable?"

I couldn't speak. Instead, I answered with my actions. I unclasped my bra and held it in place one last second before allowing it to drop to my feet.

"My God, look at you, Ellie."

Her gaze swept my skin like a thousand tiny pinpricks. My cheeks burned, and my nipples grew harder with each passing second.

She took one nipple in her mouth and tweaked the other until it was almost painful to the touch. The rush of heat between my legs wasn't unexpected. I'd felt it before when we'd kissed and touched through our clothing. But the rush of wetness was new. New and wondrous. I moaned as she continued sucking on my nipple before moving over to the other. I brought my hands to her head and pulled her tight against me.

"Daphne, I don't think I can stand any longer," I said, my voice ragged.

"Of course you can't, darling." She pushed me against the bed until I fell back and felt the cool sheets against my skin. "Why don't we shed these as well?" She hooked her thumbs into the waistband of my panties, slid them down, and tossed them onto the floor.

Before I had the chance to ask her to disrobe, she stood and moved in tantalizing slowness, baring more skin with each inching down of material. I stared at her full, round breasts. Her waist was slim and her abdomen firm, her hips perfectly curved. An image of the Venus de Milo materialised in my mind. I dropped my gaze to the patch of hair between her legs and didn't realise how long I stared until her words shook me from my stupor.

"Do you like what you see?" Her voice was low and husky.

I could only nod.

She knelt beside me on the bed and trailed her fingertips down the hollow of my throat, placing a passing glance against my chest before continuing down my legs. I shut my eyes when she touched the inside of my thighs until I felt the mattress shift as she moved on top of me.

She kissed my throat, somehow knowing how much pressure to apply with her tongue to give me the most pleasure. I stretched my neck to allow her further access and felt her smile against my skin as she moved lower, once again taking a nipple into her mouth. I arched off the bed, gasping aloud.

Her hand dipped between my legs. "Open yourself to me, my love," she said as she gently pressed my thighs apart.

I did as she asked, not thinking, only feeling. Her long fingers slid through my wetness.

"Oh, Daphne." My hips jerked at her touch.

"Tell me where it feels good."

I bit my lip hard, frightened when I tasted blood.

She rose above me, and her expression darkened with smouldering desire. She ran her fingers through my wet folds again. "Where, Ellie?"

"Oh, God, there. Please," I whimpered, knowing what I was asking for, but not too proud to beg.

She brought her lips to mine and continued her pressure below. I was building to something exquisite as the pleasure mounted.

"Trust me," Daphne whispered. And then she slid inside of me.

I had thought I would feel pain, but instead, I felt an intense need to move my hips higher. I pleaded with my body for her to go even farther.

She plunged deep inside while continuing pressure with her thumb against the other sensitive spot that only my own hand had touched before. "Let go. Let go just for me."

I grabbed hold of the sheets and balled them in my hands. Stars appeared behind my clenched eyelids. As I was about to scream out her name, Daphne thrust her tongue inside my mouth and swallowed my release.

Again and again, she moved deep inside until I slumped back against the mattress.

She slowly withdrew her fingers and lay beside me, opening her arms. "Come here, darling."

I struggled with my limp body to fall into her embrace, mortified when I burst into tears.

Daphne tensed. "Please tell me I didn't hurt you or that you didn't want—"

I placed my fingertips against her lips and shook my head into her chest.

"No. It was beautiful. I don't know what else to say except your passion takes my breath away. But I want to give you the same pleasure. Tell me how."

She kissed my forehead. "In time. For now, let me hold you."

I shifted even closer and allowed her to do just that.

Almost complete darkness greeted me when I awakened. Disoriented, I took time to adjust my eyes until I became aware of objects in the room. They appeared almost unearthly from the dim light of the candle beside the bed. The other candles had burned out during the night. Memories rushed back to me. And with the memories came an awareness of the sexual being who lay beside me.

I rose onto my elbow and looked at her face, so peaceful in repose, her full lips blowing out soft puffs of breath. My gaze dropped to her breasts. I raised a tentative hand and placed the lightest of touches on her nipple, fascinated when it grew and hardened. She murmured in her sleep and turned her head to the side, but she didn't awaken.

Emboldened now, I leaned over and took the nipple in my mouth and gently sucked, just as she'd done. I became lost in the moment and in the feelings this woman stirred deep inside me.

Fingers brushed through my hair. I stopped what I was doing and looked up at her. There was enough light for me to see the desire there.

"What do you like, Daphne?" I asked in a voice that sounded so unlike my own.

"You're doing fine," she whispered.

I ran my tongue across her nipple and held her other breast in the palm of my hand.

Daphne took my hand and pushed it lower until I felt the heat between her thighs. She opened her legs and led me to her wetness.

"Do you feel that?" she gasped.

I slipped my fingers into her folds and moaned, knowing that I had caused this reaction. My lips. My touch. Me.

Her hips rose and fell as I moved in time with her rhythm.

"Inside. Please go—"

I plunged deep inside and took her, just as she'd asked. She threw her head back, the veins pulsing in her neck as she strained for release. Enthralled, I watched the naked need play across her beautiful face.

Daphne's body tightened as she edged closer to orgasm. Unlike her, I didn't kiss her at that exact moment. I wanted to hear her. I wanted to hear her scream my name. I pushed into her one last time.

"Ellie! Oh, God, Ellie!"

I waited until she relaxed and then withdrew my hand, sliding my fingers up into her wetness again before I leaned over to give her a soft, gentle kiss. Her breathing returned to normal as I lay beside her.

"Where did you learn to do that?" she finally said.

"From you and how you make me feel. I want to give to you as much as you give to me. I… I love you, Daphne."

She stiffened then. I waited to hear the same words from her. She opened her eyes, but I wasn't certain what I saw there. I didn't have time to think about it further because in a quick move, she was on top of me. Kissing me, touching me, in such a frenetic way that my mind couldn't keep up with all of the feelings pulsing through my body.

That Daphne hadn't told me she loved me slipped into the darkness, swallowed by my cries of more… more… more…

Chapter 13

Bailey didn't wait for Eleanor to tell her to stop. She closed the diary with shaky hands and willed her heart rate to return to normal.

The only sound in the living room was the ticking of the clock. She didn't know how much time had passed until she raised her head, not daring to look at Chelsea.

"That..." Bailey stopped and cleared her throat. "That was amazing."

Eleanor wasn't looking at her, but at Chelsea. "Yes, it was. No matter how many nights we shared after that night, that one was the most remarkable. The taste of the wine, the flickering of the candles, the feel of the sheets against my skin. Everything. It's as if it were yesterday, not over sixty years ago." She turned to Bailey. "I'm sure you feel the same way about your first night together."

Bailey drew in a breath, afraid she was about to break down. She wasn't expecting this reaction, just as she wasn't expecting the touch of Chelsea's hand on hers as she intertwined their fingers.

"Are you all right?" Chelsea asked.

Bailey met her gaze and saw the woman she'd felt this same passion for. It was too much. She stood up abruptly. "I'm not sure I can do this, Eleanor." She made a quick dash to the door.

"Bailey." Chelsea rose to go after her, but Eleanor's voice kept her rooted to the spot.

"Let her go, dear."

"I should see if she's okay."

"Why don't you sit back down, and you and I can chat."

Chelsea uneasily obliged.

"Don't act like you're about to be interrogated by the CIA," Eleanor said.

"I shouldn't be leery?"

Eleanor chuckled. "I didn't say that. Maybe an hour or two on the rack will get you to open up."

Chelsea relaxed. "I get it. You're teasing me."

Eleanor's expression grew serious. "Bailey's hurting. I don't know if you've noticed."

"I'm not sure what I can do to help her."

"Do you still love her?"

Chelsea hung her head. "Sometimes love isn't enough."

"Oh, Chelsea. That sounds like a line from a grade-B movie given by a woman who doesn't believe what she's saying."

"It's true," Chelsea said with some exasperation.

"Think about that statement. Really think about it. How can love not be enough? Because if you have love, as you and Bailey did and still do, you work through all of the other malarkey."

"We tried—"

"No, I don't think you did. You took the easy way out and parted amicably, as everyone likes to say these days."

Chelsea's anger flared. "How could you know? You and Daphne were together for sixty years. You had something that's so rare."

"And you think we had it easy?" Eleanor snapped. "You think we didn't work at it? Do you think it didn't cut me to the core when she married?"

"I assumed the studio arranged the marriage as a front and that you and Daphne still saw each other."

"We'll talk more about that later when we get there in the diary." Eleanor pursed her lips. "We had such a complicated relationship, and the years were full of ups and downs, twists and turns. It was like a rollercoaster. Do you remember that exhilarated feeling you have while you're riding it? Your stomach's in your throat, and your blood's pounding in your ears. And then you step off the coaster onto solid ground. Your legs are wobbly. You're disoriented. But you remember what happens next, don't you?"

"I want to ride it again."

"Exactly. Somewhere along the way, you and she forgot to enjoy the ride. And worse, you forgot how to get back on the coaster when you thought the ride was over."

"What do we do to get back?" Chelsea asked, feeling at the moment that Eleanor held all the answers to the universe.

"You have to figure it out yourselves. Daphne and I had friends throughout the years who were there for us, encouraging us and offering support. But we were the only ones able to unlock the secret to our happiness. No one else."

Chelsea mulled over Eleanor's words.

"Try to wipe away that worried expression, young lady. You have a whole life ahead of you. You don't need the answers to everything overnight. But"—Eleanor held up an index finger—"but you don't let go of a nine-year relationship without putting up a fight, no matter when that fight might be. Eleven months ago." She smiled gently. "Or eleven months later."

Chelsea glanced at the clock. "I need to go. Even though you're not allowing us to tape our readings, I try to get everything down as quickly as possible after I leave."

Eleanor followed her to the door. "Why don't you write down some of your thoughts over what we discussed? My diary is proof that it doesn't hurt."

"That's not a bad idea."

"When you do talk with Bailey, which I hope is tonight, tell her we'll meet again Monday at nine in the morning. I trust she'll return."

Chelsea waved at Eleanor and drove away. Her thoughts returned to Bailey and the lost expression on her face as she bolted from the house. Chelsea wondered if they'd ever reconnect on the same level as when they'd met. For the first time in almost a year, she was willing to try.

* * *

Silently berating herself for her reaction at Eleanor's, Bailey tried to concentrate on her driving as she waited for Joanne to pick up on the other end of the line.

Joanne answered. "How goes it?"

Bailey stopped at a red light, checked to her left, and turned onto the main road that took her into town. "I think I want out, Joanne."

"What? You really can't sit in the same room with Chelsea and simply focus on your job?"

"No, I'm not sure I can."

There was a long pause. "At least tell me how the interview is going so far."

Bailey thought a moment before trying to describe what she and Chelsea were doing. "It's not really an interview."

"Then what is it?"

"She's asked us to read out loud from her diary."

"She has a diary?"

Bailey pictured the plump, middle-aged biographer snapping to attention with the knowledge that Eleanor had kept a journal of her life with Daphne.

"Is there any way you could convince her to take the diary with—"

"Okay. This is where Joanne Addison has entered fantasyland and left all reason behind."

"There's no need to get sarcastic."

"If you've been through what I've been through, you'd understand how ridiculous that proposition is. How much can I stress this? Eleanor Burnett is in complete control. The only way she'll allow us to interview her is if we read from her diary. At her own pace. She said once we're done, if there are any further questions, she'll let us fire away."

"That's not too unreasonable."

"It is for me. This has gotten way too personal."

"Hell, Bailey. It's not like she's allowed you to read about their first time in bed."

Bailey greeted that statement with silence.

"Oh my God. She's allowed it to get *that* personal? Is she senile?"

"Joanne, she's as far as you can get from senile. She's definitely aware of what she's doing."

"I hope you're taking notes."

"She won't let us record anything or take notes, but I've chronicled everything I can remember." Bailey pulled into the hotel parking lot and switched off the ignition. "Seeing Chelsea, reading this personal stuff aloud… brings back way too many memories. As much as I hate to say it, I think you need to get Lois to do this job."

"Bailey Hampton, I do not want anyone else doing this. That was a bluff, hoping you'd see how ludicrous that proposition is. There's a reason I asked you. Yes, some of it was because you're a lesbian, and I thought Burnett might open up more with you. But I wasn't blowing smoke up your ass when I told you you're my best. I'll ask you again. Can you at least try to set aside your feelings for the time you're there?"

Bailey felt like Joanne had asked her to move a mountain with a John Deere tractor. Apparently Joanne took the silence as her cue to keep pushing.

"If you're getting the most intimate details of Daphne's private life, it's a gold mine for me. Try not to be hasty about this. I'll offer you more money if—"

"Damn it, it's not about the money, Joanne. I mean, don't get me wrong. I'm very happy with what you're paying me. But I feel like my heart's breaking all over again. Being this close to Chelsea is like sending a five-year-old into a candy store with money and telling her she can't buy anything. Do you have any idea what this is doing to me?"

"I'm sorry," Joanne said and sounded like she meant it. "Can you at least sleep on it tonight? If you feel this strongly in the morning, I'll understand." Bailey heard a drag of smoke and an exhale. "Completely."

"I'll talk to you in the morning." Bailey flipped her phone shut. She stepped out of the Jeep and it rang again. Her heart skipped a beat. *Chelsea.*

"Hey." Bailey began walking toward the hotel.

"Bailey, I think we need to talk."

"I'm okay. We don't—"

"We do."

"I know when not to argue with you. Where do you want to meet?" Bailey said with some reluctance.

"Why don't you come over to my place? I'll give you directions, because I'm sure you still don't have a GPS."

"Nope."

"I didn't think so."

Chelsea relayed the directions and asked Bailey to meet her in about an hour. Bailey had the sudden need to get a shower and change her clothes. She rationalized it was because of the hot weather, and she needed to cool down.

Right. She punched the Up button for the elevator. Keep telling yourself that.

Chelsea heard a car door slam. She went to the window and saw Bailey striding up the sidewalk toward the house. Chelsea swung the door open.

"Bailey. Come in."

Bailey entered and stood there with her hands shoved into her jeans pockets, a move that Chelsea remembered as a sign of her nervousness. Chelsea motioned her into the living room.

"Would you like something to drink? I have Heineken."

"Sure."

Chelsea returned to the living room toting two bottles of beer. Bailey had her back to her while she checked out the photos on the fireplace mantel. She picked up one and stared at it a long time.

"Here you go."

Bailey spun around and almost dropped the glass frame. She did an admirable juggling act before replacing it on the mantel. Chelsea glanced at the photo of them, taken on their trip to Europe. She remembered how shy she'd been to ask someone to take their picture in front of the Eiffel Tower. Not Bailey. She'd grabbed the next passerby and shoved their camera into her hand. Chelsea knew French. The woman had told them they made a beautiful couple. Bailey had pestered Chelsea all afternoon to tell her what the woman had said. She told Bailey she'd get her answer in bed later that night.

Bailey took the beer. "Thanks." She gestured at the photo with the bottle. "I remember that day. I'm surprised you have it out."

Even though Bailey had every right to feel that way, the words still stung Chelsea.

"It's a happy memory." She couldn't keep the tremor from her voice.

Chelsea sat down on the couch and waited for Bailey to join her. She took a sip of her beer and set it on the end table. Tucking one leg under her, she leaned against the back of the couch so she could face Bailey.

"We haven't had much time to ourselves since we started this thing with Eleanor," Chelsea said. "Even when we went to lunch, we were interrupted."

"Did you go out on your date with the woman from the bar?" Bailey shook her head. "It's none of my business."

Instead of answering, Chelsea asked a question of her own. "Why do you care?"

"I'm not sure." Bailey wouldn't meet her eyes.

"That's a cop-out, Bailey, and you know it."

"Maybe it is. But my heart's not ready for you to shut me down," Bailey said sharply.

Chelsea sat back, a little stunned by her vehemence. "Do you think we can at least try to talk? Please."

Bailey leaned over to place her bottle on the coffee table. She laced her fingers together so tightly that her knuckles turned white. "I care because I still love you. But as you kept pointing out before you left, love wasn't enough. We drifted apart and didn't try to fix it."

"Why is that?"

Bailey captured her with an intense stare. "You tell me. Why did we give up and not talk about it until it was too late?"

Chelsea's throat tightened, seeing Bailey's hurt expression. "I think… I think I got scared. We were happy for so many years. Then we got caught up in our jobs, and you were traveling—"

"Don't try to lay this all on me again, because—"

"Please let me finish."

Bailey settled back next to her.

"You were traveling. I became more involved in my work and got calls to lecture. Then something happened one night when I was sitting in my hotel room, alone. I'd finished going over my notes and switched off the light, when it hit me. I hadn't even thought of calling you to tell you good night." Chelsea's voice shook. "I started sobbing because I realized I didn't miss you, Bailey."

"Why didn't you tell me?" Bailey's eyes filled with tears.

"How could I say that without hurting you?"

"But it hurt more not talking about it."

"I know." Chelsea sat up and moved closer to Bailey, taking her hand. "I'm so, so, sorry." Bailey looked like she could bolt at any second. Chelsea held on a little tighter. "I really am."

"I'm sorry, too. For everything." Bailey picked at her jeans. "How do you feel now?"

"I'm feeling a little mixed up. But one thing I can tell you is that until I saw you again, I didn't realize how much I missed you."

"Really?" Bailey asked, her voice small and childlike.

Chelsea reached her hand up, pulled back, and then trailed her thumb along Bailey's cheek.

Bailey searched Chelsea's eyes with the same intensity she remembered from their years together. Her gaze dropped to Chelsea's mouth and lingered there.

"Really," Chelsea said softly. She leaned forward as she anticipated the kiss, her heart pounding in her ears. But Bailey withdrew, grasped Chelsea's hand, and placed it between them.

"I've missed you, too, Chels."

She waited for Bailey to say more. Anything. Then, she accepted this night for what it was—a fresh beginning. "Tell me what you've been working on." Chelsea hoped she hid her disappointment.

"You mean besides trying to acquire the patience of Job with Eleanor?" Bailey gave her that crooked grin that always melted Chelsea's heart.

"Yes, besides that." Chelsea reached for her beer and took a swallow as she listened about Bailey's life without her. She reminded herself again that this was a beginning. Where would it end? She didn't know, but she was willing to jump aboard for the ride.

Chelsea took a long drink of her beer. Bailey's gaze traveled from the hollow of her throat down to the swell of her breasts and then up to Chelsea's face. She told Chelsea about the projects she'd worked on the past eleven months, trying her best to maintain her nonchalance. Chelsea laughed when Bailey told her about dealing with the curmudgeon of a history professor. It took every ounce of Bailey's willpower not to push Chelsea back on the couch and give her a long, bruising kiss. But she didn't.

She needed some time.

Chapter 14

Bailey pulled up and saw Chelsea lean into her car and grab her purse. She waited until Chelsea caught up with her, and they headed toward the front door.

"Good to see you again, Chelsea."

Chelsea's wide smile was a welcome sight. Saturday night had left Bailey anticipating seeing Chelsea more than at anytime since they'd separated. *Separated.* She'd not referred to their breakup as a separation until today. Their talk had planted a small kernel of hope in her heart for something that had seemed impossible only a few days ago.

"Good to see you, too, Bailey." Chelsea rang the doorbell.

Niles greeted them.

"Miss Burnett is in the gardens and has asked you to join her. If you would be so kind as to take the path around to the back."

"Did you enjoy your Sunday?" Chelsea asked as they walked around the house.

"I tried to stay busy going over my notes from these readings. Kind of had a difficult time concentrating, though."

"That's unlike you. What was the problem?"

"I found myself thinking about a certain someone."

Chelsea stared down at her feet. "You did?"

Bailey stopped walking. Chelsea went a couple of more steps before stopping and turning back.

"You're not an easy person to forget, Chelsea Parker."

A shy smile graced Chelsea's lips. Bailey remembered how timid Chelsea had always been about her own attractiveness. Heads would turn at the lesbian functions they'd attend. Later, Bailey would tease her about who had tried their best to flirt with her despite Bailey being only a few feet away, talking with another friend. Chelsea could never see it.

"You seem to be on better terms this morning." Eleanor waved them over to where she stood pruning her rose bushes.

"What beautiful roses," Chelsea said.

"Daphne bought these for me about twenty years ago. When we first met, I thought she was an avid gardener judging by the gorgeous gardens behind the mansion. She pointed to her gardener one day and said, 'I think you need to compliment Earl. If I had anything to do with these things, you'd see a pile of weeds.'"

Eleanor clipped off a perfect red bloom and handed it to Bailey. "Then she asked Earl for his shears, marched over to the garden, and cut off a red rose, just like that one. She sniffed it and studied it for a moment before giving it to me and saying, 'Roses are for our eyes to adore, but they mean nothing unless you give them to someone you love.'"

"That's beautiful," Chelsea said.

"Yes, it was, but we went through some pain before we got to that point. And then we went through the darkest time of our relationship. Come. Let's read some more, shall we?"

They walked toward the table as Niles brought out tea and coffee.

Bailey bowed and gave the rose to Chelsea before taking her seat.

"Isn't she the romantic, Doctor Parker?"

"She's always been romantic with me."

"It's nice to see you getting along now. No more arguing or fussing?"

"Chelsea and I had a good talk Saturday night."

Eleanor looked at Chelsea. "I'm glad."

"Do you mind if I ask you some questions before we get started today?" Bailey said.

"Go right ahead. You two have been patient with me thus far. It's time to reward that patience."

"What was it like trying to be discreet with Daphne when she was so well known and in such demand?"

Eleanor poured her tea before answering. "Daphne threw parties and invited over straight and gay celebrities. You see, it wasn't the actors or the actresses we had to worry about. Witch hunts were common then but not just by the government against presumed communists. The scandal magazines were out to sell a sleazy story, and suspected gay Hollywood stars came under their scrutiny."

"In my research, I saw where Daphne became a subject of the *Tinseltown Tattler*'s investigation," Chelsea said.

Eleanor's face darkened. "Don't you dare call it an

investigation. It was a witch hunt, plain and simple. That magazine ruined many lives and careers. It almost ruined our relationship."

"I'm sorry, Eleanor. It was a poor choice of words on my part."

Eleanor's tone softened. "I should apologize to you for my harshness, dear. Old wounds reopen when I remember those times."

"What were the parties like?" Bailey asked.

"They were wonderful. I can still see the food laid out on the tables, the drinks, hear the laughter."

Bailey smiled. "I would have loved to have been a little mouse at Daphne's mansion to sit back and enjoy the spectacle."

"And enjoy you would have." Eleanor's brow furrowed. "But it wasn't all fun and games."

A long pause followed her words, filled with the sound of chirping birds eating from the nearby birdfeeder.

"This is the part where we delve into some of the painful memories. Who wants to read today?"

"I'll go, if it's okay with Bailey."

Eleanor handed the diary to Bailey who passed it on to Chelsea.

"This passage is about seven weeks past our last reading. It's almost Christmas."

Chelsea opened the diary. "Saturday, 23 December 1950. I had begged Stella to let me have today off, but she said since we're closed Christmas Eve Day and Christmas, we'd be busy with customers flocking to the diner for the turkey dinner special…"

Chapter 15

Daphne told me it was okay, that there'd be other Christmas parties in our future, but I wanted to be there for the first one we'd share together.

"Table five is asking for you," Rose said as she flew past me.

I scowled. The four men at table five were more interested in getting my phone number than ordering food. So far, they'd ordered only coffee, earning Stella's ire. She'd been staring down the tallest of the group all afternoon. They'd occupied the table for over two hours, very much a nuisance and an inconvenience to the line waiting at the door.

"What can I help you with?" I asked with my hand on my hip.

"Doll, get closer so I can say this quietly."

I leaned in to listen.

"I just want your number. I'm not asking to marry you," he said.

I was about to reply when Stella interrupted me from behind.

"That's it. You four, pay your tab and leave."

"Aw, come on, Stella."

She glared at him before addressing the younger one across the booth. "And you. No more ogling my waitresses."

"What?" He raised his hands in protest.

"You think I didn't see you staring at her ass from over there?" She jerked her thumb in the direction of the kitchen. "I know what your game is. All four of you. Now pay your damn bill and get out."

After much grumbling, the taller man stood, threw down his money, and tossed a quarter in the air toward me. If I hadn't reacted so quickly, it would've struck me in the eye.

"For your troubles, doll," he said. "Come on, boys. Let's head down to Luke's Steakhouse. They've got better food anyways."

"You go ahead and do that," Stella shouted at their backs. She patted me on the shoulder on the way to the kitchen. "Sorry you had to put up with those jerks, Eleanor."

Two more hours passed with customers coming and going. Being this busy helped curb my disappointment at not sharing the evening with Daphne. By nine, the arriving patrons had died down to a trickle, but I still had two more hours to go in my twelve-hour shift. Rose must have seen me checking the time.

"I hate you couldn't go to your party. Where'd you say it was again?"

"At a friend's." I didn't offer more and was glad she didn't press.

Stella poked her head out of the kitchen. "One of you can leave early tonight. Eleanor, I think it should be you, considering the morons you put up with earlier, but I'll let the two of you work it out."

Rose lifted her chin at me. "Go on and have fun."

"You're sure you don't mind?"

"Nah. You can repay me another night when I have a date with Tim."

I didn't need her to tell me twice. I whipped off my apron and tossed it under the counter.

"Go home and make yourself beautiful, like you need to do that anyway," Rose said as I headed for the door. "Wear that blue gown again."

I waved my thanks and sprinted out the door. I didn't tell her Daphne had bought me so many other gorgeous gowns. My small closet overflowed with clothes.

I snuck in a quick bath and flipped through the dresses, settling on a red gown that fell a few inches below my knees. I'd lost my shyness with Daphne these past months and didn't mind at all that it had a plunging neckline. As I applied my makeup, I pondered how part of me longed for the day when I'd live with Daphne and part of me enjoyed my independence. I'd continued working at the diner, hoping I'd still get that big break. I made Daphne promise not to call anyone on my behalf. So far, she'd held up her end of the bargain.

I gazed at my reflection in the filmy, full-length mirror on the back of the rickety bathroom door and decided I needed some accessories. The diamond necklace Daphne had given me, along with the gold barrette, should work nicely.

I smiled at the image before me. Gone was the shy country girl from Banbury. Before me was a woman off to meet her lover.

* * *

After paying the taxi driver, I walked toward the house. Dorian greeted me with a smile and allowed me entrance through the gate. I weaved my way around the numerous cars parked in front of the mansion.

Upon entering the home, I searched for Daphne in the living room, packed with leading stars and extras, some male couples standing together, some women. I struggled through the crowd to the bar and ordered a flute of champagne, still seeking the woman I wanted most to see.

I walked outside and finished my drink as I continued to hunt down Daphne. Eventually, I deduced she must be in the house. I was about to go upstairs when someone grabbed my arm from behind.

"Eleanor, what a surprise. Daphne said you couldn't make it." Gordon gave me a tight smile and kept glancing upstairs. Quinn Tucker stood at his side.

"I didn't see Daphne in the living room or out back, so I assumed she must be upstairs somewhere." I started up the steps again, but his grip tightened.

"Why don't you stay down here and have another drink? I'll check for you." He moved to the bottom stair.

Something wasn't right. A cold, sick feeling hit me in the pit of my stomach. I yanked out of his grasp. "I'm going upstairs."

I hurried, wanting to take two steps at a time, but didn't dare chance it in my heels.

"Let me know if you find Daphne, Eleanor," Gordon shouted. "It's a little rude to be absent from her own party." Again, he shouted the words.

With each step down the hallway, dread settled on me to the point that I was barely moving when I arrived at the closed bedroom door. Our room. That's what I told myself before rapping my knuckles against the wood.

"Daph? Are you in there?"

There was rustling and cursing… and more than one voice.

"Wait, Ellie…"

I didn't. I opened the door and tried to comprehend the scene before me. A nude woman was climbing over Daphne in an obvious effort to get to her clothes. When her feet hit the floor, I saw Daphne lying there, also nude and flushed. For some unknown reason, she grabbed the sheet and brought it up past her breasts, as if I hadn't worshiped her body in the same way this woman did who was trying to flee the room.

Daphne's young, red-haired companion scrambled into her clothes. She snatched up her shoes and hastened toward the door. I recognised her then. It was Janet, the woman from my first reading.

She opened her mouth to say something, but I cut her off.

"Just go," I said in an even tone.

Janet hurried past me out of the room. I closed the door and leaned against it, angry with myself for the tears rolling down my cheeks.

"Ellie…"

Twisting around, I held up my hand to stave off her words. "Don't." After several calming breaths, I moved toward the bed. "How many?"

Daphne lowered her head. "Please don't ask me."

"How many?" I repeated, my voice rising.

"I don't know."

"There are so many, you've lost count?"

"No! Two or three, I guess. God, Ellie, why do you want to hear this?"

"Because I want to know how I rate."

She shook her head. "Please don't do this to yourself."

The sobs I'd held back escaped from my throat. Daphne started to rise.

"Stay there," I struggled to say through my sobs. "I want this image burned in my memory so I never make the same mistake again." I moved to the door, had my hand on the doorknob, but stopped and looked back at her. "I love you, but I won't be treated this way. Did you love me? Are you even capable of love?"

I didn't wait for her answer. I flung open the door and stepped into the hall. The choked "Yes" I heard cut through me like a knife. It would've been easier if she'd said nothing. I stood at the top of the stairs and wiped away my tears before attempting the gauntlet to the front door.

Rushing down the steps, I kept my head down. As I pushed my way through the crowd, I heard Gordon's deep voice. "Eleanor, wait."

I stood outside with my back to him. He walked around to face me before speaking.

"You may not believe it, but she *does* love you."

I tried to push past him. He stood his ground.

"She's scared, Eleanor."

"And deals with it by bedding other women? Is this part of

your culture? Because where I come from, it's called betrayal."

"No one has touched her like you. Here." He placed his hand over his heart. "You're the first woman she's seen more than twice. Did you know that?"

"That's supposed to make me feel better?"

"Give her a little more time."

"Time for what?" I almost shouted the words. Then I lowered my voice, knowing the door behind me was still open. "Time to break my heart again and again?" I moved past him and thought of something else. "And thank you for trying to prevent me from going upstairs," I said, not attempting to hide my sarcasm.

I stormed down the sidewalk to the gate before I broke down again.

"Miss Burnett, are you all right?" Dorian asked me.

"No. Could you call me a cab, Dorian?"

"Yes, ma'am." He stepped back into his booth and picked up the phone.

On the ride back to my apartment, I laid my head against the headrest of the taxi. The unbidden image of Daphne's and Janet's entwined bodies battered my mind.

I'd been so naïve. No more. I had willingly given my innocence to Daphne, thinking we had a future together, and it had been a lie. Just as I knew from the moment we met that I'd never be the same, I feared from this moment on, trust would be a cold-hearted enemy.

* * *

Chelsea finished reading the last line. "How did you recover from the deceit?"

Eleanor stared out at the gardens as though she hadn't heard her question.

"Eleanor?"

"Two months went by before I spoke to her. And it's not from her lack of trying. I refused another reading for one of her pictures, thinking it was a ruse to get me on the set so she could see me. Hal was so frustrated. He of course had no idea why I was turning down another opportunity. I can still hear his voice, 'Eleanor, how can you give up now?' I couldn't tell him the real reason. I couldn't betray her, despite what she'd done to me."

"What happened when you spoke to each other again?" Bailey asked.

"She surprised me one night at my apartment. She looked like hell. Believe it or not, it didn't give me much pleasure. I didn't realize how much I missed her until I saw her standing in my doorway."

"You forgave her," Chelsea said, "but I'd find that almost impossible to do. Bailey and I never cheated on each other. That's one thing I can say. We were always faithful."

Eleanor cocked her head with a knowing smile. "But you cheated each other out of time, didn't you?"

Chelsea sat back in her chair, stunned.

"Time apart can be just as much a mistress, Doctor Parker. Let's see what happens." Eleanor motioned at the diary. "Do you want to continue?"

Chelsea needed a break from the emotional reading and sought a diversion. She grabbed a shortbread cookie and shook her head. "I'm enjoying your cookies," she mumbled around a bite and pointed at Bailey.

Bailey took the diary. "Where should I start?"

"Move ahead to February 24."

"We're not missing anything, are we?" Bailey asked as she flipped the pages.

"Two months of angst, which I don't want to put you through."

Chelsea finished off the last of the cookie and brushed the crumbs from her shirt. "You remember the exact date she came to your door?"

"Wouldn't you?" Eleanor asked.

Chelsea shared a long look with Bailey. "I guess I would."

"Please start reading, Bailey."

"Here we go. Saturday, 24 February 1951. What a long day at the diner. It was my turn to repay Rose for the night at the Christmas party…"

* * *

I don't know what was going on in the area tonight, but all of the regulars showed up and it seemed they had brought as many of their friends as they could gather. My feet were killing me on my walk home from Joe's. I almost called a cab but didn't have the money. Things had been tight for me. It's not that Daphne paid for everything, but I did spend a lot of my nights and mornings eating at her place. Most of my money went for groceries now.

A nice breeze ruffled the hem of my uniform dress, but it didn't help ease the soreness of my feet. I felt the beginnings of blisters underneath my thick calluses as I walked upstairs and down the hall to my flat.

Feeling somewhat refreshed after my bath, I boiled a pot of water for tea. I brought my steaming cup to the threadbare sofa, tucked my legs under me, and tried to enjoy something that at one time gave me such pleasure. But instead, it accentuated the loneliness that had been my constant bedfellow since that fateful night. I missed the talks I shared with Daphne after making love until the early hours of the morning. Who was I kidding? I missed her.

At first, I didn't recognise the knock, thinking it was a backfire from a car passing by on the street below. But it came again. Someone was at the door. I glanced at the clock. Who would be visiting at almost midnight? Worried it might be feeble Mrs. Halberson from down the hall, I hurried to the door. I peeked through the peephole and swallowed back a gasp. *Daphne.* Wondering if it could be my vivid imagination or my fatigue conjuring up someone who wasn't there, I checked again. But there she stood.

When I opened the door, we stared at one another. Her face was devoid of makeup. Dark circles under her eyes as well as worry lines on her forehead made her appear haggard. Rather than find comfort in the fact that she must have suffered without me, I felt a deep sadness.

"Hi," she said in a timid voice. "Can I come in?"

I moved aside for her and shut the door.

"I took the chance that you might still be up. I remembered your twelve-hour shifts at the diner on Saturdays. If you're too tired, I can go."

I saw the fear in her haunted expression. Evidently fear that I would turn her out. I'd thought of this moment so many times. What I'd do. What I'd say. In my musings, I'd slam the door in her face or I'd slap her and tell her to stay out of my life forever.

But now she was a few feet away; now I smelled her unique scent and looked into those dark brown eyes that had drawn me to her so many times. The only thing I wanted to do was grab her and pull her to my chest.

"Please say something, Ellie."

"Why don't we sit down?"

She took a seat in the middle of the sofa, and I chose the chair.

"Would you like some tea?" I tried to remember the words I'd wanted to say if this moment presented itself.

"No." She ran her fingers through her hair, a move I'd seen her make so many times. Before, it was seductive. Tonight, it conveyed her nervousness.

Rather than speak, I waited.

"You're not going to make this easy, are you?" she asked.

I shifted back in my chair and crossed my legs. "Why should I?"

"I don't know what to say except if I were in your shoes, I'm not even sure I would have let me through the door. But because you did, I'm hoping I still have a chance." Daphne inflected the last word as a question.

"I thought of this moment. Thought of how I'd turn you away. But now that you're here…" I stopped as emotion overtook me.

"I'm lost without you, Ellie. I know you may not believe me, but I've not been with anyone since that night. I think about you in the morning. I think about you during filming. I go to sleep at night with your name on my lips." She slid nearer. She reached out to touch my knee, but I shifted away. "I'm so sorry," she said. "No one ever moved me like you do, and I… I got scared. I never had the feelings you stir in me. I—"

"What are those feelings?"

Daphne raised her head, as if searching for her answers from above. "That I could lose my heart to you and never regret it. That I could fall in love with you and never want to be with another woman." She looked at me then, and seeing the intensity there, my breath hitched. "That I could spend the rest of my life with you." She wiped her wet cheeks as she spoke.

"I don't understand, Daphne. How could these things be bad? How could you do what you did to me?" I shed my own tears. "You betrayed me and broke my heart."

"I was afraid of losing my freedom. But instead, when I thought about the sex with those other women…"

I flinched.

"It was just that—sex," she said hurriedly. "When I had sex with them, I was more and more alone and lost."

"How many more of these episodes did you plan to partake in before you came to this conclusion?" I let my anger show.

"I don't know."

"At least you're being honest now."

Daphne must have sensed she was losing me. She grabbed my hand. "Since that night, I realise what a colossal fool I've been. I've never been in love before. Never. When we first went to bed together, I thought this could be fun. You were young, inexperienced. I thought back to my first encounter and how she had taught me. I thought I could do the same. Stomp on your heart and move on to the next."

I yanked my hand away, but she knelt before me, took both my hands in hers, and squeezed them gently.

"But these last two months, I understood what I felt for you was love, and no matter what I might do or who I might bed, no one would be you. Only you could make me feel this way." She caressed my cheek with her fingertips. "I love you, Ellie. Can you forgive me?"

I tried to find any trace of dishonesty in her eyes. I had a decision to make. Like that first time I initiated a kiss, it was up to me if I took the next step. I loved this woman. I knew that as sure as she knelt before me. But was it enough?

God help me. It would have to be.

"It will take a lot for me to trust again. If you can live with that, then I do forgive you."

"Oh, Ellie." Daphne crushed me in a tight hug. "You won't regret this. It will never happen again. You have my word."

"Where do we go from here?"

"Spend your life with me. Leave this." She waved her hand to encompass the room. "Leave that job. Come live with me, and I'll take care of you."

"I need time," I said. "*We* need time. But…"

"But?"

"But I do love you. After I learn to trust again, yes, I'll move in with you."

She brought me to her chest for another hug.

I pushed her gently away and held onto her shoulders. "The only way this will work is if we're equals, Daphne. I know you'll always have the money, the home, the fame, but I want a say in everything we do."

"Whatever you want."

"Don't say that to make me happy. Say it because you mean it."

"I mean it with all my heart." She pressed her lips to mine.

That was my undoing. I put my hand behind her neck and pulled her forward, making the chaste kiss something much more.

We tried to catch our breath.

"You'll never be sorry," Daphne said.

I hoped she was right, because I couldn't live without her.

*   *   *

"But she hurt you again, didn't she?" Bailey asked.

"More than if she'd brought another woman to our bed."

"Yet, you still stayed together for almost sixty more years," Chelsea said.

"What did the last line of that day's entry say?" Eleanor asked her.

Bailey opened the diary and looked at the words. "That you couldn't live without her. Still…"

"Even though she did what she did to me in 1954, my love for her didn't die. Would you have let Chelsea go for this? No, wait." Eleanor tapped her temple with her index finger. "That's right. You ended your relationship because you were busy and grew apart. I believe those were the words."

"It was a difficult time for us," Bailey said. "Yes, we were busy. Incredibly busy. I was flying out of state, sometimes even leaving the country, to conduct research for weeks at a time. Chelsea had her own obligations. She's very well respected in her field."

"You're in gender studies at the university, correct?" Eleanor asked Chelsea who raised her eyebrows. "Don't look so surprised that an old woman knows how to use a computer."

"My core concentration is lesbian feminism and film."

"That's right. You've had several books published. And one of your biographies was up for an award. The one on Marlene Dietrich? About two years ago?"

"Yes."

"Outstanding work, Doctor Parker."

Chelsea's face reddened.

"No need to be embarrassed." Eleanor turned to Bailey. "And you. You've done some remarkable work with Ms. Addison."

Bailey tried to hide her surprise that Eleanor checked into her credentials, but she wasn't successful.

"Like I said, I may be eighty-one, but I do know how to, what's the word? Surf? Ms. Addison speaks highly of you on her website." Eleanor stood up and stretched. "I think that's enough for the day." She reached for her cup. Bailey didn't miss the tremor in her hand as she placed the cup on the tray. "Why don't we take a break tomorrow? That will give you time to go over anything you may want to discuss. Perhaps together?"

Bailey chuckled. "You aren't going to give up, are you?"

"Not where you two are concerned. I'll see you day after tomorrow. Come a little later next time, say around ten?"

Bailey and Chelsea agreed and watched as she entered her home.

"I wonder how much Daphne's death has taken out of her," Chelsea said. "Over sixty years together. I can't imagine..."

"Can't imagine what, Chels?"

"I can't imagine how I'd be if something were to happen to you." The wind ruffled her hair, carrying the soft scent of the roses up from the gardens.

Seeing the sun sparkle in Chelsea's eyes, Bailey had a rush of memory from their college days. "Let's go to the lake tomorrow."

"The lake? You mean Lake Monroe?"

"Yeah. Let's pack a picnic lunch and head down there. We can take our notes if you want, since Eleanor mentioned that. Or we can go and talk and..." Bailey tried to read Chelsea's expression and thought she saw hesitation. "Or we don't have to. It was just an idea."

Chelsea smiled, bringing out her dimples. "I think that sounds like fun."

"You do?"

"Why don't you pick me up tomorrow at eleven since you know where I'm at? Would that work for you?"

A trembling hit Bailey's stomach that she hadn't experienced since their first dates together. "I think I can arrange that, Doctor Parker."

Chelsea slapped her arm on their way around the house. "Don't you start. One person giving me a hard time is enough."

Chapter 16

Chelsea added Cokes to the two sandwiches she'd already packed. She set the cooler by the door, next to the bag containing a blanket and a bottle of sunscreen. A car door slammed outside. Peeking through the blinds, she smiled when she saw Bailey bend over to check out her hair in the Jeep's side-view mirror.

She opened the door before Bailey had a chance to knock.

"Ready?" Bailey asked.

"Just need to grab the cooler and—"

"Let me." Bailey picked up the cooler and bag. "You might have to remind me how to get there. It's been awhile."

Chelsea followed her to the Jeep and enjoyed the way Bailey's cargo shorts showed off her tight butt. She realized Bailey had said something but had no idea what it was. "I'm sorry, what?"

Bailey opened the back, put everything inside, and slammed the door shut. "Lake Monroe. I'm a little rusty on directions," she said as she slid into the driver's seat.

"No problem. It's pretty easy."

Bailey fastened her seatbelt and gave Chelsea a curious look. "Everything okay?"

"Fine. I'm fine." Chelsea ran the palms of her hands over her thighs in an effort to calm her nerves. "Traffic should be light right now, not that this is a huge metropolis." Bailey hadn't started the engine. Chelsea noticed Bailey's slight smile. "What?"

"Nothing." Bailey started to turn the key.

Chelsea grabbed her wrist. "No, what?"

"This reminds me of when we first dated. I'd come by the place you were renting and pick you up. We'd go down to the lake and hang out for the day. Do you remember?"

Chelsea felt relieved that Bailey was just as nostalgic about their outing. "I remember."

Bailey keyed the ignition and pulled out onto the street. "This is where you let me know where I need to go."

Chelsea gave her directions as they drove. The lake was just south of Bloomington, but with the winding back-country roads, it took about thirty minutes to get there.

"Do you want to go to our usual spot?"

"If we could," Chelsea answered with a hopeful tone.

"Absolutely." Bailey paid the fee at the entrance to Hoosier National Forest and drove for several minutes. "Isn't this the way?"

"I think so."

Bailey followed a gravel road, the tires kicking up more dust the farther they traveled down the incline. "Think anyone else has found our secret hiding place?"

"It's been almost ten years, but maybe we'll get lucky." Chelsea meant every word. She wanted as much privacy as possible to enjoy the outing.

They arrived at the opening in the trees, and the lake appeared below. Sunlight danced across the water, reflecting off the hulls of the speedboats and fishing trawlers out for pleasure or a day's catch. No one sat on the grassy hillside overlooking the lake.

"We got our wish," Bailey said as she pulled to a stop. She brought the cooler and bag midway down the hill.

Chelsea reached inside the bag for the blanket and laid it out. "Are you ready to eat now or did you—"

"Let's sit and enjoy the view a little before we eat." Bailey held out her hand to help Chelsea to the blanket and sat down beside her. They faced the water with their legs stretched out in front of them as they leaned back on their hands. Birds chirped in the trees, and boat engines whined below. An occasional loud laugh carried across the water.

Bailey had her face tilted toward the sun. Chelsea liked the way it highlighted the blonde in her hair. She seemed more rested since that first meeting at Eleanor's. The lines around her mouth were faint, and the dark circles had all but faded. Bailey turned toward her. Chelsea's heart skipped a beat. Bailey hadn't looked at her with such directness for a long time. Their last months together had been so difficult. They'd danced around their feelings. Chelsea had been afraid to show Bailey how lost she'd felt and wondered if Bailey's reluctance to meet her eyes had been for the same reason.

"What are you thinking?" Bailey asked her.

"That it's been so long since you looked at me that way."

Bailey scooted next to Chelsea and gently touched her cheek. She stared down at her lips and then up at Chelsea as if asking permission.

Chelsea waited for the kiss that had haunted her nights since they parted. Bailey's lips touched hers lightly, soft and tentative. The kiss was gentle and giving, a reminder of all she'd left behind.

Bailey lingered. She relished the touch of Chelsea's lips against hers, remembering the newness of their first time together, yet feeling like she'd found her way home.

She pulled back and ran her thumb along Chelsea's jaw. "You don't mind if we go slow do you?"

Chelsea held Bailey's palm against her cheek. "I think we both need slow."

They shared a long look. "How about those sandwiches you promised?" Bailey finally asked.

"Sure." Chelsea opened the cooler, handed her a sandwich, and peeled back the cellophane on hers.

Bailey chuckled when she lifted the bread to see what Chelsea had packed for her. "Peanut butter and jelly. My favorite." She took a big bite and gestured at the cooler. "What else do you have in there?"

Chelsea retrieved a Coke and handed it to Bailey. She grabbed the other Coke, popped the lid, and took several sips.

How much Bailey had missed sharing moments like this. When was the last time they'd stolen away and spent the afternoon together?

Chelsea broke into Bailey's thoughts. "What do you think of Eleanor Burnett?"

"I think she's one fascinating, stubborn, beautiful, sad, remarkable old woman."

Chelsea laughed. "Gee, Bailey, how do you really feel?"

"You have to admit you've never met anyone like her."

"No, and I doubt we'll ever meet anyone like her again."

"How much would you love to steal that diary of hers and stay holed up for weeks reading it?"

Chelsea pointed at her with the last remnant of her sandwich. "You know me too well."

"And then there are the other diaries to come."

"I'm sure she'll bring those out as we go along." Chelsea popped the last bite in her mouth and brushed the crumbs off her hands. She gazed out at the lake with her brow furrowed.

"What are you pondering in that little head of yours?"

"It has nothing to do with the diary." She shifted to face Bailey. "Why don't you check out of the hotel and stay with me?"

Bailey couldn't have been more shocked at the turn in conversation if Chelsea had asked her to join her on a trip to the International Space Station.

Chelsea broke eye contact. "It was just a thought."

Bailey touched Chelsea's cheek until she looked up. "It's a wonderful thought. You took me by surprise. Are you sure this is what you want? We said we'd take it slow."

"We can still take it slow. You can stay in the spare room. There's a desk in there where you can work on your notes. I think it's such a waste of money to have you stay in the hotel. I'm sure Joanne is paying for it, but why not take advantage of a place to stay that won't cost her anything?"

Bailey tried to hide her disappointment. "That's the only reason for me to stay with you? To save Joanne some money?"

"No, no. I didn't mean it like that," Chelsea said in a rush of words. "It didn't come out right." She ran her hand over her face. "Why is this so difficult?"

"It's okay. I think maybe we should keep things as they are." Bailey rose to her feet. She knew she was being too sensitive, but it seemed everything said between them had to be weighed and measured before spoken aloud. If not, it resulted in hurt feelings.

"I didn't mean to upset you," Chelsea said and stood up. She kept her head down as she spoke, and her chin quivered.

"Hey." Bailey tilted her chin up with her fingertips. "Don't mind me. I'm being a shit about this. We said we'd take it slow, and you're trying to do that, plus make it easier on me. I'm sorry."

Chelsea nodded her head slightly.

"I *am* really sorry," Bailey repeated. "I don't want to stop this before it even has a chance to get started again." She kissed her, pleased when Chelsea responded to the touch. "Ask me again."

Chelsea smiled. "Bailey, why don't you stay with me at the house?"

"What a great idea, Chels. When do you want me to come over?"

"You mean it?" Chelsea looked like a kid who'd gotten a shiny new toy for Christmas.

"I never say something I don't mean—" Bailey couldn't get out another word because Chelsea wrapped her arms around her in a tight embrace.

"You won't be sorry," Chelsea whispered in her ear.

If there was one thing Bailey was certain of, it was the sincerity of Chelsea's words. "I believe you, honey."

* * *

Later in the evening, after Bailey had gathered her belongings and checked out of the hotel, they carried her bags and laptop into the spare room. Chelsea hoped she found it suitable enough. A queen-size bed sat against the wall to the right of the door. A desk sat against the far wall on one side of the window with a dresser on the other side.

"You can put your clothes in this closet," Chelsea said as she opened the door. To make room, she pushed aside the few winter clothes she'd stored there. Bailey pressed into her from behind and slipped her arms around her waist. Chelsea leaned back into the embrace.

"This is perfect, Chels. Thank you."

Chelsea shifted in her arms and fought the urge to take Bailey's hand and lead her to the bed. She knew this was more than about sex. It was about getting to know each other again and working through the issues that had led them to separate in the first place. Although at that exact moment, Chelsea was finding it hard to remember just what those issues had been.

"You're welcome," she said, moving out of Bailey's arms. "Well, I'll let you get settled in for the night." She backed out of the room and shut the door. "Slow, remember, Chelsea?" she muttered on her way down the hall.

* * *

The aroma of fresh-brewed coffee wafted under Chelsea's door. At first, her foggy mind had trouble comprehending how her coffeemaker had switched itself on without being preprogrammed. She sat up, rested against the headboard, and yawned. A smile made its way across her lips when it dawned on her that Bailey was in her house. In her kitchen.

She glanced down at her ratty gym shorts and thin gray T-shirt. She debated about taking a shower and dressing before venturing out to the kitchen. But the smell of the coffee and the pull of seeing Bailey in the morning made up her mind.

Chelsea stood in the entryway of the dining room. Bailey munched on a piece of toast as she read the paper. Her hair was slicked back from her shower, and she'd dressed casually in a pair of cargo shorts and a Colorado Rockies T-shirt. She pursed her lips over something she was reading, unaware of Chelsea's scrutiny. She looked up. Her gaze quickly turned heated as it traveled down Chelsea's body and back up to her face and almost made Chelsea's knees buckle.

"I forgot how damn sexy you are in the morning," Bailey said in a husky voice.

"I could say the same." Chelsea tried to appear nonchalant as she padded across the cool tile floor to the cabinet. She reached for a mug, filled it, and joined Bailey at the table.

Bailey motioned at the coffee. "I don't remember you drinking this early."

"I need something to wake me up." Chelsea took a cautious sip.

"You didn't sleep well?"

Chelsea almost told her the truth—she'd awakened at least four times from erotic dreams involving the two of them. "I slept okay."

They enjoyed their coffee together as they chatted about what Eleanor might have in store for them today. Chelsea excused herself to take a shower. She decided on casual as well and threw on an IU T-shirt and a pair of white shorts. She brushed her hair back from her face and pulled it into a ponytail.

She had her head lowered as she walked down the hall to the front door. Glancing up, she caught the full brunt of Bailey's stare and almost stumbled in her gait.

"Ready?" she squeaked out.

"Yes." Bailey held the door open for her. "You look fantastic."

She gave Bailey a quick kiss before stepping outside. "Let's go visit our friend."

* * *

"Well, well, well. What do we have here?" Eleanor asked as they got out of the Jeep.

Not giving Chelsea a chance to reply, Bailey said, "We have two women deciding to conserve on gas and drive over together."

"Don't pull an old woman's leg, Bailey. Our fair doctor has a spring to her step that wasn't there when we first met."

"Maybe I do," Chelsea said. She held out her hand for Bailey to take.

A little surprised at the show of affection in front of Eleanor, Bailey took it, and they walked to the front door together.

"You're giving me hope, aren't you?" Eleanor asked.

They stepped into the foyer. "We're giving each other hope,"

Chelsea said and squeezed Bailey's hand.

They followed Eleanor into the living room where shortbread cookies, tea, and coffee were already prepared.

"I thought we'd talk in here today. The heat's a little too much for me." Eleanor took her customary seat by the mantel. "We'll move ahead a few months to April, and before you ask, Bailey, you're not missing anything. We'll pick up on a trip that Daphne and I went on to her hometown, which is..."

"Bloomington," Bailey said.

"Right. Contrary to her studio biography that had her birthplace as New York City. Back then, they tried their best to spruce up things. But another reason for the name change was to keep her father out of the picture.

"I never read much on him." Chelsea reached for a cookie and polished it off quickly.

"The reason you've never read much on him is because he wasn't a very nice man. When we came to visit in 1951, it was to visit her mother."

"How was your presence explained to her mother?" Bailey asked.

"I thought she'd introduce me as her traveling secretary, but she didn't. Later, her mother and I had a talk, which we'll get into shortly. Because of the scarcity of beds, we slept together. But that was all."

"Had you two... you know..." Chelsea said.

"No. I had to trust her again. We were close, but I couldn't make love with her until I knew in my heart she wouldn't betray me." Eleanor looked up at the painting. "She was a fantastic lover. But our relationship had to be built on something more than that." She turned back to Chelsea. "Why don't you read today?"

Chelsea picked up the diary and opened to the marked page.

"Saturday, 7 April 1951. We arrived by train in Chicago at seven this morning. From there, we changed trains to the Monon Railroad, which briefly stopped in the town of Monon in Indiana. It then continued on to Bloomington..."

Chapter 17

I didn't know what to expect when we started on this journey. Farmland stretched for miles outside the window of the coach. Daphne said we'd stay with her mother. I had asked about her father, but Daphne became evasive and only offered that he wasn't in town.

When we chugged into the Bloomington railway station, I noticed a tall woman standing next to a Ford Woody station wagon. She had to be Daphne's mother. The resemblance was unmistakable.

No one seemed to recognise Daphne as we followed the porter with our luggage to the car. Either they didn't know she was a movie star, or they thought of her as family—someone who'd left the small town to make her way to stardom.

I stood back as Daphne embraced the woman.

"Mom. It's so good to see you."

Her mother held her at arm's length. "You're not getting enough rest," she said as she caressed Daphne's cheek.

"I'm fine." Daphne led her to me. "Mom, I'd like you to meet a very special friend of mine, Eleanor Burnett. Eleanor, this is my mother, Margaret O'Shea."

I held out my hand, surprised at the firm grip I received. "It's very nice to meet you, Mrs. O'Shea." Same dark brown eyes. Same defined cheekbones. Her hair, pulled off her face, held a few grey hairs but not enough to think this could be Daphne's mother. She looked more like an older sister.

"Please, Eleanor. Call me Margaret."

I waited for her to ask why I'd joined Daphne on her trip, but no question was forthcoming.

The porter loaded our bags into the station wagon. Daphne gave him such a large tip I thought the poor man might have a heart attack.

Daphne fell into an easy conversation with her mother about

their family and neighbours. I focused on the homes we passed and gawked at the stateliness of some of them. We eventually hit dirt and gravel roads until Margaret turned into a long drive that led us to a well-kept, two-story farmhouse. We carried our bags into the home and walked into a large entryway leading into the living room. Shiny wood floors and pastel-coloured walls made it feel like home. The smell permeating from the back of the house made my mouth water.

"I've seen that same expression from my Daphne many times, Eleanor," Margaret said. "How would you like a home-cooked meal? I've kept it warming in the oven."

After we put our bags upstairs in the small bedroom at the end of the hall, Daphne led us back downstairs to the dining room. Margaret had already set the table. It appeared she'd laid out her finest china along with sparkling silverware for the occasion.

"Mom, you didn't have to go to all this trouble."

"Nonsense. How often do you come home? Once, maybe twice a year? Always the best for my girl."

Daphne helped Margaret bring out the food—pork chops, mashed potatoes with gravy, green beans, dinner rolls that smelled heavenly. Good Lord. I hoped she didn't expect me to eat all of this. It looked like enough food for eight people.

"Expecting company?" Daphne asked in a teasing tone.

"Oh, hush and sit down."

Margaret reached for my hand and Daphne's and stared at Daphne until she reached her other hand across the table to me. Margaret bowed her head.

"Dear Lord, we thank you for the safe travel of Daphne and Eleanor, and we thank you for the abundance of our blessings. Amen."

"Amen," I murmured.

Margaret passed me the pork chops. I scanned the meat and tried to find the smallest one. She didn't pass the mashed potatoes. Instead, she ladled out a large scoop onto my plate. I again wondered how she expected me to eat all the food. I took the bowl of beans offered by Daphne and dished some onto my plate.

I was the only one who wasn't eating, so I cut into my pork chop and took a bite. It was just as tasty as its aroma promised. I paid no attention to the conversation between Daphne and her mother as I devoured my food. When I noticed a lull, I looked up.

Daphne grinned at me. "How do you like my mother's cooking?"

Embarrassed, I apologised, but her mother stopped me.

"No need to say you're sorry, Eleanor. It's a compliment to see someone enjoy my food as much as you have."

I glanced down at my plate, a little horrified to find only a smattering of mashed potatoes and a dribble of gravy left standing.

"It's quite good, Margaret. Well, *was* quite good."

She stood up. "I hope you saved room for my apple pie," she said as she headed to the kitchen.

Daphne gazed at me from across the table. "Thank you."

"For what?"

"For coming here and meeting my mother."

I was about to ask about her father again, but the front door flew open and banged against the wall in the living room. I jumped at the sound.

"I hear my daughter's back in town," a voice boomed from the front of the home. Heavy, stomping footsteps approached the dining room. A large man with greying, mussed hair filled the entryway with his bulk. The red veins in his nose stood out prominently, and his cheeks were flushed. A thin sheen of sweat dappled his bushy moustache. Alcohol fumes pervaded the small room. He swayed and placed his thick hand on the plastered wall. Steadied somewhat, he still looked as though he would fall over at any moment. Lifting his chin at Daphne, he slurred, "An' there she be."

Daphne seemed humiliated at the sudden appearance of her father. I wanted to go comfort her.

"Patrick O'Shea, what in God's name are you doing here?" Margaret shouted.

Turning to the sound of Margaret's voice, I got a glimpse of where Daphne inherited some of her spunk. Margaret didn't seem in the least frightened at the appearance of this bear of a man. To the contrary, I thought she could throttle him.

"I came to greet my daughter. Since she can't see fit to seek me out on her own, I thought I'd find her." He lurched over to Daphne.

Daphne stood up. "I haven't wanted to see you, Dad. I've told you that. You've not changed, and I'll no longer subject myself to your abuse."

His face contorted in anger. He raised his meaty paw and slapped her face hard. She grabbed the back of her chair but was unable to catch her balance. She tumbled to the floor, and the chair landed on top of her.

"Daphne!" I jumped to my feet, moved the chair out of the way, and knelt at her side, holding back a gasp. Her cheek had already swelled with an angry red welt.

I shot up from my kneeling position and moved toward him. "I don't know you, and I'm a guest in this home, but don't think for one minute I'll allow you to hit her again."

He squinted in an obvious effort to focus on me.

"And who might you be? Her British whore?"

Daphne had struggled to her feet. "You'll not talk to her that way."

"Or what?" He bellowed. "What'll you do, Daphne Katherine O'Shea? And it *is* O'Shea, despite what those bastards decided to name you. Do you think you can do something about it?"

A loud click sounded behind us. I'd heard that noise on one other occasion in my life when I'd accompanied my father on a hunting trip. I turned to see Margaret aiming a shotgun barrel at her husband's chest.

"She may not be able to do something about it, but I will."

The ruddiness drained from his cheeks, leaving his face a pasty white. "Now, Maggie. Don't go doing something stupid."

"This?" Margaret asked and waved the gun slightly. "This would be the smartest thing I've done. I told you when I kicked you out of this home that if you ever came back and laid a hand on me, I'd take care of it. That also includes laying a hand on our daughter. Your days of violence are over, Patrick. Get the hell out. If you ever so much as allow your shadow to pass through that door, I'll blow your damn brains out. There'll be no blathering beforehand, either."

Daphne grasped my elbow and pulled me back to stand behind Margaret.

"Fuckin' bitches," her father muttered. But the bluster had disappeared from his demeanour. He made a hasty retreat to the door and left, slamming it shut.

Margaret leaned the shotgun against the wall. She cupped Daphne's face and tilted it toward her. "The bastard. Let me get you a towel and some ice."

I led Daphne to the living room and sat next to her on the sofa. Tears streamed down her face.

"I guess you know now why I don't visit that often." She sniffed and ran the back of her hand along her nose. "And why my name is DeMonet rather than O'Shea. Why my bio lists my birthplace as New York City and not Bloomington, Indiana. My agent and the studio didn't want to chance the press hunting down this story."

"I'm so sorry, Daphne." I gently caressed her cheek and wiped away another tear.

"I didn't leave to find fame and fortune, Ellie. I left to get as far away from that son of a bitch as I could. I became a different person and tried to leave this life behind."

Seeing her so vulnerable and so open to her feelings, I knew what made her such a good actress. She'd recreated herself and, by doing so, entered a new world where imagination and subterfuge reigned supreme.

Margaret entered the room and offered the dish towel full of ice to Daphne. "Here, honey. Put this to your face. It'll help the bruising and swelling."

Daphne took the towel and held it to her cheek. "Come to Los Angeles, Mom. Get out of this town and start a new life with us."

Trying to discern if Margaret knew what "us" really meant, I watched her reaction. Her eyes darted to mine.

"No. You have your life to live now, Daphne. You don't need me there to muck everything up."

"Don't be ridiculous."

"Sweetheart, this is the first time you've brought a friend home. I believe I understand how special Eleanor is to you. I also know you need your privacy. Besides, this is my home. I was born in this town, and I'll die here. Don't worry about your father. He's not come to this house in months."

"But—"

Margaret shook her head. "No more discussion. Why don't you both get some rest? I'm sure you're exhausted from your travel. And it'd be best for you if you lie down, Daphne."

Daphne and I rose and started for the stairs.

"Eleanor, if you don't mind, before you go up, I'd like to have a word with you."

Daphne hesitated.

"Honey, don't worry," Margaret said. "I won't browbeat the poor child. I only want to talk with her briefly."

"It's okay," I told Daphne. "Go on. I'll join you soon."

Daphne gave her mom one more look before going upstairs.

"Sit with me. Please." Margaret moved to the sofa.

I sat down and smoothed out my trousers, unsure of where to put my hands.

"How long have you known my daughter?" Margaret asked as she settled back into the cushion.

I tried to do the same but still felt on edge. "We met last August at the studio. I had a small part in one of her movies."

Margaret didn't speak right away but observed me for a long while. "You're different than the others."

I wasn't sure how to respond to that, uncertain if her mother knew the extent of Daphne's affection toward women.

"It's okay, dear. I've had my suspicions about Daphne since she was a teenager in high school."

I found my voice. "And you approve?"

"I wouldn't go that far. But I do want my daughter happy. Seeing the two of you together seems to do the trick. I noticed how she watched you throughout dinner."

"Daphne means the world to me."

"Enough that you'll promise me two things?"

"What are they?"

"Smart girl. Let's hear the terms first."

"Well—"

"I understand. Here they are. Promise me you'll never break her heart, and promise me you'll never give up on her."

I didn't answer right away, choosing to let the gravity of her words sink in. "She's already broken my heart, Margaret."

"And this is where I'd ask you to not give up on her."

I gazed down at my hands. "If she ever betrays me like that again, I'm not sure."

"She's a complicated young woman, my Daphne. She's also been a lost spirit since she left home right out of high school. But with you, I've seen something in my daughter I've never seen before."

I raised my head.

"She loves you," Margaret said.

"She's said as much. And I love her."

"I know I'm asking a lot of you in staying with her through thick and thin, but she'll come around some day and quit her foolish ways."

"I can't believe I'm having this conversation with you."

"You didn't think you'd hear these words from a simple bumpkin from Bloomington, Indiana?"

I smiled. "And I'm a simple bumpkin from Banbury, Oxfordshire."

She returned my smile. "So?"

"I promise I'll try, Margaret. It's the best I can offer."

The stairs creaked. Daphne stood halfway down the stairs with her hand on the banister. "Is everything all right?"

"I think it is," Margaret said. "Don't you, Eleanor?"

"Yes, ma'am."

Margaret rose. "You go on now. I'll clean up the dishes."

I rose, too. "You're sure you don't need me to help?"

"No, I think you have more pressing matters upstairs." She tilted her head toward Daphne.

I stood there and watched her leave, trying to grasp the enormity of our conversation. Daphne's voice cut into my musings.

"Are you coming, Ellie?"

In answer, I went to the stairs and followed her to our room.

"The bath's across the hall if you'd like to freshen up before you lie down."

I touched her cheek, which already sported a slight bruising. She flinched.

"I hate that he hit you."

"It's not the first time, but it's the first in a very long while. I've avoided him in my other trips home. I thought he'd left town, but I was mistaken."

I stripped away my clothes until I was down to my undergarments.

"What are you doing?" she asked.

"I'm taking you to bed." I caught the expression on her face. "And, no, not what you're thinking. I want to lie with you and hold you."

She slipped off her robe, still dressed in her undergarments. I led her to the bed, we lay down, and I held my arms open for her. She threw one leg over mine and wrapped her arm around my waist.

"You're not making this easy on me," I said.

"Whatever do you mean?" She batted her eyelashes.

I stifled a giggle. "You're incorrigible. You do know that, don't you?"

"I've been called worse in my life."

I kissed her forehead. "We'll make love again, Daph. Soon. But for now, I want to hold you, tell you I love you, and let you know I'm sorry about your father."

"He's not a bad man when he doesn't drink. But that's just it. He's rarely sober. I couldn't stay any longer and watch him beat my mother. He would hit me on occasion, but he took most of his anger out on her. I tried to get her to leave with me, and I've tried over the years to convince her to move to California. She's always refused."

"It's her life and her decision to make."

Daphne leaned up on her elbow. "What did you and my mother talk about?"

"She wanted to let me know she approved of her daughter's choice."

Daphne sat up suddenly and propped her back against the headboard. "She what?"

"She knows about the two of us, Daph."

Daphne blinked in obvious startlement. "She does?"

I joined her in sitting up. "I guess it's not too difficult to see. Especially for a mother."

"And she approves?"

"She didn't say that exactly. She said she wants you to be happy and can tell that you are with me."

Daphne let a few seconds pass. "Imagine that," she said, with a touch of wonder in her voice. "What else did you talk about?"

"Wasn't that enough?" I tried to inject humour in my tone. I didn't add the other words her mother and I had shared.

"I guess so."

"Why don't you get that rest your mother asked you to?"

"Will you stay?"

In answer, I moved back down into the bed and pulled her with me. I draped my arm around her and tugged her to my body.

Daphne eventually drifted off to sleep. I petted her hair as the shadows lengthened and engulfed the room. My thoughts drifted back to her mother's request.

"I'll do it, Margaret," I whispered. "But she has to meet me halfway."

Chapter 18

"Having Daphne's mother know about her daughter's sexual orientation had to be a shock," Chelsea said as she closed the diary.

"Shocking indeed."

"Did you and Daphne ever talk anymore about her father?" Bailey asked.

"We never talked about his behavior that weekend. The only other time we spoke of him was when she told me he was in hospital four months later with a bad liver. Daphne never went to see him while he was there. Her mother visited once, I suppose to say her final goodbye. He died a week later."

"Did she go back for the funeral?" Bailey asked.

"I wouldn't say she went back for the funeral. She went back for her mother. I joined her, and not a tear was shed."

"How was your relationship with Daphne when you returned to Los Angeles?"

Eleanor turned to Chelsea. "You mean, when did we make love again?"

"Yes."

"The night we returned from Indiana." Eleanor put her cup on the tray. "I think we'll stop there and pick up again a few years later in the diary. What you read next will be very hard for me to hear again. I'd rather get a restful night's sleep before that happens." She rose from her chair. "Come back again tomorrow morning, but be prepared to stay longer. You can show yourselves out."

Chelsea and Bailey watched her retreat down the hall.

"This next one will be the hardest," Chelsea said as they walked to the front door. "I bet she has us reading about Daphne's marriage."

"I'm sure that's it, too." They got into the Jeep. "Where do you need to go?"

"I should head into the office for a few hours."

"I guess I can give Joanne a call after jotting down today's notes."

Chelsea put her hand on Bailey's thigh. "Why don't we have a nice quiet dinner tonight at the house?"

"That sounds wonderful."

* * *

Chelsea parked her car at Memorial Hall. She grabbed her briefcase from the backseat and shut the door. Keeping her head down, she stepped up the curb to the sidewalk and about jumped out of her skin. Rebecca stood right in front of her.

"Don't scare me like that, Rebecca." Chelsea walked toward the building.

Rebecca caught up with her. "How've you been, Chelsea? I haven't seen you around the office lately."

Chelsea opened the door. "I'm fine. I've been busy with the Eleanor Burnett project." She started up the stairs. Like before, she set a brisk pace, hoping Rebecca would get the hint that she wasn't interested in any further conversation.

"Hey, I have tickets tonight for *Arsenic and Old Lace* at the Auditorium. Would you like to come?"

"That's nice, but I already have plans." They arrived at Chelsea's office. She unlocked the door and stepped inside, dismayed that Rebecca didn't leave her. Chelsea powered up her computer and pulled her notes from her briefcase.

"Oh?" Rebecca leaned against the doorframe with her arms crossed.

Chelsea wasn't going to offer more.

"With Bailey?"

"That's none of your business."

"Hey, I'm sorry. I'll let you go." Rebecca huffed off.

Chelsea sat down and opened the document where she'd compiled her notes. She tried to decipher her own poor handwriting so she could add the new ones to the file but found it difficult to concentrate. She got up and shut the door in case Rebecca decided to return.

As she worked, her mind drifted to thoughts of Bailey. She pictured her with her head tilted toward the sun as they sat on the hill overlooking Lake Monroe. Chelsea leaned back in her chair and swiveled to face the window. The breeze rippled the leaves of the large oak tree, and she tried to remember when she'd last taken time to relax like that. To really relax and enjoy nature at its finest. A slow smile crept across her lips.

And enjoy Bailey at hers.

* * *

Bailey punched in Joanne's number.

"Hello, Bailey. How goes things in the land of Hoosiers?"

Bailey held the cell phone against her shoulder as she typed up her latest thought before she lost it. "It goes well."

"Oh? You've decided to stick it out?"

She hit Control S to save her work. "Chelsea and I are good."

"That sounds interesting. Do tell."

"We're doing much better. We've talked some things out and… well…"

"Yes?"

"I'm staying here with her."

"Whoa. You're staying at her home?"

"It's not what you think, Joanne. She thought it'd save you some money and—"

Joanne snorted on the other end of the line. "Right." She drew out the word. "I think I might have heard that line from my first boyfriend when he suggested we move in together in college."

"I won't lie and tell you that we haven't gotten close again. It's weird. Reading this diary seems to have smoothed out so many rough things between us. But we've agreed to take it slow and talk things through."

"Good for you—and for her. I hated that you two gave up so easily. It was difficult to watch."

Bailey was a little surprised. Joanne had never expressed that much interest in her private life other than the little bit Bailey had shared. Her silence must have spurred Joanne to say more.

"I'm not a heartless ogre, Bailey. You're not only a researcher to me. I consider you a friend."

"Thanks, Joanne. I appreciate that."

"Okay, on to our subject matter. One Ms. Eleanor Burnett. How has that been going?"

"Very well. I'm typing up several pages of notes tonight. I'll e-mail them to you in a couple of hours." She looked at the clock. "How about six my time, which would be four for you?"

"That'll work."

"Take it easy, Joanne. I'll talk to you soon."

"You take it easy, too. And good luck with Chelsea."

"Thanks." She ended the call, waited a few minutes, and gave her friend Tara a call.

"Yo, Hampton. I wondered when you'd check in." Bailey at first thought she heard the TV in the background. A few giggles close to the phone let her know she was wrong. The sound became muffled, but Bailey heard Tara saying, "Nat, baby, give me a minute, okay?"

"Am I interrupting something? And where are you, by the way?" Bailey asked with a frown. "You're not in my bed, are you?"

"N-no. I told you I wouldn't do that." Another muffled giggle. "Wait, Nat. Can you wait two minutes?"

"Don't leave her waiting too long, Romeo."

"You have my undivided attention. How are things in Bloomington?"

"Definitely interesting. Research is going well. Oh, and I'm staying with Chelsea now."

A loud thud reverberated from the other end of the line.

"Jesus Christ, Tara!" a high-pitched voice screeched. "You didn't have to throw me on the floor."

"I'm sorry, Nat." Bailey heard more fumbling. "Wait! Don't go." There was a slamming of what Bailey assumed was her door.

"There's still glass in my front door, right?"

"Yes. Goddammit, Bailey, give me some warning before springing shit like that on me."

"Now you know how I felt when Chelsea showed up on my first day of interviewing Eleanor Burnett."

"And you didn't call me until now?" Tara sounded hurt.

"Hey, I'm sorry, but I didn't know if I was coming or going since I got here."

"So, you're staying with her?"

"I'm staying in the spare bedroom."

"Oh, man, Bailey. Do I need to fly out there and give you pointers? You haven't lost it this fast, have you?"

"I'm not here to bed Chelsea." Not that the thought hadn't crossed her mind. Damn. The way Chelsea looked in the morning...

"Hello? Are you listening to me?"

"Sorry, Tara. Did you ask me something?"

"Yeah. If there was some hope of the two of you patching everything up."

Bailey hesitated.

"I'm sorry I asked."

"No, no. It's not that. I was thinking how I'd answer. Let's just say we're taking things slow. We've... um... kissed a couple of times. But we—"

"Wait. You've kissed? That's fantastic!"

Bailey smiled at Tara's enthusiasm. "I have to admit, it was nice." Bailey recognized the creaking of her screen door on the other end as it opened and slammed shut.

"Nat, give me another minute."

"You said two minutes five minutes ago," Nat whined.

Bailey cringed. "God, Tara, how do you put up with that voice?"

"It ain't the voice, my friend," Tara said, low enough that Bailey was sure she was the only one who heard. "It's that mouth."

"I don't need to know. Forget I asked. Listen, I'll let you go and catch you later."

"Call back with all the details. And don't wait so long next time."

"Have fun. And remember. Stay. Off. My. Bed." She hung up the phone with the sound of Tara's laughter in her ear.

*　*　*

Chelsea unlocked her front door. "Bailey, I'm sorry I'm so late," she said in a loud voice. "I got caught up in my notes."

Bailey walked around the corner of the hallway, her hair mussed up. Chelsea had seen this look before. When Bailey worked on her research, she would run her fingers through her hair while concentrating on what she was doing.

"Busy?" Chelsea asked, quirking her mouth up.

"Huh?"

Chelsea walked over to her and smoothed down her hair. "I seem to remember this."

Bailey met her eyes.

"Uh." Chelsea cleared her throat and took a step back. She walked to the kitchen. "What sounds good to you?" she asked with her back to the entryway. She opened up the pantry and debated what she'd throw together as she tried to slow down her uneven breathing.

"I don't know. How about we order pizza?"

Chelsea jumped at the sound of Bailey's voice close behind her, and she spun around. Bailey was leaning back against the counter.

"Sure. I'll get the number off the fridge." Chelsea walked past

Bailey, a little too skittish to venture another glance her way. "If I remember right, you like pepperoni and black olives with extra cheese." She grabbed the portable to dial the number.

"You remember correctly," Bailey said and left the kitchen.

Chelsea placed the order and added breadsticks to the pizza. "Want something to drink?" she shouted.

"How about a Heineken?"

Chelsea grabbed two beers and walked back to the living room. Bailey was standing at her bookshelf, running her fingers along the spines.

"See anything that interests you?" Chelsea asked.

Bailey grinned. "Yeah, but it isn't one of these books."

Trying not to appear flustered, Chelsea handed her a bottle of Heineken and sat on the couch.

"I'm sorry, Chels. I bet you're rethinking letting me stay here." Bailey sat down next to her. She picked at the label of her bottle. "I keep making these comments."

Chelsea touched her hand that fidgeted with the paper. "I'm flattered, so don't apologize." Bailey still wouldn't look at her. "Hey, it's okay."

Bailey raised her head. They gazed at each other until Chelsea blinked and took a long drag of her beer.

"You all right, Chels?"

"You need to quit staring at me like that."

Bailey laughed. She held up her hand when Chelsea glared at her. "I won't apologize for how I look at you. You're so damn beautiful. You always have been."

Chelsea set her bottle on the coffee table. "How about we move on to safer ground and talk about something else? Were you able to reach Joanne?"

Bailey leaned over and set her bottle beside Chelsea's. "Yeah. I told her it was going well and typed up my notes for the last couple of hours. I e-mailed them right before you walked through the door."

Chelsea hated the absence of playfulness in Bailey's voice and that she was responsible for cooling the sparks between them. But it was probably for the best. For the next thirty minutes, they discussed the most recent readings of Eleanor's diary.

Bailey took a sip of her second beer. "How about you? How'd you do at your office? Get much done?"

"I did."

"You don't seem too pleased. Something happen?"

"Rebecca was there and—"

Bailey stiffened. "Do I need to talk to her?"

"No. Everything's fine."

"It doesn't seem fine. Did she hit on you again?"

Chelsea debated lying, but thought better of it. "Kind of."

"Either she did or she didn't."

Chelsea chuckled. "Wow, Bailey. Are you going all cavewoman on me?" She regretted her words when she saw Bailey's hurt expression. "Hey, I didn't mean anything by it. She asked me out again, and I turned her down. Then she asked if I was seeing you. I told her it was none of her business."

"Good for you. Because it isn't any of her business, and if I need to have a talk with her, I'd be more than happy to. She doesn't seem capable of taking a hint. It'd be no problem if I—"

"Bailey, I've got it covered."

"You're sure?"

Chelsea suppressed a smile. "I'm sure. I'll let you know, though, if she gets to be a problem. I've missed this. I always loved it when you were so protective."

"You're not just saying that?"

"No," she whispered. She stared at Bailey's mouth and then leaned forward. She meant to place a chaste kiss. But Bailey parted her lips, inviting Chelsea to make the next move. She slid her tongue inside, and Bailey claimed it with a hunger that almost melted Chelsea on the spot. She wasn't aware that Bailey had pushed her prone onto the couch until she felt the cushion under her back. Their breasts pressed together. Chelsea moaned as her nipples hardened against the cotton of her blouse.

She wrenched her mouth away, grabbed Bailey's hand, and moved it under her T-shirt. "Touch me," she rasped. "God, Bailey, touch me."

Bailey cupped her breast and rubbed her thumb across Chelsea's nipple. She pressed her mouth into the pulse point of Chelsea's neck.

"You make me so wet. Every time. It hasn't changed." Chelsea gasped as she turned her head to grant Bailey even more access. Her mind was spinning. Her blood pounded in her ears. At least that's what she thought until the pounding became so loud that it sunk in someone was banging on her front door. "Honey. It's the door." Bailey wasn't stopping. Chelsea put her hands on her shoulders and gently pushed her back. Bailey looked at her in confusion. "The door?"

"Shit," Bailey muttered as she sat up.

The rapping at the door became even louder. Chelsea rose and tried to smooth out her clothes. She hoped she didn't look like Bailey had just kissed her senseless.

"Coming!" she shouted and winced at her choice of words. Bailey's snickering didn't help. She pointed at her before she opened the door. "Stop it."

She paid the teenager for the pizza and gave him a five-dollar tip, sure her lightheadedness contributed to her generosity. She was about to ask Bailey if she wanted another beer, but she stopped when she saw Bailey's troubled expression.

"What's wrong?" Chelsea set the pizza box on the coffee table.

"Nothing."

Chelsea sat down in the chair beside the couch, suddenly feeling a distance between them. "Please, Bailey. Tell me."

Bailey scrubbed her hand over her face in obvious frustration. "I think maybe we got a little carried away. We said we'd go slow and…"

Her remark hit Chelsea like a bucket of ice water. Her next words rushed out of her mouth. "I get it. We'll cool it. My fault." She jumped to her feet. "Why don't you enjoy the pizza? I'm going to bed to read over my notes."

"Chelsea, wait." Bailey stood up.

"I'll see you in the morning." Chelsea hurried to her bedroom and shut the door. She sank to the mattress and drummed her hands against her head. "Chelsea, how could you be so stupid?"

"Damn it." Bailey walked to the bedroom door and tapped on it. "Chels, come on. Open the door."

"I'm fine." Her voice sounded strained. "Don't let the pizza go to waste."

Bailey held her palm against the door and stood there for a minute longer. She finally gave up and went back to the living room. She flipped the pizza box open. "Fine," she said as she picked up a slice. "I hate that frigging word."

Chapter 19

They drove to Eleanor's house in strained silence. Chelsea thought back to last night and agonized that, once again, they'd failed to talk. She was responsible for her share of the silence between them, but she wouldn't have shut down if Bailey hadn't done the same.

They were approaching the front door when they heard music floating outside.

"Guess we'll find her out back," Chelsea said. She stuttered to a stop when they got to the backyard. She hesitated to intrude on a private moment. Eleanor was dancing to a slow tune, her eyes closed, one hand held up high, the other low as if she were in the arms of her lover.

Chelsea was entranced. So much so, she almost didn't realize Bailey had cleared her throat until Eleanor stopped and turned to face them.

"Caught me reminiscing." She switched off the CD player.

"You dance beautifully," Chelsea said, as they sat down at the table.

"Poo." Eleanor gave a dismissive wave. "My Daphne. Now there was a woman who could dance. She and Gordon were quite the pair when they'd dance at the studio functions. And on film, of course."

"But how about the two of you?" Bailey asked. She poured coffee into their mugs and tea into Eleanor's cup.

"Thank you, dear. The two of us dancing? With the press of her body against mine and the rhythm of the music pulsing through my veins? It was magic. God, I miss her."

A breeze rustled through the trees, carrying with it a soft murmuring that, to Chelsea's ears, sounded like unintelligible, whispered words. A chill coursed through her. Certain it had been her imagination, she glanced over at Bailey whose face had paled.

"You weren't hearing things, Chelsea," Eleanor said.

"Daphne's spoken to me a few times since she left."

If the sensation hadn't stirred Chelsea's awareness, she'd have thought Eleanor had gone off the deep end. Chelsea rubbed her hands over her arms, trying to rid them of the goose bumps. "H-how often?"

"The first night after she died, she visited me in our bedroom. I'd cried myself into a fitful sleep and awakened, sobbing, in the middle of the night. I felt a light touch on my hand and a whispered, 'I'm here, darling. I'll never leave you.' At first, I thought I was losing my mind. Then a warmth enveloped my body, and her love surrounded me." Another breeze blew gently across the patio.

"But today, we're going to hear about the darkest days of our relationship." She pushed the diary to Chelsea. "Why don't you read for us? Bailey can pick up later."

"Where are we starting today?" Chelsea asked as she took the diary.

"We're jumping to 1954. I told you from the beginning that we'd hit highlights. This is one of the most important periods of our lives together."

Chelsea opened the diary. "Thursday, 25 March 1954. The weather has been cool these past couple of weeks, but I still worked in the garden every day…"

* * *

As I knelt in the soft, wet dirt, weeding and pruning, memories of my family's garden in England flooded over me. I hadn't had much contact with my father or my brothers these past two years. My relationship with Daphne seemed to consume all my time. I tried not to contemplate where I was and who I was with, frightened that if I did so, everything would vanish around me like the screen fading to black after the closing credits.

Daphne appreciated my love for the garden, almost amused that I didn't feel the need for a gardener to tend to the grounds as long as I was there. A warm air blew in and rippled the scarf tied around my head.

Daphne was at the studio filming a scene in her latest romance with Gordon. After that night in the limousine, Gordon and I had become fast friends—this despite the night he'd tried to warn Daphne of my presence in the mansion. I had to smile as I remembered the jealousy I'd felt at the premiere of The Brave Few, seeing Daphne and Gordon together.

Caught up in my work, I didn't realise for a moment that the intercom near the back door was buzzing. It connected to the guardhouse out front. Frequently, we spent our time in the backyard as we enjoyed walks through the gardens. The intercom came in handy during those times.

I reached the intercom and punched the button. "Yes, Dorian?"

"Miss Burnett, there is a gentleman here to see Miss DeMonet. He said he works with her agent, Victor Shannon, and has something he needs to discuss with her. I told him she was at the studio, but he insisted he speak with you." His voice sounded tight and strained.

"Send him back." I wondered why someone who worked with Daphne's agent would make an appearance here. I wiped my hands on the rag tucked in the back pocket of my jeans. Glancing down at the front of my shirt and my knees, I winced. Wet splotches of dirt adorned my clothing. I feared I was about to make a poor impression.

A man in a black suit and tie approached me. He had a pasty face that almost matched the colour of his starched-white shirt.

His gaze dropped to my dirty jeans and top. He held out his hand. "Miss Burnett, I'm Fred Martin, a reporter with the *Tinseltown Tattler.*"

I had taken his hand but dropped it immediately once he identified himself. His palm was cold and clammy, and I felt the sudden need to wipe my hand again.

"I'd like to speak with Miss DeMonet, but I understand she's at the studio. Do you know when she might be returning home?"

"No. You have no right to be here, and you need to leave."

Without any further preamble, he asked, "What is the nature of your relationship with Miss DeMonet?"

My stomach lurched. "I'm a good friend."

"A good friend?" Martin smirked. "As a good friend, do you often work in her garden? Or do you live here with her?"

"I… well, I…"

Daphne's husky voice interrupted me from behind. "Miss Burnett is a good friend and my private secretary. She also works in the garden because it's something she enjoys doing, not because I've asked her to do so." She strode over to where we stood, her face an ugly red. I'd seen her this way only one other time when she'd thrown a drunken actor out of our home. He'd made a pass at me during one of our parties. "I'm sorry I wasn't available earlier, but I just finished filming for the day. Who are you and what are you doing on my private property?" I noticed she never answered his question as to if I lived there. I didn't think it escaped Martin's attention, either.

"I'm Fred Martin with the *Tinseltown Tattler*."

The colour drained from Daphne's face.

"I see you've heard of me," Martin said with a triumphant expression.

"I've heard of you. I also know how you've ruined the lives of many of my friends." Although Daphne appeared to put up a brave front, her hands trembled as she pushed back a lock of wind-blown hair.

"Any lives that have been ruined, as you put it, were the sole fault of those individuals whom I've investigated." Martin's voice was devoid of emotion, and his speech sounded well-rehearsed. "You still haven't answered my question about Miss Burnett. Does she live in your home?"

"This is where I ask you to please leave. I need to call my attorney."

"Miss DeMonet, you're only making this more difficult—"

"Please leave," Daphne repeated.

Martin stared at her. The tension crackled around us like static air during a thunderstorm. "Fine. We'll do it the hard way. I'm not going to let this drop." His gaze shifted over to me as he handed his card to Daphne. "Call me."

Daphne took the card. He strolled down the pathway around the house as if he'd lived there for years.

"Daphne, I'm so sorry. I didn't know what else to do. He told Dorian he worked with your agent. I told him he had to leave once I knew who he was."

She gave me a tight smile, her jaws still clenched in anger. "You didn't do anything wrong, Ellie. You know how these people are and how they operate. They're out for blood and don't care who they hurt in the process. Listen, why don't you go back to gardening? I'll call my lawyer and Victor."

Victor Shannon was a man I despised. Daphne, on the other hand, trusted him with her life—or at least her career. He knew of her sexual preferences and arranged for Gordon to accompany her as often as possible, wherever he thought cameras might be present. Me, he tolerated. He'd been used to Daphne's dalliances and one-night stands, but I was certain he saw me as a liability, or at the very least, a constant threat to Daphne's privacy.

Daphne didn't wait for my response but pivoted on her heel

and hurried into the house. Kneeling again to weed the daffodils, I thought of the volatile times we lived in. Beginning in 1947, the House Committee on Un-American Activities had called actors, actresses, screenwriters, and directors to Washington, D.C., and forced them to testify about their colleagues and their supposed communist leanings. If they refused, they were cited for contempt of Congress and ultimately blacklisted. And now scandal sheets like the *Tinseltown Tattler* fed off the prevalent fear and tried to expose suspected homosexual actors and actresses. It had been agony for Daphne to sit by and watch her friends victimised by a witch hunt. Now the witch hunt had arrived at our door.

Monday, 29 March 1954. Daphne had left for her attorney, Ralph Edmonton's, office. Victor was to join them to discuss how to proceed. I wanted to be with her, but I knew that was impossible. I was the main reason the reporter had asked to see her.

The front door slammed. I was sitting in the den in a feeble attempt to read a magazine, but I'd read the same paragraph five times without retaining any of the content.

Around the corner, Daphne went to the bar and banged around awhile. I heard ice dropping into a glass.

"Daph? I'm in here."

She entered the den. Her eyes were red-rimmed, and her makeup, which usually was impeccable, had smeared. She tilted her head back and downed the drink. She set the glass on the table and sat beside me on the sofa.

"You look like you've been through the wringer," I said.

"I've never been so humiliated, Ellie. This Martin contacted Victor and asked about my relationships with women I can't even remember. Someone had to have talked. I know how this works. They browbeat someone else into giving up a friend. I don't know who it was, but they knew enough about me to question my sexuality. And they asked about you." Daphne's lost and defeated expression frightened me.

"What are you going to do?"

Her chin trembled. "This is the part that's so hard for me to tell you."

I reached for her hand. "Daphne, look at me."

She raised her head. Her dark eyes pooled with tears. "I... I have to get married."

I felt as though someone had sucked all the air out of the room. I struggled to breathe. "What do you mean?" I didn't recognise my voice as my own.

"Victor thinks if I'm married, it'll quell this talk about me being a homosexual. People are naïve enough to think that as long as a couple's married, there's no possibility one of them could be a homosexual."

I felt I was about to be sick but waited for her to continue.

"He thinks Gordon would be the perfect one for me to marry. It would help both of us stay off their radar. Especially since we've already been linked romantically."

"But... but what about me? What about us?"

Daphne squeezed my hand. "We'll still be together, darling. You won't be able to live in the house, but we can get you an apartment nearby. I'll come there to stay with you at night, or you can come here. The only difference is that, legally, your address will change."

"And you agreed to this?" The reality of the situation hit me full force then.

"Don't you see? I have to."

I wrenched my hand out of hers. "You don't have to do anything you don't want to do."

"Please don't be this way. I'll never be able to work again if I don't go through with the marriage. When everything eventually blows over—and it will, I'm certain of it—you and I can go back to how we are now."

I rose and stared down at her. Did I even know the woman sitting there? "Our relationship will be a lie."

She stood up. "No, it won't. I still love you, Ellie." She reached to touch my face, but I stepped back. Her expression changed to one of hurt. "Don't pull away. Please."

"Me? You're telling me not to pull away? I'm not the one who's talking of marrying a man. And a man who's also homosexual at that. You're both hypocrites."

"No, we're both realists. We're doing what has to be done. You need to remember where I get my pay cheque. The studio and every gaffer, cameraman, and electrician—all of the employees—depend on Gordon and me to keep those box office receipts rolling in. You know that as well as I."

"I'll tell you what I do know, Daphne. It's that it's quite obvious your career means more to you than our relationship."

Her face flushed. "That's not fair."

"Fair? Oh, that's bloody rich." I thought of something else. "And your fans. You can't live without them, can you?"

She looked away, which gave me my answer.

I sucked in a breath. "Your career. Your fans. Thank you, Daphne. Thank you for letting me know where I fall in the pecking order."

She took a step toward me and held out her hand in a beseeching gesture. "Please be reasonable."

"Don't even talk to me about being reasonable. I will not be your concubine."

"You know damn well that's not how it would be."

"Then what exactly would you label it? You want to put me up in an apartment while you play house with Gordon. You want me at your beck and call. That is the very definition of a concubine."

Daphne folded her arms across her chest. "Now, you're just being ridiculous."

I took in her defiant pose and the stubborn set of her jaw… and I knew I couldn't stay.

"I'm going home." I started for the living room.

"What do you mean you're going home?" Her footsteps followed close behind.

"I mean just that. You and Gordon can live out your idyllic fake marriage in your home, but I don't have to watch it. I'll make it easy for you. I'll go back to England."

Her voice shook. "You can't mean that, Ellie."

"Watch me." I stomped upstairs. Daphne continued to follow me as I hurried down the hallway and into our bedroom. I flung the closet door open and pulled down my suitcase. I threw it on the mattress and haphazardly tossed clothes into it.

She grabbed my hands as I reached for more hangers. "You can't do this."

"I can, and I am. If you think I can live under these conditions, you're delusional. Let go of me. Now."

She released my wrists. It didn't take long to finish packing; I had no intention of taking all the dresses she had bought me. I snapped the suitcase shut and carried it down the hallway. Daphne grabbed it from behind, causing me to stumble.

"What will I do without you?" she sobbed. She held onto the suitcase as if for dear life.

"You'll survive like you always have, Daphne. That's what you do. I only hope for your sake Gordon and your fans keep you warm at night." I tore the suitcase from her grip and marched downstairs. "Can you ask Perkins to take me to the airport? Or do I need to call a cab?"

"Ellie, please…"

"Fine. I'll call a cab." I went to the phone and put my hand on the receiver. She reached from behind and placed her hand over mine.

"I'll ask Perkins to take you."

Perkins pulled the limousine around in record time. He took my suitcase, stored it in the trunk, and opened the back door for me, avoiding eye contact.

Daphne rushed forward and flung herself on my neck. "I love you."

I stood limp in her arms. "I love you, too, Daphne. But I love myself enough to know I can't stay."

I withdrew from her embrace and slid into the backseat. Perkins shut the door. Daphne held one hand to her mouth and the other flat against the glass of the window. Her sobs penetrated the well-insulated car and mixed with my own. Perkins didn't linger long.

As we drove away, I resisted the urge to look back at her one last time. My heart couldn't take it.

Chapter 20

With a shaky hand, Chelsea set the diary on the table.

At some point, Eleanor had pulled out a handkerchief. "I didn't know it would affect me so to hear those words again. I've not read that passage in years." She dabbed her cheeks.

"How did you survive?" Chelsea asked.

"I could ask you the same thing, my dear. How did you survive being separated from Bailey?"

Chelsea thought back to the lonely nights, the empty days, when she could barely summon the strength to get out of bed. She'd cry herself to sleep only to awaken in the middle of the night and sob from the remembrance of a vivid dream of Bailey making love to her.

She met Bailey's eyes when answering Eleanor's question. "I honestly don't know. I was so lost."

"Much of this mirrors our own lives," Bailey said in a soft, but sure voice. "I kept traveling with my research, clueless to the damage I was inflicting on our relationship. I was so damn selfish."

Chelsea gripped her arm. "Stop. We've talked about this. It wasn't just you." She glanced toward Eleanor. "I kept letting the months go by, afraid to say anything, until it was too late."

"As you will learn, it's never too late," Eleanor said. "I used my savings and the remaining money my father had sent me and bought my plane ticket for the long trip home to England. I had no idea what I'd do when I arrived. I'd corresponded with my father but not to the extent where he'd welcome me into his home while I tried to get my feet back on the ground."

"You had to be frightened," Bailey said.

"Oh, I was terrified. Not because I had to face my father again, but because I was alone for the first time in four years. That was daunting. You see, I didn't think we'd ever get back together. Not after this."

"What happened when you returned to England?"

"I stayed with my father and stepmother for a few weeks while I worked at a bookstore in town until I had enough saved to rent a small cottage. The lease agreement stipulated I was to keep up the garden, which wasn't a hardship at all."

Bailey asked the question that was on Chelsea's lips. "Did Daphne ever try to contact you?"

"She sent a slew of letters to my father's home for about eight months after I moved out. I read them all. Each one of them begged me to come back. Once they trickled down to nothing, I received a visit from Gordon. He'd located me through my father. He told me Daphne was heartbroken and could barely work. He asked me to reconsider and travel back to California with him. I, of course, refused. After that, I didn't hear from them during their marriage."

Her expression saddened. "But I'll admit to grabbing every piece of press ever written about them. There were plenty of photos—they were the darlings of Hollywood, after all. In those photos, I saw the life that she and I could never have. Let's continue. Bailey, I think it's your turn."

Chelsea scooted the diary across the table to her.

"You'll find I've marked a place in 1955."

Bailey opened the book and began reading.

"Wednesday, 13 April 1955. Work has occupied my time, and for that, I'm grateful. I've made a good friend at the bookstore. Her name is Helen…"

* * *

We've worked the same hours at times and, afterward, have ventured down to the pub to have a pint or two. She's a remarkable woman. Blonde, blue-eyed. Very Scandinavian in her appearance. At the store, when arising from placing a book on the bottom shelf, I've caught her watching me from the register. Her cheeks would redden, and she'd immediately focus again on the customer. When we've gone to the pub, she sits closer to me than what's necessary, pressing her knee against mine under the table. I haven't been sure what to do in these instances, so I've left them alone.

She's asked me to accompany her to a film Friday night and join her at her flat afterward for drinks. While apprehensive, I'm also curious and a little excited at the attention she's paid me.

Friday, 15 April 1955. Helen and I left from work to enjoy dinner together and then walked on to the cinema. *The Country Girl* was a wonderful picture. I've always loved William Holden, especially after meeting him once at a party at Daphne's. He was such a gentleman. During the movie, Helen rested her hand on mine. I shot her a quick look, but she continued to watch the movie as if nothing were amiss. I had to admit that I enjoyed the touch of a woman again.

We strolled down to her flat, which was a few blocks from the cinema. She switched on the light as we entered, illuminating a small, but well-kept living area.

"What would you like to drink?" she asked as I sat down.

"What do you have?"

"Cream soda and Coca Cola."

"Cream soda's fine."

She popped the lids off two cream sodas, handed me one, and sat beside me on the sofa, draping her arm across the back. She took a sip and watched me over the bottle.

"How have you fancied moving back to England?"

I studied the bottle, not looking up. "I'm doing okay."

"I can't help but notice a little sadness with you, Eleanor. As if a part of you died when you returned from the States."

It surprised me how many people were aware I'd returned from the States after living there for four years. I'd assumed it had been because of my father sharing the information, but apparently, people had noticed my two appearances in Daphne's films and talked them up.

Not knowing what to say to her keen observation, I kept silent.

Helen shifted so that her knee pressed into mine. "I hope I haven't gotten the wrong signals from you," she said. "You've not pushed me away when I've sat close, nor did you pull your hand away tonight at the cinema. If I'm misreading your body language, please stop me."

She shifted nearer. Then she touched her lips to mine.

Uncertain of what I was feeling, I didn't react at first. But her kiss became more ardent. I parted my lips, and she dipped her tongue inside. She pushed me into the arm of the sofa and draped her body on top of me. Our kiss became even more intense. She brushed her lips against my neck on the way up to my ear.

"Ellie," she whispered as she cupped my breast.

Daphne, I've missed you. But then it struck me that it wasn't Daphne's husky voice speaking. I pulled away.

"No. Stop, please."

She sat up and straightened her dress. "I'm sorry, I thought…"

I also smoothed my dress. "Don't apologise, Helen. You did nothing wrong. It's just that—"

"Your heart belongs to another. A Yank, I suspect." There was no accusation in her tone. She smiled gently as she spoke the words.

"I guess it still does. I didn't mean to lead you on."

"I know, Eleanor. And I want to apologise for calling you Ellie, but I was lost in the moment. You're such a lovely woman."

"I think you're beautiful."

She laughed. "There you have it. We both think the other is quite the catch."

"Yes, I guess we do."

She held out her hand. "Friends?"

"I wouldn't want it any other way." I checked the time. "Well, it's getting on, and I should start for home."

She walked me to the door. Then she leaned in and kissed my cheek. "Whoever she is was a fool to let you go."

A rush of emotion flooded my senses. "Thank you for those words."

"Don't thank me for something that's so plain to see."

"I'll see you at work tomorrow morning."

A drizzle had started, and she peered up at the light mist. "Hold on. Let me get you my brolly." She hurried inside and came back with her umbrella. "You can return it to me tomorrow."

"Thank you."

"Good night, Eleanor."

"Good night."

On the way to my cottage, I thought of the evening's events, thought of Helen's lips pressed against mine. And I thought of Daphne and how much I missed her. I didn't realise I was crying until tasting the salty tears that trickled down my cheeks.

* * *

Eleanor interrupted Bailey before she could continue to the next passage. "That was such an odd feeling, kissing a woman other than Daphne. It was soft and supple but not the same. And having someone else call me 'Ellie,' well, that just wouldn't do. I don't know if either of you experienced that during your separation." She looked at Chelsea. "Perhaps I'm wrong about that."

Bailey noticed Chelsea's flushed face, and a sharp pang of jealousy shot through her. Was it Rebecca? She didn't like the woman anyway. Now she had the overwhelming desire to crack something hard over Rebecca's head.

"Go to the next marked passage, Bailey, which is about a year later, in May 1956."

Relieved that she had something else to focus on other than an image of Rebecca kissing Chelsea, Bailey flipped to the next bookmark.

"Saturday, 19 May 1956. Today was our spring inventory at the bookshop. The job was tedious, but I enjoyed going through the stacks, ensuring all was as it should be. Somehow it was a comfort since I felt my own life was lacking in order…"

* * *

Helen and I had been cracking jokes all day, much to the chagrin of our dowdy manager, Mrs. Baldwin. She never found the humour in anything we'd say and didn't understand how we could possibly perform our jobs if we were cutting up together.

Six o'clock arrived. It was my turn to balance the register, but Helen shooed me out the door.

"You've done this a million times for me, Eleanor. Go home and enjoy what's left of the weekend."

I stopped by the bakery on the way to the cottage to buy some bread and a Danish roll for my morning tea. Rain greeted me as I left the store. I pushed open my brolly and glanced up at the dark clouds overhead. The weather was about to get ugly fast.

I hastened home and walked through the front door before the deluge. Still, I had managed to step in all the puddles on the way home, despite my best efforts not to do so. My shoes were soaked through, clear to my stockings. A hot bath and a warm fire were in order.

A shiver ran through me as I gathered the firewood stacked beside the stone fireplace. After getting the fire started, I drew a hot bath—as hot as I could stand it—stripped down, and slid into the water. I stayed there, removing the plug and twisting the hot water spigot every so often, until I was becoming a prune. With great reluctance, I stepped out of the tub, dried, and dressed in my flannel pyjamas and robe. I entered the living room, pleased to find the fire going full force.

I made a sandwich from leftover fish and sat with my back against the cushions of the sofa, my stockinged feet pointed toward the warmth of the fire. I watched the flames and became drowsier by the second. Not wanting to leave the cosy living room yet, I curled up onto the sofa and pulled a thick quilt over my body. I drifted off into a restless dream about storms and scary branches banging against my windows. The banging increased in volume. Disoriented, I jerked awake. Was that someone at my door? No, it couldn't be. Who would be about at night in this dreadful weather? Another knock told me I was wrong.

With my heart pounding in my ears, I approached the door and chastised myself for not insisting the landlord put in a peephole.

"Who is it?" I asked but couldn't make out the response. If I wanted to find out who my nocturnal visitor was, I'd have to chance it and open the solid wooden door. Hesitating for a split second longer, I unlatched the bolt and cracked open the door. A gust of wind and rain blew in, stinging my face. I blinked several times, finally able to focus on the forlorn, soaked person before me.

Daphne.

Drenched, her long dark hair clung to her face. Visibly shaking, she hugged her body. Her teeth chattered so much that what was probably intended as a smile became a grimace.

Jolted out of my stupor, I opened the door farther, pulled her inside, and shut the door with great effort against another gust of wind. I turned around and had to swallow my nervousness before I spoke.

"What... what are you doing here? And how did you find me?"

"Gordon."

"You mean your husband." The hurt and anger returned in an instant.

"No, I mean Gordon. He told me where he'd hunted you down before. I hoped I'd get lucky and you hadn't moved." She kept shaking as water pooled around her feet from her coat.

"Here. Take that off and stand by the fire."

She stood placidly, allowing me to undo her coat and slide it off her shoulders. My fingers trembled as I undid each button. I tried to blame it on the draft that had rushed into the cottage from the open door. But I knew better.

Daphne moved to the fire and held her hands toward the flame as she rubbed them together.

"We've divorced," she said in a voice so quiet, I wasn't sure I'd heard correctly.

"Divorced?"

She remained facing the fire. "Yes."

"What about your career and the possibility of being blackballed?"

"We've been married long enough that there's no speculation anymore about our sexuality. The press now sees us like any other troubled Hollywood couple. We're no longer together but remain friends. We'll always be friends."

Not sure how to take this bit of news, I just stood there.

She turned toward me. "It's you, Ellie. It's you I love. You're the one who haunts my dreams. You're the one I've yearned for these years apart."

Glad I stood by a chair, I gripped the cushion tight between my fingers and dug into the soft material in an effort to control my emotions.

"You have a funny way of showing it, Daphne. And forgive me, but I think I've heard this speech before."

She took a step toward me, but I made no effort to move toward her. I couldn't. It wouldn't be that easy.

"Marrying Gordon was—"

"A move to save your career."

She lowered her head. "Yes. It was."

"It was something I couldn't stay and watch, despite how much I loved you." How much I still love you, I added silently.

"I understand." She looked up at me. "Is there any chance for us, Ellie?"

I wanted to say no. Wanted to have the strength to send her on her way, back to the States, back to Los Angeles. But the word died on my lips.

Daphne's face fell. "I guess… I guess I should leave you in peace." She took a step toward her coat but staggered. I hurried to her and gripped her elbow to keep her from sinking to the floor.

"God, Daphne, you're ice cold. You can't leave like this. Let me draw you a bath."

She allowed me to lead her to the bathroom and stood silently as I filled the tub with hot water. I heard her teeth clattering together. She seemed to be in a daze and made no move to shed her clothes.

I unbuttoned her blouse and tried not to notice her nipples pushing against her wet bra. I unsnapped her trousers and let them drop to her feet.

"I'll let you do the rest."

I walked to the door and was about to leave the room when I heard her whimpering. I turned. She sat on the edge of the tub, hugging her body and rocking.

My heart went to my throat. I couldn't watch this. I went to her and unsnapped her bra. "Stand up and lean on me," I said in a gentle voice. Pulling down her underwear, I tried to keep my eyes averted while helping her into the tub. "Do you think you'll be okay?"

She barely nodded.

"I'll be right outside the door."

I shut it and leaned against it, the image of her rain-soaked nude body planted firmly in my brain. I sat down on the closest chair. I couldn't allow her to leave tonight. Not in her state of mind or physical condition.

About fifteen minutes passed when I heard her muffled voice. "Ellie, do you have any dry clothes I can wear? I left my luggage at the inn."

I went to my bedroom for an extra pair of pyjamas, cracked open the bathroom door, and offered them to her. "Here."

She took them from me. "But these are pyjamas."

"You're in no shape to leave tonight. Get dressed and come out."

A few minutes later, she opened the door. The clothing, oversized for me, fit her perfectly.

I held out my hand, not thinking anymore about what she meant to me, but rather how I could help her get warm. We went unspeaking into the bedroom. I turned back the covers and helped her to the bed. She shifted onto her side with the covers pulled up to her chin. I lay behind her and wrapped my arm around her waist. Her cold hand tugged me tighter to her body.

Lying there in the dark with her familiar body pressed against mine, I waited for her breathing to become deeper. As hers did, I relaxed and drifted off.

I awakened sometime in the night with the front of my pyjamas drenched from holding her. I put my hand to her forehead, alarmed when I found her burning up.

"Daphne." I tried to nudge her awake. "Daphne?"

She turned to me. In the dim lighting, I could see her eyes were glassy with fever. She tried to lift her hand to my face, but it dropped weakly to her side. I took her wrist and checked her pulse. It was rapid, a possible sign of a spiked temperature.

I got aspirin and a glass of water and helped her sit up to take the pills. She seemed unaware of her surroundings.

"Ellie?" Her voice was raspy. She began coughing for several minutes. When she was able to take a breath, I offered her more water.

"I think you have a fever, Daphne. I'm going into town in the morning to get Doctor Grayson."

Without protest, she fell back onto the bed and shivered. I pulled the covers up past her shoulders, now truly worried. This could easily go into pneumonia.

Sunday, 20 May 1956. After staying up most of the night watching over Daphne, I made sure she was sleeping before I left for the doctor. It was Sunday, but Doctor Grayson had been practising in town since I was a small child. He always considered himself "on call."

He met me at his door, dishevelled and still in his robe.

"Can you come to my cottage, Doctor? My… my friend who's staying with me is quite ill. I would wait until tomorrow, but I'm afraid she has a high fever."

"Of course." He dressed and grabbed his medical satchel.

When we got to the cottage, I took him into my bedroom and roused Daphne.

"Daphne, the doctor's here to see you."

She looked at me as though she didn't recognise me but permitted Doctor Grayson to perform a thorough examination. The last thing he did was take her temperature. He raised his eyebrows when he looked at the reading. He nodded toward the hallway, and I followed him.

"Miss DeMonet is very ill." He must have noticed my surprise. "She's still very recognisable, Eleanor, despite her sickness. Her temperature is extremely high. I strongly suggest we admit her to hospital."

Thoughts raced through my mind, one of which was if I should call her mother. Maybe her agent or even Gordon.

"And I suggest we admit her today," he stressed.

I agreed. As he was making arrangements over the phone for an ambulance, I went to the bedroom to check on Daphne. She seemed a little more aware as I approached the bed.

"We need to get you in hospital, Daphne. Is there anyone I should call? Your mother?"

"No, please. She's been in poor health the past two years. I don't want to worry her."

"Your agent or Gordon? Someone in the States needs to know."

"Call Gordon. I don't want Victor to make this into a publicity stunt."

She gave me Gordon's number just as the ambulance arrived.

She reached her hand toward me as they wheeled her on the gurney.

"Please don't leave me."

"I'll follow you with Doctor Grayson." They pushed her into the back of the ambulance and shut the doors.

* * *

Bailey looked up from her reading. "That had to be scary watching the medics put Daphne into the ambulance."

"Oh, I was indeed frightened. Not just of her state of health, but that I might lose her before we had a chance to start over."

"So, even though you didn't tell her that night, you thought you might get back together?" Chelsea asked.

"I put up a brave front when she arrived at my doorstep, but seeing her so ill made me realize again how much I still loved her."

"Did you call Gordon?" Bailey asked.

"Yes. He thought it best that he stay in the States. Of course, he knew why Daphne had come to England. He confirmed that her mother wasn't well. He said he'd let her know of Daphne's illness and assure her she was getting proper medical treatment. As for Victor and the studio, Gordon told them Daphne would be out of the country for a while. If I had known when I talked to him just how much worse she'd be, I might have handled things differently." She pointed at the diary. "Let's see what happens in the next passage."

Bailey picked up where she left off. "Friday, 25 May 1956. Doctor Grayson met with me today. His worried expression did nothing to quell my anxiety…"

* * *

"Eleanor," Doctor Grayson said, "I don't understand why she hasn't responded to antibiotics as she should. It's almost as though she's given up."

We stood in the hallway outside Daphne's hospital room. She'd been in and out of a fevered state for almost a week. Through the doorway, I could see her in the hospital bed, and my heart went out to her.

"We'll try a different round of antibiotics today. It's all we can do." He patted my shoulder and walked away.

I entered her room and pulled a chair beside her bed. I smoothed the wet tendrils of hair from her forehead and kissed the overly warm skin.

"Don't you dare leave me, Daphne."

Tuesday, 29 May 1956. Another four days passed. Another four days of worry. She'd been unresponsive since they'd brought her in. And here I sat in the same place as Friday night. I took her hand in mine.

"I don't know where you are right now, but you listen to me. You have too much to live for. Do you hear me? You fight, damn it. You fight and…" I leaned over the bed as my shoulders shook with sobs. At first I didn't notice the soft touch of her fingers in my hair. I raised my head. "Daphne?"

She smiled weakly. "Don't cry, darling."

"Still trying to tell me what to do, are you?" I answered her smile with one of my own.

She started coughing. I quickly got her water and held the straw while she drank. She collapsed back on the bed after she finished.

"I take it I'm still in the hospital."

"And you'll stay here if you don't fight to get well."

"Now who's the bossy one?"

Hearing her tease me was a breath of fresh air.

Friday, 1 June 1956. Daphne showed enough improvement since Tuesday that Doctor Grayson released her from Horton General Hospital into my care today. Once I got her home, she called Gordon and her mother to let them know she was out of hospital and recuperating.

As she talked on the phone, I noted that colour had returned to her cheeks. She was to take it easy for the near future. This meant she'd be in Banbury a few more days. How much longer, I'm sure, depended on me.

Daphne hung up from her call and went into the living room. "Come. Let's talk."

I sat down on the sofa and faced her. "Daph, I know you want—"

"Wait. Let me say this before you say anything, please?" She waited until I nodded. "What I did to you two years ago was completely selfish. As you pointed out at the time, I was afraid of losing the adulation of the fans I'd grown to love over the years. I was afraid I'd lose my identity if that happened. But what I really found is none of it mattered without you. None of it."

I thought I'd get some satisfaction out of hearing those words, but "I told you so" was such a hollow sentiment.

"I have no right to be here begging for your forgiveness, Ellie, but that's precisely why I came. If you need more time, I understand. But I'll wait the rest of my life if I have to."

I took a moment before replying. "You did hurt me, Daphne, deeper than if you'd bedded another woman. Your actions told me our relationship meant nothing to you." She started to speak, but I held up my hand to stop her. "I still have strong feelings for you. But give me the time you've promised. Stay with me while you recuperate, and we'll see where we stand."

Her eyes brimmed with tears. "Thank you."

Saturday, 16 June 1956. For two weeks, Daphne stayed at my home while I went to work. I had the inn deliver her luggage here while she was in hospital, so she had plenty of clothes. She insisted on keeping the place tidy, telling me it was the least she could do. She made several calls to the States. I overheard a heated conversation between her and Victor about her decision to stay in England for the near future. I asked her about it and told her I didn't want to cause any friction, but she told me not to worry.

Tonight, after an evening of reading, Daphne rose and said she was going to bed. After much argument, I had insisted she take the bedroom and I had stayed on the sofa. We'd maintained this sleeping arrangement in the weeks she'd been there. I think every night, she hoped I'd join her because, just like tonight, she paused at the entrance to the hallway before going to the bedroom. She didn't know how many nights I came close to getting into bed with her.

I'd dozed off with my book still on my lap, but a noise awakened me. Daphne was crying out in her sleep. I hurried to the bedroom. Without thinking, I crawled into the bed behind her and pulled her close.

"I'm here," I whispered into her hair.

"Do you still love me?" she asked in a shaky voice.

"Shh. You need to sleep and get your rest."

"But…"

"Try to sleep, Daph."

She eventually eased into a restful slumber. A short time later, I joined her.

A soft breath puffed against my face and awakened me. I suddenly remembered what had happened and who lay beside me. Daphne still slept, but she faced me now. I brushed back a lock of hair, and my fingers caressed her cheek, still just as soft.

Her eyes fluttered opened, and I thought back to how her lips felt against mine. She lay still, as though sensing how tenuous this night could be.

I gave her one last look before I touched my lips to hers. We were cautious, like teenagers experiencing our first kiss together. Entwining my fingers into the back of her hair, I ran my tongue along her lips and pressed into her mouth. Her tongue met mine. I wasn't sure who moaned, whether it was she or I. Or both of us. The kiss grew in intensity.

With no thought as to what I was doing, I began unbuttoning her pyjama top. I slipped my hand inside and cupped her breast. Her fingers fumbled with my top, but I pushed them aside, rose to my knees and peeled the top off, never losing eye contact with her. I yanked off her pyjama bottoms, did the same with mine, and lay on top of her.

I took her nipple in my mouth, and this time, the moaning was mine. She squirmed under me and tried to touch me, but I put her hands above her head and held her wrists with a tight grip.

I didn't speak as I dropped my other hand lower and dipped into her wetness. I'd never been the aggressor in our relationship, had never made the first move. But tonight was different. Tonight I was reclaiming what was mine.

"Inside," she gasped. "I need you, Ellie."

I pushed my fingers into her and moved my body up so I could use my thigh to press even harder with each thrust. I stroked her clitoris with my thumb, remembering how she responded to the touch.

"You say you need me, Daphne?"

"Yes!"

"Open your eyes and look at me, love." I was close to orgasm, and she must have sensed it.

"Let me touch you," she whispered.

I released her wrists and shifted so her fingers could slide into me, knowing right where to go. Knowing how much pressure to give.

"Tell me you love me, Ellie. Please."

"I love you, I love you, I love you." I started sliding over the edge. She was close, and I thrust into her until she tightened and spasmed around my fingers. "I never stopped loving you."

She plunged her fingers into me, bringing me to a crashing climax.

I lay beside her, and her body shook as she sobbed. I opened my arms. "Come here."

Daphne pressed her face into my shoulder. "Don't ever leave me again," she whimpered. "Please. I couldn't survive if you did."

"Never, my love." I rocked her in my arms as I kissed her hair and stroked her back. "Never again."

In the quiet darkness of my room, holding my only true love in my arms, I lived in that moment—that precise moment when I knew with absolute certainty that we would be together until our dying days.

* * *

Chelsea choked up as she listened to Eleanor's words. She wanted this. With all of her heart, she wanted the same love Eleanor and Daphne shared. They'd overcome difficulties, and she was sure there would be more in the pages to follow. But they had gotten back together and stayed that way. Their love gave her hope.

"Hey, are you all right?" Bailey rubbed her shoulder.

Chelsea didn't trust herself to speak, so she nodded.

"It all ends well, Doctor Parker." Eleanor's voice was gentle and reassuring. "We'll stop for the day."

Chelsea tried to hide her disappointment but must not have pulled it off.

"Don't worry," Eleanor said. "This is where I trust you with my treasures." She rose from her chair. "I'll be right back."

"Do you think she's about to allow us to take the other diaries to read?" Bailey asked.

Chelsea was still lost in the last reading.

"Chels? The diaries?"

"I don't know. She mentioned letting us take them when we first started."

Eleanor returned carrying a stack of books. "These lead up to the last book which we'll read together. You may take these with you and go through the years. Read what you think is relevant. When you're finished, give me a call, and I'll be ready."

Bailey took the books from her. "You're sure, Eleanor?"

Eleanor cupped Bailey's cheek. "I trust you both. See what you can learn from our lives." She turned to Chelsea. "And what you can learn about your own."

Eleanor walked back into the home. Her shoulders were a little more stooped, her gait a little slower than at other times.

"What has listening to certain snippets of her life cost her?" Chelsea murmured aloud.

Bailey moved to her side. "I was wondering the same thing."

"Have we pushed too hard?"

"Maybe," Bailey said as they walked back to the Jeep. "But remember, it was her arrangement. There was a reason she did it this way."

On the drive home, Chelsea thought about Bailey's words. Bailey parked in front of the house.

"Why don't we take a walk before going inside?" Chelsea asked as they strolled down the tree-lined avenue. "You realize why Eleanor made this arrangement, don't you? Especially after hearing about Daphne putting her career first."

"I do believe Ms. Burnett has been playing matchmaker. I mean, I think we pissed her off with our reason for separating, especially with all she and Daphne went through. But I also like to think she saw something between us that shouldn't die." Bailey stopped beside a bench and pulled Chelsea down beside her. "And I don't want it to die. I did a poor job of communicating last night, but I promise I'll work harder to tell you how I feel."

Chelsea shifted closer, and Bailey put her arm around her shoulders. "I saw you shut down," Chelsea said, "and I went into my shell and did the same. But that has to stop if we want this to work. Eleanor is giving us a gift, a blueprint for making a relationship last."

"That's a good way to look at it. Thank God for her meddling ways."

At length, Bailey asked, "I wonder what else she has in store for us?"

"I don't know. But what I do know is this makes a heck of a story, doesn't it?"

"I can't wait to call Joanne, but…"

"What, sweetheart?"

Bailey's face softened. "God, I missed hearing you call me that." She kissed Chelsea lightly on the lips. "I wonder about us telling their story. It's like we're invading their privacy or intruding on a fairytale."

"I've wondered the same thing. Eleanor's entrusted us with this huge opportunity to delve into the private life of Daphne DeMonet, but at what price?"

"Exactly."

"Do you think we shouldn't report it? Or maybe not all of it?"

"Tell you what. Why don't we make a pact? We'll go on, read these diaries, and see what else happens. When we're done, we'll call Eleanor like she requested. Then we'll go from there. How does that sound?"

"Sounds good."

Chapter 21

Bailey called Joanne to give her an update, told her they now had possession of several diaries, and would go over them for however long it took. Joanne, of course, wanted her hands on the diaries and asked Bailey to send them to her overnight. Eleanor Burnett would be none the wiser, she assured Bailey. Bailey shot her down in rapid fashion.

She and Chelsea settled into a routine, each studying the next diary to decide what was pertinent as they took notes.

Daphne remained in England for the next five years. She bought the cottage from the landlord and took a hiatus from films. Frank Teller and Victor Shannon inundated her with scripts, but she turned down every one of them. Eleanor tried to convince her to go back to Hollywood and continue her career, but she wouldn't hear of it.

Daphne even got a job working in the cinema selling tickets. Eleanor wrote that some of the townspeople didn't recognize Daphne from the big screen, but those who did accepted that she had private reasons for leaving Hollywood, and they left her alone. It was almost too surreal to read.

Bailey had tried to research this period of Daphne's life before, but found nothing other than she had stepped out of the limelight and moved to England.

Chelsea was preparing dinner when Bailey came upon a crucial date.

"Hey, Chels. Come in here when you have a minute." Bailey had propped her back against the arm of the couch and stretched her legs out while she read the diary and took notes.

"Let me get the chicken into the oven," Chelsea said from the kitchen.

Bailey waited until she joined her.

"This is the day when the director, Frank Teller, and her agent, Victor Shannon, come to Banbury and bring the script to *A*

Sheltered Heart."

"Didn't she win the Movieland Film Award for that?"

"Yeah. They still had to do a lot of convincing, I guess. Do you want me to read it to you?" Bailey asked.

"Why change a good thing? We have about an hour before the chicken's ready." Chelsea motioned to Bailey's lap. "May I?"

In answer, Bailey shifted on the couch to sit upright, and Chelsea settled her head in Bailey's lap.

"Sunday, 29 October 1961. A cold rain fell throughout the day. Daphne and I remained in bed until we came out for sustenance around seven-thirty to dine on grapes and an old bottle of champagne I'd rustled up from my batch…"

* * *

"What a glorious day," Daphne said with a sated grin. She sat next to me at our modest table. In our modest home. I still found it hard to believe she'd been here for five years and claimed to have not missed Hollywood at all.

I plucked another grape from the bunch and fed it to her. Her lips lingered on my fingers in a move that radiated all the way to my groin.

"If you're not careful, we'll end up right back in bed," I said with a groan.

"And you see this as a problem?"

I kissed her. "Not at all, love, but it might not be a bad idea to go out tomorrow."

A sharp knocking at the door interrupted our conversation.

"Now, who can that be?" I checked my robe to ensure the sash was secure and glanced back at Daphne. She shrugged and popped another grape into her mouth. I opened the door. My stomach dropped when I saw who was standing there.

Frank Teller and Victor Shannon. They held brollies over their heads, but the rain had morphed into a deluge, and it hadn't spared them.

I glanced back at Daphne.

"Eleanor," Frank said.

Daphne's face paled the instant she saw who our visitors were. She jumped up from the table and hurried over. "What are you doing here?"

"Please, come in out of the weather." I moved aside for them to enter.

Frank and Victor leaned their brollies against the wall and brushed off their drenched raincoats.

"I apologise," Frank said. "We're causing a mess."

Victor frowned at him like he had no reason to apologise. His reaction reminded me how much I despised the man—especially after the marriage fiasco. It was all I could do to keep from shoving him back out into the rain.

"Don't worry about it. Let me have your coats, and we'll dry them by the fire. Please, sit down."

Frank pulled out a bound stack of papers from under his raincoat. He and Victor moved to the sofa while I draped their coats on the hooks near the mantel. Daphne sat down in one of the chairs. I was about to take the other, but she smiled and beckoned me over. I sat on the arm as she took my hand in hers.

Frank acted as if nothing were amiss. Victor, however, stared up at the ceiling. Good Lord, what did she see in him as an agent?

"To what do we owe this visit?" Daphne asked, not hiding her displeasure.

"Daphne, I realise you've been happy in England with Eleanor," Frank said. "I've tried talking you into projects that have crossed my desk and thought you'd want. But I've never visited you in person, have I?"

"No."

He scooted up to perch on the edge of the cushion, obviously anxious to tell her about the project. "This script I have is perfect for you." He held it up in the air. "Absolutely perfect. I've tried to think of other actresses who could play this part, but you're the only one who stands out for me. Please—"

"No," Daphne said evenly. "I'm not coming back."

"Honey, why don't you hear him out?"

She looked up at me. "Because I'm very happy where I am. I have no desire to return to California. Ever."

"At least hear what Frank has to say about the script, Daph," Victor said in his nasally voice.

I never noticed until now how over-groomed he was. He was dressed in a fine silk suit. His hair was perfectly styled, and despite the horrid weather, not one strand was out of place. I glanced at his fingernails that were manicured and shiny from a fresh buffing. He looked like an agent to a movie star of Daphne's quality, and I couldn't help but wonder how much money she'd made him over the years. His referring to Daphne as "Daph" got under my skin even more.

Frank jumped in before Daphne had a chance to refuse Victor's request.

"The preliminary title is *A Sheltered Heart*. The premise is about a Midwestern gal who leaves home to try to make it in Hollywood. She works her way to the top, but throughout the story, she has a drinking problem. One she doesn't overcome until she loses the man she loved most in the world." He rushed his words as though he feared she'd cut him off at any second. "She goes through a difficult rehab and leaves Hollywood behind to move back home to Ohio. And since it's a love story, her man searches for her, and they live happily ever after. But at the meat of the script are her rehab scenes, complete with detox and DTs."

Daphne squeezed my hand tighter and tighter with each word Frank spoke.

"I can't play a part like that," Daphne said in an almost whisper. She turned to Victor. "You of all people should know this."

Victor shifted on the sofa. "I know about your family history, but listen to Frank. This part's perfect for your comeback."

Daphne jumped to her feet. "I don't need to make a goddamn comeback, Victor."

"Darling—" I said.

She cut me off with a curt wave. "No, Ellie. I'm not doing it."

Victor's face reddened. He stood up. "You need to quit hiding in the English countryside and get your ass back to Los Angeles. You're an actress, Daphne. When you come back—and you *will* come back—she stays here." He thrust his bony finger at me.

Daphne lunged toward him, but I gripped her arm to hold her back.

"Don't you dare speak to me that way and don't you dare think you have a say-so in my private life anymore. You're fired, Victor. I can't believe I've waited until now to do this. I was a fool to listen to you seven years ago. I almost lost the woman of my dreams because I listened to your meddling advice. No more. Get out." She marched over to his coat by the mantel and tossed it in his face. "Take your fucking coat and get out of our house and out of my life."

I thought his face had reddened before, but now it turned an ugly purple. "You can't fire me," he shouted. "We have a contract."

"Which I'm sure my lawyer can take care of. He's gotten me out of worse situations."

She grabbed him by the elbow and pushed him toward the

door.

"But… but," he sputtered.

She threw the door open, shoved him into the rain, then grabbed his brolly and tossed it at him. He fumbled with it for a few seconds before catching it and flipping it open. With one last glare at me, he disappeared into the darkness. Daphne slammed the door shut. She stood there, her head lowered, her back rising and falling. I wanted to go to her, but something told me to let her blow off the rest of her anger.

She regained her composure and turned around.

"Frank, I'm not angry with you."

"Well, that's good, because I've been on the receiving end of one of your rants before. I'd rather not have that happen again."

She gave him a tired smile. "I know you mean well, but I really don't think I can take the part. Not only that, I don't think I want to."

He walked over to get his coat and placed the script on the mantel.

"Listen, I know we barged in without warning. It's a lot to take in. At least do me a favour. At least look it over and think about it." He patted the script and then addressed me. "Both of you."

Daphne's expression softened when he included me in on the discussion.

"I'm staying at the inn attached to the pub down the street. Victor and I were booked until tomorrow. I hope he got the hint and heads back tonight. If he's not on his way when I get to the inn, I'll see he makes it to the airport. I don't leave until tomorrow afternoon. If you change your mind, and I hope you do, please come and talk with me. If I don't see you by noon, I'll know I have your answer." He walked to me and pulled me close as he kissed my cheek. "No matter what, take care of my girl," he whispered in my ear. He moved toward the door, embracing Daphne before grabbing his brolly. "If I don't see you tomorrow, I wish you both the best."

After he left, we stood there staring at the door as if it might pop back open at any moment with yet another surprise visitor for the evening.

"Tell me what I can gain by doing the film, Ellie."

"Let's go to the bedroom so I can hold you while we talk." I led her to the bed. "What are you so afraid of, love?" I asked.

She played with the lapel of my robe as if it had all the answers in the world. "It brings up so much for me. You met my father, Ellie. You know what killed him. I'm not sure I can open myself to that kind of raw emotion."

"There's that. But what's the other reason? Why have you avoided going back to the States? I've told you many times that we could move back and keep this place as our second home. You've always sidestepped my questions as to why we can't go back. Since you've never answered me, I think I'll answer for you. You're afraid to return to Los Angeles because you're afraid for us. Afraid that hectic life will tear our relationship apart."

She jerked her head up. "How did you know?"

I caressed her cheek. "Because I know how much you love me and how much you want our love to last. I know you don't want to take any more chances. You feel you've done that twice now, and you're afraid the next will doom us." I searched her face. "Tell me I'm wrong."

"No," she said softly. "That's it exactly."

"You needn't be afraid. You've shown your love to me these past five years. And there is no doubt"—I wiped away a tear—"no doubt that we'll be together for the rest of our lives. Please don't let the reason you've given up your career, given up something you're so damn good at, be because of this fear. Because the fear has no foundation, Daph. I love you." I leaned in and gave her the gentlest of kisses. "I want you to do what you were born to do. And that is to work in front of those cameras and give pleasure to your fans who have missed you."

She gazed at me a long while in the dusky darkness of our room. "Do you think I can do this film?" she asked.

In answer, I pushed her down on the bed and laid my body across hers, hoping I conveyed everything I felt in my expression. "I think you can do anything you set your heart to. I have a good feeling about the part. A really good feeling."

She tugged open the sash of my robe. "Take this off. Now."

We hurriedly undressed but made love almost in slow motion, grazing our fingertips across each other's skin, touching all of the intimate places we'd memorised in our time together.

An hour later, I held her in my arms. I'd almost drifted off when her voice nudged me from my languidness.

"I guess we'll be seeing Frank tomorrow morning." She shifted closer.

"I guess so."

"Ellie?"

"Hmm?"

"I want you with me always, especially on the set for this one."

"If that's what you want, that's where I'll be."

She tightened her hold and kissed my shoulder. "Good."

* * *

"I'm glad she fired Victor," Chelsea said.

Bailey set the diary aside. "Me, too. The bastard." She raised her nose in the air. "Mmm. I think dinner's ready."

Chelsea stood up and pulled Bailey to her feet. "Come on. Let's eat and maybe watch a movie. I want to wind down before going to bed."

After they'd finished dinner, Chelsea went to her DVD collection and held up *The Ghost and Mrs. Muir.* "What do you think?"

"I think that's a perfect movie to end the day."

They cuddled on the couch and got lost in the film.

Bailey awakened to the butterfly flitting across the blank television screen. She tried to make out the small numbers on the cable box digital clock. It was after midnight. Chelsea had fallen asleep in her lap. Bailey stroked her back.

"Hon, it's late. Let's go to bed."

Chelsea squirmed and mumbled but didn't awaken. Bailey nudged her a little harder this time.

"Chels, come on."

Chelsea slowly awakened, rose, and stretched. "I didn't mean to doze off on you."

"Don't apologize. I did the same thing. Just woke up." Bailey switched off the DVD player and television. She turned around and found Chelsea looking at her intently.

"Do you remember when we first watched this movie together?" Chelsea walked slowly toward her and placed her hands on her chest. "Do you remember that night?"

Bailey swallowed hard when Chelsea's eyes darkened with desire. "How could I forget? When you told that story to Eleanor, it brought it all back to me."

"And now?"

"Now I want nothing more than to take you to bed. I think I know the way this time, though," Bailey said with a smile. She led them down the hall to the bedroom.

Chelsea switched on the bedside lamp. The want in Bailey's

eyes made the throbbing between her legs almost painful.

"I know we said we'd go slow. If you don't want to do this, tell me to stop," Bailey whispered as she hooked her thumbs under Chelsea's T-shirt.

Chelsea's answer was to push Bailey's hands away and tug the T-shirt off. Bailey reached around and unhooked her bra. She stepped back and gazed at Chelsea's breasts.

"Oh, God, Chels." Bailey took a nipple in her mouth. Chelsea put her hand behind Bailey's head and pulled her in even tighter.

"Bailey, please…"

Bailey pushed her back to the bed and slid off Chelsea's shorts and panties. She quickly undressed.

Chelsea stared at the lean body of the woman she knew so well. Bailey's breasts were as firm and high as Chelsea remembered.

Bailey lay on top of her, and Chelsea got even wetter as their nipples pressed together. Bailey reclaimed Chelsea's mouth and delved inside with her tongue. She didn't stay there long, moving down to Chelsea's breast, again running her tongue around her nipple.

"I need," Chelsea tried to say between gasps of breath, "I need…" She grabbed Bailey's hand and pulled it down between her legs. "Here. I need you here."

Bailey ran her fingers through Chelsea's wetness. "I'm going inside now."

Chelsea cried out when Bailey's fingers pushed into her and her thumb pressed against her clitoris. "Oh, God, Bailey. You know just what to do."

"I've never forgotten you, and I've never forgotten your body." Bailey took Chelsea's nipple in her mouth again and sucked as she continued the rhythmic motion of her hand.

"I'm so close," Chelsea's hips jerked with each movement.

Bailey plunged deep inside. Chelsea slammed her eyes shut as her orgasm coursed through every fiber of her body. She clung to Bailey and held on until the last throbbing pulse subsided.

Bailey withdrew her hand. She moved her lips up Chelsea's chest until she gave her the gentlest of kisses, just as Chelsea remembered each time after Bailey made love to her. A drop of water hit her cheek. Bailey was crying. Chelsea didn't realize she was crying herself until tears spilled out and streamed down her face.

"Don't cry, baby." Chelsea sniffled.

Bailey wiped away one of Chelsea's stray tears with her thumb.

"I could say the same to you." She lay down beside her and held her.

"I love you," Chelsea whispered as she ran her fingers between Bailey's breasts.

"Love you, too, Chels." Bailey kissed the top of her head.

"You wiped me out. I don't think I can—"

"Shh. We have plenty of time."

They both grew quiet. Chelsea listened to the chirping of the crickets outside the open window for several minutes before breaking the silence. "What are we going to do?"

"About…"

"About us. I mean this is wonderful. It was always wonderful. But what about—"

"What about the other stuff? The time away from each other?"

Chelsea leaned up on her elbow to try to read Bailey's expression.

"We'll work it out. Nothing's worth losing you again." Bailey's voice sounded firm in its resolve. "Nothing. I don't care what I have to do. If I have to change jobs so we have more time together, I'm willing to do that."

Chelsea kissed her. "No one is giving up their job. It would cause resentment, and we wouldn't last long at all. You're good at what you do. I'd never ask you to give it up."

"I feel the same way."

"We'll make this work. We'll communicate like we said we'd do," Chelsea added with equal conviction. "Because I never want to be without you again, either."

"That's wonderful to hear. I don't think I could survive another separation. As to where we live? My job allows me to live anywhere. I don't want you giving up your position at the university. You're on tenure track, and I won't have you risking it."

"What about the house in Denver?"

"We'll sell it or we'll rent it out, and I'll move here. Tara's always been in love with it. She told me once if we ever thought of selling, to let her know first."

Chelsea lay back down in Bailey's arms. "I love it when you get all butch on me."

"Oh, so that's what I'm doing, is it?"

Chelsea slapped her lightly on the stomach. "You know what I mean. I agree with everything you're saying, but sometimes it's nice having you voice your opinion before I do." She grew quiet and listened to the sound of Bailey's heartbeat. Her breathing had evened out to the point that Chelsea thought she'd drifted off to sleep. "Bailey?"

"Hmm?"

"Do you think we should have talked more before we made love?"

Bailey chuckled. "Probably."

Chelsea snuggled even closer. "Doesn't matter," she murmured as her eyelids grew heavier with each passing second.

Bailey blinked a few times and tried to take in her surroundings. The pale light filtering through the blinds announced the impending sunrise. She smiled as she felt the warm body stir beside her. Bailey's muscles ached for all the right reasons.

She had wondered if she'd wake up in the morning and question her judgment. But feeling Chelsea's body pressed next to her had righted everything in Bailey's world. During their separation, it was as though she'd pictured life around her in muted colors. Being with Chelsea had brought everything back into sharp, crystal focus.

"What are you thinking?" Chelsea asked, her voice muffled.

"I'm thinking that I've been a damn fool for these past eleven months."

"Don't say that. We're both one hundred percent responsible for our fifty percent of this relationship. Nothing more, nothing less. Which means we were both at fault."

"What makes you so smart?"

"Well..." Chelsea swung her leg over Bailey and straddled her. "I do have those three degrees."

"Mmm hmm." Bailey stroked her hands up and down Chelsea's sides.

Chelsea leaned over so her nipples brushed against Bailey's. "But I've learned a lot in the nine plus years I've known you."

Bailey pulled her down. "What's the most important thing you've learned?"

"That my body molds into yours like a hand to a glove. But even more than that..." Chelsea placed her hand over Bailey's heart. "Our hearts are meant to beat together, not apart. I'm lost without you, Bailey." She touched her lips against Bailey's, and the kiss quickly ignited their passion.

"God, how I've missed you," Bailey said as Chelsea took her nipple in her mouth while rubbing the other nipple hard with her thumb.

Chelsea kissed a path down Bailey's stomach. She planted a light kiss on her mound. Bailey remembered that signal well, and she willingly opened her legs. Chelsea spread apart her folds and gave her one last smoldering look before she lowered her mouth to Bailey's wetness. She took her time as she ran her tongue along Bailey's clit, never taking her fully.

"Please, Chelsea." Bailey raised her hips, trying to push against Chelsea's lips.

Chelsea answered her plea and sucked on her clit, not stopping her assault until Bailey climaxed.

Bailey weakly tugged on Chelsea's head. "Okay, stop." Chelsea gave her one last swipe of her tongue. "Jesus," Bailey hissed.

Chelsea crawled back up Bailey's body, leaned over her and kissed Bailey long and hard. "I forgot how good you taste, but thank you for reminding me," she said with a sexy smile.

"Come here, you." Bailey pulled her to her side. She brushed her fingers through Chelsea's soft hair. Bailey had been wrong. Not only had everything righted itself in her world. The entire universe had shifted back into place.

Bailey must have drifted off, because when she checked the time, an hour had passed.

"I love watching you sleep." Chelsea ran her fingertips along the side of Bailey's face. "So at peace."

"You. You're my peace, Chels." Bailey gave her a gentle kiss. "What do you have to do today?"

"I'd love to stay in bed with you, but I need to go into the office and work on some stuff for the semester."

"I'll catch up on my notes and jump ahead in the diary. I think the next important date would be when they start filming *A Sheltered Heart*. I'll see if I'm right. Do you want to keep reading to each other?"

"I enjoy it, don't you?" Chelsea asked.

"Of course."

"Then let's keep at it."

Chapter 22

Chelsea parked in the university parking lot. The lot was almost empty, which wasn't unusual for a weekday morning in the summer.

After entering her office, she powered up her computer and thumbed through the mail stacked in her in-box. Nothing of any importance. She took her flash drive from her briefcase and plugged it into a USB slot.

For the next two hours, she concentrated on her work and didn't hear someone step into her doorway.

"Chelsea, good to see you."

Chelsea didn't look up from the computer screen. "Hey, Rebecca."

Rebecca stood over her. "So, how's it going?"

Chelsea leaned back in her chair. "I'm doing well."

"Haven't seen you much these past few weeks."

"No. Been busy with the Burnett project. I came in to catch up on school stuff."

Rebecca stared down at the floor. "Um… so, how are you and Bailey?"

Bailey decided she'd surprise Chelsea with a visit to her office. They could get lunch at the Union Building and enjoy the beautiful weather under one of the old trees on campus. She found Chelsea's campus address and was about to enter her office when she heard someone else speaking.

Rebecca. Asking about her. Bailey stopped outside the door. She gave in to the temptation to eavesdrop; she wanted to hear Chelsea's answer to Rebecca's question.

"We're doing great, Rebecca. Better than great, actually."

Bailey couldn't hold back a satisfied grin.

"Chelsea, I know the two of you were together before, but you seemed so unhappy when you got here."

"I was unhappy. More than anything because I felt I'd given up too easily on the best thing that ever happened to me."

"There had to be a reason you split up."

Bailey leaned forward. She was anticipating Chelsea's answer probably as much as Rebecca.

"We didn't communicate like we should have. We'd been so good at it throughout the beginning of our relationship that I think we took it for granted. But these past few weeks, we've found out how much we've missed each other and how precious our love really is." Chelsea's voice was thick with emotion. "And how we'll never make the same mistake again."

"Guess that means no more dating."

"But we can still be friends and colleagues, Rebecca."

"I'd like that."

Bailey tapped on the doorframe. "Hey, Chels." Was the burst of love she felt for Chelsea obvious on her face? Seeing Chelsea's expression, she guessed it was.

"Hey, hon."

Bailey entered and held out her hand to Rebecca. "How's it going?"

Rebecca clasped her hand and this time didn't attempt the death grip like she had at the pub. "I'm good. I need to let you get back to work, Chelsea." She made a beeline for the door and left.

Chelsea grinned at Bailey.

"What?"

"How long had you been standing out there?"

"Uh…"

Chelsea giggled. "It's okay. I'm glad you heard it."

"I'm sorry. I know I shouldn't have—"

"No, Bailey. It's fine." She grabbed the hem of Bailey's T-shirt and pulled her down for a kiss. "I see you didn't have trouble finding my office."

Bailey leaned her hip against the desk. "Not at all. I was a student here once, remember?" She held up the diary. "Want to grab lunch at the Union and then read some more?"

"I'd love to."

*   *   *

After they'd eaten, Bailey brought a blanket from her Jeep and carried it to what had been one of their favorite spots on campus— one of the giant oak trees by the Jordan "River," which was really a stream that wended its way through the campus.

They settled on the blanket. Bailey leaned her back against the big tree trunk and patted her lap.

"Why don't you lay your head down, and I'll pick up where I think we need to go next."

Chelsea got comfortable. "Is it when Daphne's working on *A Sheltered Heart*?"

"Yes. I'll admit to cheating a little and reading ahead, but this is good, like we thought it would be." Bailey flipped to the marked passage. As she stroked Chelsea's hair, she began reading.

"Wednesday, 14 March 1962. Daphne and I had been back in the States five months, and I was becoming acclimated again to the way of life here. Filming of *A Sheltered Heart* was going strong. As I promised, I was on the set every day…"

* * *

As expected, this wasn't an easy part for Daphne. I watched as she struggled through some of the scenes with Gordon. When Frank would call "cut," I'd hurry to her side and take her to a private area where only the two of us could sit. She'd sometimes cry, agonizing whether she'd made the right decision in taking the part.

Today would be even more emotional for her. The scene called for her character, in a drunken stupor, to lash out at Gordon's character and force him to make the difficult decision to leave her. She'd gone ahead of me to the studio. I arrived just as Frank yelled, "Action!" I stood back in the shadows and watched her work, mesmerised as the scene unfolded.

Daphne staggered to the liquor cabinet and poured bourbon into a tumbler of ice.

Gordon shouted at her from where he stood as he gripped the chair in front of him. "That's your answer to everything, isn't it, Erica? Booze. Like drinking yourself into oblivion will solve all your problems."

Daphne twisted around, her drink splashing over the glass to the carpet below. I had to keep from gasping aloud over the transformation. Her hair was unkempt. Her dark eyes, ablaze in anger, glared at Gordon. "Who are you to tell me wha' to do?" she slurred. She took a drink and swept it in front of her in a grand motion, spilling more bourbon on the carpet. "Whose money bought this place? Whose money pays the bills? You're nothing, Phillip. *Nothing* without me."

He lowered his head, his knuckles white as his fingers dug into the cushion. "I can't watch this anymore." His voice cracked with emotion. He made a move toward the door, but she blocked his path.

"That's it. Leave like all the other people in my life. Leave like the coward I always knew you were."

He pushed her aside, and she staggered backward. He slammed the door so hard, the pictures rattled on the walls.

"Go!" Daphne screamed and threw her glass against the door. It shattered in tiny pieces, and the liquid dripped down the wood. "You think I can't make it without you?" She stepped backwards, lost her balance, and fell to her knees. I held back from running to her side. She swiped at the tears that ran down her cheeks. Her face, streaked with mascara, contorted in complete anguish. "I can make it." She sank into a heap on the floor and buried her head in her arms. In a gritty voice that seemed torn from her soul, she spoke once more. "I can make it."

The set was deathly quiet. Frank shook his head, as if finally realizing his place. "Cut!" He stood up, walked over to Daphne, and helped her to her feet. "Remarkable, Daphne. Simply remarkable."

A makeup woman ran over and handed Daphne a towel to wipe her face.

"Thank you," she said quietly.

The door flung open and Gordon lumbered inside. "Goddamn, woman, you can act." He hugged Daphne.

She broke out of the embrace and visibly relaxed when she saw me. "This is it for the day, Frank?"

"Yes. We have the hospital scenes next week to finish everything up."

They'd already shot the reunion scene between Erica and Phillip the week before. I'd never gotten used to the fact that movies filmed out of sequence.

Everyone dispersed, and I made my way to her. "How are you doing?" I asked in a hushed voice.

She shook her head slightly. "Let's get out of here."

On our way home, Daphne was quiet, her forehead pressed against the window glass.

When we arrived at the mansion, she tugged me to the back of the house. "Come on, Ellie, let's go out to the garden."

We walked to one of the benches. Our bench.

"Do you remember when we first kissed?" She stared out at the surrounding flowers.

"How could I forget? You changed my life that night."

"And you mine." She turned to me. "I don't think you realise how much you've altered my whole universe. The way I look at everything around me."

We sat for a few minutes, blanketed by the intoxicating scent of flowers.

"How are you really?" I asked.

"I'll be glad when we finish this damn movie."

"I'm sorry I ever suggested we return and for you take the part if—"

"No, don't apologise. You were right. I was hiding away from my life and what I'd felt called to do. This picture has emphasised that point. Sometimes you pick the part and you go through the motions during filming. But sometimes, on one or two rare occasions, the part picks you. It's what happened on this one."

"I'm not sure if it'll make you feel any better, but you've been amazing to watch, Daph. I can't keep my eyes off you. I mean, I can never keep my eyes off you. But this is different. It's as if I'm drawn to you, watching your every move, listening to every word you speak. I think you have an award-winning performance here."

She blushed. "I don't know about that."

"I do. Mark my words, Daphne DeMonet. You'll be accepting one of those ugly little gold trophies they hand out for the best at your craft."

She laughed. "Ugly little gold trophies?" She leaned in and kissed me. "I love you so much."

"I love you, too."

Her expression grew serious. "Promise you'll be there next week."

"Right by your side," I said and kissed her again.

Friday, 23 March 1962. It was a difficult week for Daphne. The shooting of the rehab hospital scene proved more traumatic than even I had pictured. I still felt a lot of guilt since I had suggested she take the part. Watching her these past few days had been heart-wrenching.

She had to be on the set at eight this morning and told me to sleep in. I'd lain in the bed for an hour before taking a shower and asking Perkins to drive me to the studio.

I entered the studio and made my way to the set. I stayed behind Frank and out of Daphne's line of sight as I watched the scene unfold.

Daphne lay curled up on a small cot in what was supposed to be a patient's room at the rehabilitation hospital. White walls and stark, bright lighting made her appear even paler. I worried that the dark circles under her eyes weren't from makeup but from genuine lack of sleep. She balled her fists tight against her stomach. Her wailing cut me to the core.

"A drink!" she cried, repeatedly. Daphne lurched to her feet, staggered to the door, and pounded on the glass. "You have to give me a drink! Please, oh God, please. It hurts. It hurts so much." She bolted for the toilet in the corner of the room and fell to her knees. With her back to the camera, she made loud retching noises. She stood and wiped her mouth with the back of her hand. She threw herself at the door again, pounding and pounding. She'd scraped her knuckles in the process. Splotches of blood dotted the white door. She slid to the floor and held her head in her hands as she sobbed.

Frank yelled, "Cut!"

Without a thought, I ran to her and knelt with her on the floor. She wasn't acting. This was real, raw emotion spilling over. Emotion compiled from her years of living with an abusive, alcoholic father. Taking her in my arms, I whispered so that only she heard how much I loved her. She clung to me, and I held her tighter.

"That's a wrap, everyone," Frank said. "Let's give Daphne some privacy."

The crew made a quick exit, and soon, it was just the two of us.

"Let me see your hands, love."

Daphne stretched them out. I gently flipped them over and winced when I saw the scraped knuckles. Taking my handkerchief out of my pocket, I held it against the small cuts to staunch the bleeding.

"Come on." I helped her to her feet, and we sat down on the cot. I rocked her gently, still whispering endearments.

She sniffled as she fingered my blouse. "I got you all wet."

"Don't even worry about it, Daph. The important thing is you're okay. That's all that matters to me." I tilted her chin up. "*Are you okay?*"

She nodded, but her bottom lip quivered. "I think so." More tears flowed. "I hope this is the last of it, Ellie. I don't think I could handle another scene."

"I don't know if you heard Frank, but he wrapped it."

Relief flooded her face. "Oh, thank God."

"Why don't we get you home and into a nice hot bath?" I

guided us toward the exit. Frank stopped us before we got too far.

He embraced Daphne. "I've never been so proud of any actor or actress I've worked with as I am of you. It's been a privilege directing you these past few months."

"And now it's time for her to get some rest," I said pointedly.

"Yes. I'll let you both go. I'll call you Monday once I go over the dailies, Daphne, but your work is done on this one."

Daphne nodded and thanked him.

We stepped outside and looked for the limousine. Perkins pulled up, got out of the car, and opened the back door. I slid in first and stayed next to Daphne when she sat down. She collapsed into me.

"Home, please, Perkins," I told him.

As we drove, I stroked Daphne's hair. Although the filming had taken its toll on her, I thought it had almost been a cleansing—as if she'd exorcised her childhood demons on that set. Only time would tell if I was right.

* * *

Chelsea was so caught up in visualizing Daphne on the set, she was surprised Bailey had stopped speaking. "Aren't you going to read more?"

"Pushy little thing today, aren't you?"

Chelsea grabbed Bailey in the side where she knew she was ticklish.

Bailey swatted her hand away, laughing. "Wait, wait! Give me a minute and I'll find the next passage I thought we should read."

"That's more like it."

"You're such a slave driver." Bailey flipped through the pages. "Okay, here we are."

"Are you going to tell me what we're about to hear?"

"No."

Chelsea started to tickle her again, but Bailey intercepted her attempt. "Do you want me to read, or not?"

"Go on, spoilsport."

"Monday, 8 April 1963. Tonight, at the Santa Monica City Auditorium, they'll coronate Daphne at the thirty-fifth annual Movieland Film Awards. I was certain of it, just as certain as I knew I wouldn't be there to see it. Only Daphne wasn't aware of this yet…

* * *

She rushed past me on her way to one of her jewellery boxes. She held up a delicate strand of pearls. Ones that I had bought her.

"I think these will look lovely with my burgundy gown, don't you?" Daphne frowned. "Why are you still sitting on the bed, and why aren't you dressed?"

"I'm not coming."

Her arm dropped to her side. "What do you mean you're not coming?"

"Exactly what I said."

"Why?" she asked with a tremor in her voice.

"They're expecting you to show up with Gordon, as always. The divorced couple who are still such good friends. You know the drill." I tried to hide my distaste for the whole charade but didn't think I was successful.

She sat beside me on the end of the bed. "Yes, Gordon will be there, but so will you."

I shook my head. "No, Daph. It'll be better for you this way."

"That's where you're wrong. What is right for me is for you to be there, too."

"I don't think—"

She pressed her fingers to my lips. "This is where I think for you, my darling. And my thoughts are that you need to slip into that gown I bought you last week and come with me."

I gazed into her eyes, pleading with mine for a "yes."

"Please," Daphne whispered, caressing my cheek.

"The black one?"

She clapped her hands in pleasure. "Yes. Come on, I'll help you dress."

We picked Gordon up at his home, and he slid into the backseat with Daphne between us.

"I'm still not sure this is a good idea," I said.

"Come on, Eleanor." Gordon patted my leg. "Tonight's Daphne's night and it's also yours. You deserve this just as much, and don't you forget it."

"He's right, Ellie." Daphne leaned over and kissed me on the cheek. She used her thumb to wipe away the lipstick.

We arrived at the City Auditorium. Perkins hopped out and opened the back door. Gordon stood and offered Daphne his hand. Flashbulbs went off around us. He tucked Daphne's hand in his elbow and led her over to the fans draped across the red velvet ropes. I hung back while she worked down the line and signed the books thrust in her face.

She signed the last one and moved toward the red carpet. But before she set one foot on it, she did a remarkable thing. She held out her hand and motioned me to her with a dazzling smile and a lift of her chin.

I shot nervous glances at the cameras surrounding us and took her hand.

And that's how she walked down the carpet—with one arm tucked into the crook of Gordon's elbow and the other in mine.

We took our seats and sat through the other award presentations until it was time for the reading of the nominees in the Best Actress category. Even though I had every confidence that she'd win, the competition was tough this year. Shirley Morrison had been especially outstanding in *A Rose by Any Other Name*, as had Andrea Louis in *Going Home*. I held my breath after Richard Patton had finished reading the nominees and tore open the envelope. "And the winner is…" He grinned, obviously pleased with who had won. "Daphne DeMonet for *A Sheltered Heart*."

Shouts rang out around us, and everyone rose to their feet. Daphne stood and accepted Gordon's embrace and kiss.

"Congratulations, kid," he said as he applauded with everyone else.

Before Daphne walked to the stage, she squeezed my arm and gave me a look I'll never forget. One just for me—a combination of gratitude and a smouldering promise of what lay ahead for our evening.

She stepped up on stage and took the award from Richard before addressing the crowd.

"I have so many people to thank. Frank Teller, thank you for bringing this part to me and urging me to take it no matter how many times I tried to turn it down. To Gordon." She pointed the statue toward him. "You're proof that, yes, an ex-husband can indeed still be a good friend." Laughter rippled throughout the auditorium. "To my mother back home. I love you." She paused. "And a very special thank-you to a dear, dear companion. I couldn't have done this without you." Her voice broke as she met my eyes briefly before following Richard off stage.

No, she didn't say she loved me for everyone to hear, but it didn't matter. We knew.

The evening concluded with Frank winning Best Director and

A Sheltering Heart winning Best Picture. The only travesty was they hadn't nominated Gordon for his outstanding portrayal of Phillip, but he was so happy for Daphne, you'd never know if he was disappointed at the slight.

After posing with the other winners and after many congratulatory embraces, we piled into the limousine. As soon as we were a safe distance away, Daphne pulled me in for a passionate kiss. "There'll be more of that later after our party."

"What party?"

"You didn't tell her?" Gordon asked.

"No. I wanted it to be a surprise and didn't want to jinx it tonight. We're having a party at the mansion, but only friends and colleagues of our persuasion are invited," she said with a wicked grin.

"How did you pull that off without my knowing?"

Gordon leaned forward to look at me. "Eleanor, you need to give me a little credit. We gay men live to plan parties."

Champagne flowed as we all danced to the hired band—also of our persuasion, as Daphne had put it. She and I swayed to a wonderful rendition of Elvis Presley's "Can't Help Falling in Love." Her hands swept down to my hips and then back up to my bare shoulders. She whispered in my ear, "Why don't we slip upstairs? No one will notice."

I glanced around at the crowd of friends. She was probably right. It was late—well past midnight. Everyone was pretty well inebriated as they laughed and tipped back their glasses.

Without another word, she took me to the stairway and we slowly made our journey upstairs. I gazed below us. Gordon and Quinn held up their champagne glasses in a salute.

Daphne led me down the hall to our bedroom and closed the door. We undressed without speaking, each sensing the heated urgency between us. She pushed me onto the bed and draped her body over mine. Her dark hair spilled down like a curtain, enshrouding us as she leaned in to capture my lips.

"Do you know how much I love you?" she asked.

I couldn't answer because her lips now encircled my nipple. I entwined my fingers into her thick hair while she tugged and nibbled, knowing what I liked. She looked up at me and her eyes simmered with desire and purpose.

She began her journey down my stomach to the *V* of my legs. She planted light kisses along the inside of my thighs and gently pushed my legs farther apart. I resisted, but she continued the pressure with her hands.

"Let me, Ellie. Please."

This had always been one aspect of our lovemaking I'd resisted. I'd shown my love to her this way many times, but I'd never let her reciprocate. It frightened me… a fear of the unknown.

"Trust me," she whispered, just as she said when she made love to me for the first time. Her dark gaze held mine, and what I saw there was a promise that she wouldn't hurt me.

I lay back and squeezed my eyes shut. Her fingers spread my wet folds apart. The first touch of her lips to my sodden heat was like the call of a siren. I couldn't resist the pull as she took me in her mouth and brought me higher with each loving stroke of her tongue. My hips flew off the bed, but she held me tight. She would take me to the point where I felt like I'd explode and then retreat to give me soft kisses where I needed her most.

I grabbed her head and pushed her hard into me. "God, Daphne, please…"

I felt her mouth pull into a smile. She took my clitoris into her lips and tugged with purpose. A purpose I knew wouldn't end until I was spent.

"Oh God!" I cried out. When I thought it couldn't get any better, she slipped two fingers deep inside. I grabbed hold of the sheets and held them tight in my fists as she brought me to a pounding release.

Daphne kept her mouth against me and stayed inside until my last throbbing spasm had subsided. She slid out her fingers, kissed her way back up my body, and held me in her arms.

"I should… you need…" I stopped, realising I was incapable of speaking. "Oh, bloody hell."

"Now, that wasn't so bad, was it?" she asked, her voice teasing and light.

I feebly smacked her stomach before cupping her breast.

"Sleep, darling," she said as I gave in to the blessed exhaustion. "We have all night."

* * *

"God almighty," Bailey croaked and shut the diary. "They sure had a passionate relationship."

"Reminds me of another couple I know." Chelsea peered up at Bailey through the late afternoon sunlight shooting through the trees. "Don't you agree?"

"Yeah, I agree." Bailey brushed her fingers through Chelsea's hair.

Chelsea's body warmed to Bailey's touch. "Feels nice."

"We could sit here longer and enjoy the mild weather, or we could head home and enjoy our bed."

"Home. I like the sound of that," Chelsea said as she rose to her feet. "I especially love the 'enjoy our bed' part."

* * *

"What are you thinking?" Bailey asked her.

They'd come home, stripped off their clothes, and giggled and groped each other on the way to the bedroom.

Chelsea stroked Bailey's nipple. "That I can't wait until you move here permanently."

Bailey stopped the motion of her fingers. "I can't talk if you're doing that."

"I don't know. You did a lot of talking earlier when I was doing this. I believe the word 'harder' came up a time or two."

"Ha ha."

"Oh, all right. I'll be good." Chelsea pushed her pillows up and leaned against them next to Bailey. "Can you talk now?"

"Sorry, but you do things to me. Believe me, I'm not complaining."

"Good. I'm glad. Seriously, though, when do you think we can get you moved?"

"I haven't talked to Tara yet. I mean, I have, but not about this. Like I told you, she always said she'd buy the house if we ever wanted to sell."

Chelsea remembered the discussion they'd had about the house before she'd left. Bailey had wanted to sell. She insisted on paying Chelsea her half of the money. But Chelsea had balked. As long as they shared the house, she shared a part of Bailey. Over the course of the almost year apart, Bailey had inquired by e-mail on occasion about selling it. Every time, Chelsea had a feeble excuse why it wasn't a good idea.

"It's okay. I really didn't want to sell at the time, either," Bailey said. "I think I just wanted you to tell me you felt the same way without actually saying it."

Chelsea caught Bailey's smile.

"How did you—"

"I can still read you, Chels. Why don't I give Tara a call tonight and see what she says?"

"Do you really want to live here, Bailey?" No matter how close they'd become again over the past few weeks, Chelsea still had a little insecurity.

Bailey put her mind at ease. "I wouldn't want to live another day away from you." She gave Chelsea a long, lingering kiss. "How about we go raid the fridge?"

After they'd finished snacking on leftover pizza over a couple of beers, Bailey called Tara. Bailey gave her the news, and they chatted for a few more minutes.

"She wants to talk to you." Bailey handed Chelsea the phone and went into the kitchen.

"Hey, Tara." Chelsea nodded her thanks at Bailey when she returned with another beer.

"You cannot believe how happy I am about the two of you," Tara said.

"No more than I."

"Are you serious that you'd want to sell the house? After all you put into it?"

"My job's in Bloomington, and Bailey can do her research from anywhere, so it works out for both of us. I'm renting this place. Maybe we'll get a house together in the future, but we have lots of time to decide that."

Bailey had already given Tara the price of the house, which Tara had agreed to, so they spent the next several minutes catching up on everything. Chelsea finished with a promise they'd be in touch soon.

She held up her bottle to Bailey. "Here's to saying goodbye to our old home..."

"And hello to our new," Bailey finished for her.

Chapter 23

Through the next week, they pored over the diaries to find pertinent dates. They discovered that Eleanor didn't write every day. In fact, months passed in between some journal entries.

Daphne stayed active in her career after winning the Movieland Film Award. From 1963 to 1974, she made twelve films, garnering two more nominations, one for Best Supporting Actress and one for Best Actress. But health concerns caused her to slow down in 1975.

After sending Joanne her most recent notes, Bailey drove to the campus to meet Chelsea for lunch and another reading. They sat down again under their favorite tree.

"My turn," Chelsea said.

Bailey handed her the diary and motioned to Chelsea's lap. "My turn?" she asked.

"Sure."

Bailey laid her head down, and Chelsea started reading.

"Saturday, 14 June 1975. It was a mild day with temperatures in the seventies. Daphne and I decided to enjoy the pool…"

* * *

We have a gorgeous outdoor pool that we rarely use. Daphne had been so busy with her career since we returned to the States, she was usually exhausted when she arrived home from the studio.

I drifted on a raft and enjoyed the warmth of the sun on my skin. Daphne splashed nearby. I admired her muscled back as she touched the other side of the pool and swam toward me. She had always been a strong swimmer, which was another reason it was a shame we'd wasted this beautiful pool.

I closed my eyes and thought she'd continued to the other side until light droplets of water sprinkled my face. I peeked at her. She was grinning as she treaded water beside me.

"Do you mind?" I asked with exaggerated annoyance.

"What? Is this bothering you?" She cupped water in her hand and sloshed it onto my stomach.

"Hey!"

Daphne leaned her elbows on the raft and gave me a curious look.

"What's on your mind, Miss DeMonet?"

"You and me naked."

I laughed. "That's always on your mind. I guess my question should have been 'do you have something new on your mind?'"

"You and me naked while Douglas Roman paints our portrait."

I sat up suddenly. The raft rocked precariously and almost threw me in the pool. "Are you insane?"

"Some have thought I am, although I don't think I've exhibited the symptoms over the years. It depends on which director you ask." She stroked my thigh in lazy circles with her fingertips. "Ellie, I want us to have a portrait done, and Douglas is the perfect one to do it. He's talented and sought out by people all over town. And he's gay."

"Like that makes all the difference in the world."

"Well, it should somewhat. It should at least make it a little easier."

"Daphne, you know how shy I am, and you expect me to pose nude?"

"Do it for me. I have a birthday coming up next month. This would make a perfect gift."

I groaned. "Can't I get you something a little more practical, like a necklace or a bracelet?"

She stuck her bottom lip out in her cutest pout. The one that made me give in every time.

"Pretty, pretty please?"

"I can't believe I'm going along with this."

"You mean it? You'll do it for me?"

"Yes, for your birthday. And remember this one in the years to come because, trust me, I'll frequently remind you."

"Come in here with me, darling," she said with a sexy purr.

I tilted the raft and slid into the water. She pulled me toward the shallow end and pushed me against the side of the pool. Then she gave me one of her toe-curling, blood-boiling kisses, nipping and tugging on my lips. I put my hands around her neck and yanked her forward, prolonging the moment.

She leaned her forehead against mine. "Thank you."

"Anything for you, love."

She kissed the tip of my nose. "I'll go make that call to Douglas before you get cold feet." She stepped up the ladder.

I draped my arms over the side of the pool and admired Daphne's still firm and sleek body in her black one-piece bathing suit. Then I cringed as I thought about what I'd agreed to do.

Thursday, 19 June 1975. We arrived at Douglas's studio to pose. He couldn't have been more gracious and understanding. I'd met the man at one of our parties. Tall and thin with wispy blond hair, his relaxed air set me at ease immediately. When he shook my hand, I noticed his long, tapered fingers—definitely the hand of an artist.

He directed us behind a partition where we'd shed our clothes and slip on two rather thin satin robes.

I fingered the material. "Daphne, I'm not sure I can do this."

"Sweetheart, I understand if you can't. Let me go out and tell him no. Maybe he can paint us wearing these." She turned to leave.

"Wait." I grabbed her arm. I knew how much this meant to her. She'd been talking about it nonstop since last week. "I'll try. That's all I can promise."

We undressed, put on the robes, and approached the dais he'd set up in the middle of the loft.

"Daphne, I want you to sit with your legs stretched out," Douglas said. "Once you're seated comfortably"—he pointed at me—"I'd like you between her legs with your knees drawn up to your chest." He demonstrated the position to us. "Daphne, you'll drape your arms across her chest."

He walked back to his easel and readied his pencil. He'd already explained to us that he would start with a rough sketch and then would begin filling in with oil. He kept his face averted as we prepared to disrobe.

"Ready?" Daphne asked. Without any further pretence, she dropped her robe and posed the way that Douglas had asked.

I let my robe slide to the floor and settled between Daphne's legs.

She leaned in and whispered into my ear, "I have to say I don't mind this at all."

I was too nervous to respond. Douglas came over and manipulated me into the position he wanted. When he finished and Daphne draped her arms around my neck, I saw the look he was going for. Yes, we were nude, but the way he posed us, no one studying the painting would see anything but what their imagination wanted them to see.

Douglas walked back to his easel and started sketching. "Perfect, Eleanor, perfect. That shy expression is what I want to capture."

I wanted to tell him it wouldn't take much effort to maintain it.

"And Daphne. Perfect. Like you're the cat that swallowed the canary."

For the next hour, he sketched, his brow creased in concentration. He let us take a break while he readied his paints. After another fifteen minutes, he had us back on the dais. He painted for another hour. Sweat trickled down my back. I hoped against hope he'd stop soon.

"I think I have what I need," he finally said as he set his brush aside.

I groaned at my cramped muscles and reached for my robe to slip it back on. Daphne did the same. She walked toward the canvas, but he held up his hand like a crossing guard.

"No."

"No?" Daphne asked as her gait hitched.

I almost laughed aloud. No one usually said that word to Daphne in such a forceful manner.

"Not until I'm finished. Give me a few weeks to work on the painting. When I'm done, I'll call you."

"Oh, Dougie, come on." Daphne took a couple more steps.

"I said no, Daphne. That may be a foreign concept to you, but it's how I work. If you take one more step, I'll refuse to finish it."

She quirked one dark eyebrow. This time I couldn't help it. I burst out laughing.

"Douglas, you are a dear man," I said. "Come on, Daph. I'm stiff and tired and would like to go home. Let him do his work."

She mumbled all the way to the partition and even as she dressed.

I zipped up my trousers. "Do you want the painting or don't you?"

"Fine." Daphne finished buttoning her blouse.

I tipped up her chin and gave her a light kiss. "When you say that word, I know it's time to go home and have a cocktail. Which is exactly what we're going to do."

Wednesday, 9 July 1975. We received the call from Douglas this morning that he'd finished the painting, two days before Daphne's fifty-fourth birthday. I finished dressing. Daphne had already showered and dressed before me and was downstairs waiting. I knew she was anxious to see the finished work.

I hurried down the stairs, expecting to find her in the living room, but she wasn't there.

"Daph?" I walked around the corner into the kitchen and cried out. She lay on the kitchen floor. A cup of coffee had shattered around her. "Daphne!" I ran to her and knelt in the ceramic shards, not caring if I cut my knees. "Oh my God." I pulled her up, rested her head in my lap, and pushed her hair back from her face, which was pale and drawn.

When she opened her eyes, her gaze was unfocused. "Wh-what happened?"

"I don't know. I came downstairs and found you on the floor. I think you fainted."

She tried to sit up but fell back into my arms.

"Easy," I said in a soft voice. "Not so fast. Wait until you get your bearings." I kept brushing her hair with my fingertips until she seemed a little more focused.

"I think I can sit up now." She grabbed her head. "Oh, God, my head's killing me."

"Did you hit it? Let me feel." I rubbed around her scalp but didn't find any lumps.

"Help me up."

I debated whether it was a good idea, but I helped her to her feet and led her into the living room to the sofa.

"Let me get you something." I returned from the kitchen with a glass of water. "Drink a little."

Daphne took a few sips. "I'm feeling better. The headache's going away." She gave me a weak smile. "I think we can leave for Douglas's now."

"Oh, no, we're not. I'll call him and let him know we'll come over tomorrow. I'm taking you to the hospital." I intended to jump to my feet to get my purse, but she grabbed my arm.

"Ellie, it's no big deal. I probably had a drop in blood sugar or something. I've not eaten anything yet this morning."

"Don't try to talk me out of it."

"How about we compromise and you call Doctor Barry? Will that make you happy? Because I'm not going to the hospital. Period."

Daphne had that stubborn set to her mouth that I'd seen from her so many times when she worked on a film. It drove Frank Teller and the other directors crazy. But she was usually right about the direction she wanted the film to go in. I hoped she was right this time. Knowing I didn't have a choice, I went to the address book and made the call. I wasn't fond of Doctor Barry, mainly because he seemed to give into Daphne's wishes so many times over the years.

Since he was Daphne's personal physician, we had no trouble having him agree to come to the house. I hung up and phoned Douglas to tell him we'd see him tomorrow.

About an hour later, Doctor Barry arrived. He was a short, balding man who, because of his eyebrows that pointed straight up to his forehead, always looked like he was in a perpetual state of surprise. He checked Daphne's blood pressure and her reflexes, which seemed to be a little sluggish. His brow furrowed as he flashed his penlight into her eyes. After he listened to her heart, he leaned back in his chair and asked her questions about what she remembered last and when she'd eaten.

He put away his instruments and motioned for me to take a seat next to Daphne. We awaited his prognosis.

"Daphne, I think you experienced a spell of hypoglycaemia."

"How will you be able to know for sure?" I asked. "Shouldn't she come in for some tests?"

"Yes. We need to do some blood work to check her glucose levels. I don't think it's anything more serious than that."

I remained sceptical. "But it wouldn't hurt to check for any other reason, would it?"

Daphne shot me a look.

"That's up to Daphne, but I don't see any other problems. She hasn't presented enough symptoms for it to be a mild stroke or anything of that nature. Her speech isn't slurred, and she's coherent."

Daphne stood up and walked him to the door. "Thank you for coming on such short notice, Richard. I'll visit your office early next week for the test to check my glucose levels."

After he left, she talked before I even had a chance to object.

"I know you think I need more tests, but I trust Richard. If he says it's nothing major, I'll trust his judgment."

"Daph…"

"No, Ellie. I feel fine now. A little tired, but that's all."

I wasn't going to win this argument. Despite the nagging feeling in the pit of my stomach, I gave in.

Thursday, 10 July 1975. We arrived at Douglas's apartment loft in the afternoon after a lunch at our favourite restaurant. He ushered us inside. He'd set the painting on his easel in the centre of the room and had draped it with a cloth.

"I think you'll be pleased. It captures your essence as a couple." He grabbed the bottom of the cloth and tossed it back with a dramatic flourish.

I stared at the painting, stunned at what I was seeing. Daphne was glorious, a goddess with an impish smile. He was right. He'd captured my shyness perfectly, even the blushing of my cheeks.

"Douglas, you've outdone yourself," Daphne said as she approached the painting. She reached out to touch it, but stopped short of the canvas. "Amazing."

He turned to me. "Eleanor?"

"Since it will be the one and only time I'll ever pose nude, I'm honoured that you made it such a work of art."

Douglas beamed with pride. "I'm glad you approve. And how's your health, Daphne?"

"The doctor thinks it's low blood sugar."

"Can they tell for sure?"

"No. I need to have a blood test next week." She looked drained.

"I think we should get you home, Daph."

"Of course," Douglas said. "I'll bring this over to you tomorrow morning in my truck. Would that be okay?"

"That's perfect," I answered.

On our way home, Daphne was quiet. When we got inside, she said, "I think I'll go upstairs and take a nap."

"I'll join you."

We undressed and stretched out under the covers. Lying on my side, I asked, "Are you sure you still want to have this party tomorrow night?"

"Yes. It's a tradition with our friends, just as yours is next month. I want them to see Douglas's painting."

"I'm not sure about others seeing—"

"Eleanor Burnett, you are one gorgeous forty-five-year-old woman who should not be ashamed of her body. In the least."

I felt the flush rise to my cheeks.

"I can see that blush even in the dim lighting." She leaned over, kissed me, and cupped my breast. "Why don't you let me worship that forty-five-year-old body for the next several hours?"

Which is exactly what she did.

* * *

"I hate to read this about the doctor misdiagnosing her stroke." Chelsea closed the diary. "I know what's coming later, and I hate it."

Bailey's cell phone rang. She checked the caller ID and pointed at the diary. "It's our friend." She flipped the phone open. "Hello, Eleanor. How are you?"

"I'm doing well. My question is how are you and the fine doctor? And how have you come along in your reading?"

"We've progressed to July 1975."

"Daphne's first stroke. Which that quack completely missed."

"We were saying how we hate knowing what will come later."

"No more than I." Eleanor sniffed. "I believe you have a few readings before your next visit. When you get to the end of what interests you, call me. As I said, we'll finish the readings here."

"Of course."

"And say hello to Chelsea."

"Will do. Bye." Bailey flipped the phone shut. "She says hello."

"How is she?"

"She sounds okay except when I talked about the stroke. I could've kicked myself."

Chelsea stood and folded up the blanket. On the way to the car, she said, "I can't imagine being without someone I'd been in love with for over sixty years. There has to be such a void in her life."

"I think she's feeling it." Bailey keyed the ignition. "I'm curious as to why she wanted us to read all of this by ourselves."

Chelsea stroked her leg. "I think she had an inkling that you and I would grow closer with each reading. Perhaps she thought she was a distraction."

Bailey considered that. "Maybe you're right, but I don't think of her as a distraction. To me, she's our guardian angel who stepped into our lives right when we needed her most."

"Bailey Hampton, you're so romantic. But I already knew that." Chelsea leaned across the seat and kissed her.

After they got to the house, Chelsea suggested hamburgers on the grill, designating Bailey as the chef.

"Ah, I see. Only butches can grill burgers."

Chelsea patted her shoulder on the way to the kitchen. "Yup."

"Cute."

Chelsea prepared the patties. While Bailey fired up the grill, she lit the citronella torches around the patio. Bailey had the burgers going in no time, and within a half an hour, they were enjoying their dinner.

"What do you think of reading another passage tonight before we go to sleep?" Bailey asked around a bite of burger.

"I like the idea."

Chelsea had already taken a shower and was flipping through the diary while Bailey stripped down.

"See what interests you next." Bailey unsnapped her bra and stepped out of her panties.

Chelsea was concentrating on the diary. "I think there's a date in 1979 that's good. You might disagree, but you can—" Chelsea glanced up and watched Bailey collect her boxers and tank top on her way to the bathroom. "Damn."

Bailey gave her a cocky grin. "Yes?"

"And you expect me to want to read this?" Chelsea shouted at her back after she'd left the room. Bailey's laughter drifted through to her.

Twenty minutes later, Bailey walked in with her hair slicked back. Her nipples pressed against her tank top, and her thigh muscles rippled as she walked toward the bed.

"Why don't you go ahead and read?" Bailey slid into the bed next to her.

Chelsea was finding it difficult to swallow, much less read from the diary.

"Chels?"

"Read. Right. Sure." She opened the book. "Thursday, 5 July 1979. We flew to England after the Independence Day holiday in the States. We'd visited our cottage over the years, but I wanted this trip to be special for Daphne…"

* * *

She needed a break. She just finished a draining shoot in the heat of Arizona. I'd joined her and was there every night at the hotel when she returned from the set. She never complained, but I noticed the strain and weariness on her face that she tried to hide from me.

I picked Studland Bay on the Dorset coast in southernmost England. I could have selected any one of several outstanding inns, but I chose the Gentry House for its cliff-side view of the sea and for its beautiful gardens.

We drove down from London and enjoyed the lush countryside

along the way. I looked over at Daphne as I drove, pleased to see the tension in her face had already dissipated.

"I'm so glad filming's done," she said, smiling. "You always know when we need to get away, don't you?"

"I'm pretty in tune with you, Daph. Haven't you noticed over the years?"

"Oh, I've noticed. More than you'll ever know," she said softly.

We arrived at the Gentry House in the late afternoon. The two-story Gothic-style building immediately charmed Daphne, which in turn pleased me. When we followed the hotel staff members who had taken charge of our bags, we both faltered in our gait as we ogled the opulent lobby. Built in 1923, the place retained the original darkened wood and elegant chandelier from that era. With the solicitous staff dressed in old-fashioned red bellmen uniforms, I had the eerie feeling of stepping back in time. The desk clerk gave us our key, and we followed the two young men who carried our luggage to our room.

After giving them a generous tip, I admired our accommodations. The room was painted a light, cheery yellow. A king-size, four-post, cherrywood bed sat against the wall to the left of the door. A matching cherrywood wardrobe sat against the wall to the right. Beyond that was the doorway leading into what I assumed was the bathroom.

Daphne stood in front of the bay window. I walked up beside her, pulled her close, and looked out at the bay that led to the great expanse of sea beyond. Sunlight twinkled like thousands of fireflies skimming across the blue water. Daphne relaxed under my fingertips, which relaxed me. I'd wanted her to love this place as much as I thought she would.

"Ellie, it's breathtaking," she said as she rested her head on my shoulder. "Can we change clothes and go down to the beach?"

"Whatever you desire."

We changed into Capris and sleeveless blouses, slid our sunglasses in place, and strolled down the path to the beach below. It wasn't a steep walk, but the ground was uneven, so we took our time.

Not many populated the beach, much to my relief. Waves swooshed into the white sand as we strolled side by side. I longed to reach for Daphne's hand and interlace my fingers in hers. She glanced at me as if she knew what I was thinking. She reached over, gave my hand a quick squeeze, and released it.

We walked to the edge of the water. She bent over and slid off her sandals, and I did the same. Wading into the shallows, we let the warm water slosh over our bare feet. I breathed in the cleansing, salty air. Yes, Daphne needed this break, but so did I.

Sailboats glided across the water farther in the distance, and I thought how carefree it must feel to have the sea mist tingle your skin as the wind whipped through your hair. I became aware that Daphne was staring at me.

"Have I told you enough how beautiful you are, Ellie?" she asked.

I turned to her and basked in the love I saw there. "Every time you look at me, I feel beautiful." I touched her cheek. "But you? You took my breath away the first time we met, and that hasn't changed."

We were content watching the sailboats until the breeze chilled us.

"Hungry?" I asked as we made our way back up the path.

"Now that you mention it, yes. I'm starving."

"They have a restaurant at the hotel that's of five-star quality. Will that do?"

"Or we could go to our room, make love, and order room service."

I laughed. "There's always that."

Sunday, 8 July 1979. I awakened early and reached beside me for Daphne but found only cool sheets. I arose and stepped over to the bay window. In the dim light of the sunrise, I saw a lone figure seated on a large cliff-side rock.

I dressed in a pair of jeans and sweater and grabbed Daphne's jacket on the chair, thinking she might have forgotten how cool the mornings can be here—especially with the wind coming off the water.

I approached her and had to catch my breath. The green of the lawn that led to the rocks was a vivid contrast to the white of the cliffs. The view was so beautiful, it was almost too painful to look at.

"Good morning," Daphne said as a breeze blew up from below and swept her hair away from her face.

"Good morning. I thought you might need this." I handed her the jacket.

"Thank you." She slipped it over her cotton shirt.

"I missed you."

"Sorry. I couldn't sleep any longer, and the sea beckoned me."

"It does seem to have that magical quality. How long have you been out here?" I sat down beside her on the cool stone.

"What time is it?"

"Seven."

"About an hour I guess. It's so peaceful. I feel like I belong. My family's from Ireland, as you know. The first O'Sheas lived along the coast before settling in Durrow. I think that's why I feel such a pull here." She smiled at me. "And because of you. I found myself again when we lived in Banbury those five years. You gave me my life back, Ellie."

I took her hand in both of mine. "I'd say we gave each other our lives back."

She seemed content in not speaking for several minutes but was the first to break the silence.

"The only green that comes close to matching this for me is the green grass of my old home in Bloomington." A tinge of sadness cloaked her words. Her mother had died of a massive stroke a year ago. Over the course of the year, we'd gone back and forth between the house there and ours in California, as if she couldn't let it go. But at the same time, it caused her pain when we were there. "I've been thinking I'd like to tear that house down."

"Your mother's house?" I asked, not hiding my surprise.

"Yes. I don't have many fond memories of the place, but I do love the peace and slowed down life in Indiana. What would you think if we were to tear it down and build a house matching ours in Beverly Hills?"

It made sense. She could enjoy the solitude of the countryside away from the hustle and bustle of Los Angeles. She would do so by razing the house that had brought her misery and building anew.

"I think it's a wonderful idea."

"You do?" Her face brightened.

"Of course, Daph. I want what makes you happy. And you know wherever you are is my home."

She embraced me in a tight hug. "Let's start when we get to the States."

"Whatever you say."

We turned at the dissonant cries of gulls below us.

"Ellie, will you promise me something?" she asked as we watched the birds on their quest for their early morning food.

"Anything."

She turned to look directly at me. "When I die, I want to be cremated and I want my ashes scattered over these cliffs."

"Daphne, don't talk of—"

She cupped my cheek. "But it's something we *should* talk about. We need to face the fact that I'll likely go before you."

I didn't even want to think of such things, but she seemed determined, so I listened.

"Scatter my ashes here," she repeated.

"Only if I can join you."

"But who'll do that for us?"

I brushed my lips against hers. "God will provide, love."

* * *

Bailey lay on her side as she listened to Chelsea. "I guess that's why the house doesn't fit in with the rest of the houses on that road."

Chelsea set the diary on the bedside table. "Yeah, I guess so."

"What are you thinking about?" Bailey asked.

"How hard it must have been for Eleanor to talk about Daphne dying before her." Chelsea moved into Bailey's arms. "Did you ever notice the oak box on top of the mantel?"

"No."

"I bet it contains Daphne's ashes."

Bailey tried to visualize the box Chelsea was talking about but could only see the painting above the mantel.

"They had such a connection between them. I can understand why she hasn't let her go yet," Chelsea said and yawned.

"Hey, it's late. Why don't we pick up again tomorrow?"

"Sure. Do you want to get away for our reading?"

"What did you have in mind?" Bailey asked.

"I don't know… the lake again? Maybe rent a boat?"

"I'd love to."

Chapter 24

On the drive to the lake, they made plans about when to travel to Denver and start the house sale. Chelsea would help get things packed for the move then travel back to Bloomington and prepare for Bailey's arrival. They'd already agreed they'd sell most of the furniture, maybe to Tara if she was interested. They would pack books, clothes, and other personal items and rent a moving van.

They entered Hoosier National Forest, drove down to the docks, and pulled into the parking lot of the rental building.

Bailey jumped out of the Jeep. "Why don't you go ahead and get changed? I'll get us a pontoon boat for the day and join you in the dressing room." She walked up to the counter but craned her neck to watch Chelsea retreat into the back, already picturing how Chelsea would look in her bathing suit.

"Can I help you?" The woman behind the counter sounded annoyed. Bailey wondered how long she'd stood there ogling Chelsea.

"We'd like to rent one of your pontoon boats for the day."

The blonde shoved the paperwork in front of Bailey, asked for her driver's license, and went back to watching the soap opera on the small black and white TV behind her. Bailey filled out everything and slid the clipboard back inside. After paying the fee, she went to find Chelsea.

She rounded the corner of the dressing area and stopped short. Chelsea was bent over, rubbing suntan lotion on her legs. Her emerald green one-piece bathing suit looked as though someone had airbrushed it on her body.

Chelsea turned her head and jerked. "God, Bailey, you scared me."

"S-sorry." Bailey's gaze started at Chelsea's bare feet, raked across her toned legs and her chest where her nipples pressed against the material, and then up to her face which sported a full blush. "Goddamn, Chels," was all Bailey could think to say.

Chelsea ducked her head. Bailey glanced around them and saw they were still alone. She tipped Chelsea's chin up and kissed her gently. "Don't ever be embarrassed about how beautiful you are."

"I've only believed that coming from you." Chelsea gave her another kiss. "Get changed."

Bailey retrieved her blue Speedo one-piece from her bag and stepped into one of the curtained-off changing rooms. She tugged at the material after she put it on. She definitely wasn't pulling off the same look as Chelsea.

Bailey yanked the curtain back and pulled at the material again around her stomach. "I don't know if this fits right. I haven't worn it since last summer," she said as she kept her head down. When she raised her head, she had to swallow at the expression on Chelsea's face.

"Oh, you most certainly fill it out just fine," Chelsea said with a raspy voice.

Bailey shifted in place.

Chelsea giggled. "Talk about someone who's not aware of their own beauty. You are one handsome woman."

Bailey cleared her throat. "Uh, how about getting on that boat?"

Thirty minutes later, they found a quiet little cove to anchor in. Chelsea took a Coke out of the cooler and held it up to Bailey.

"Here you go, my captain." Chelsea popped the lid on hers and went to her duffle bag. She removed the diary she'd encased in a protective plastic bag and waved it at Bailey. "Would you like to read?"

After spreading out their beach towels, they sank back into the cushions at the front of the boat.

"I think the next passages we should look at concern Gordon Scott," Chelsea said. "You'll see where I marked them. I think we're at the end of what we need to read without Eleanor. She writes sporadically after these entries. I assume she has what she wants us to read next at the house."

Bailey opened to the marked page.

"Wednesday, 6 June 1984. Today dawned sunny and happy. We enjoyed the pool until ten o'clock when the phone rang inside. Daphne was floating in the middle of the pool on the raft, so I volunteered to answer it…"

* * *

"If it's the studio, tell them I'm indisposed," Daphne said in her most put-upon voice.

"I will, your highness." I yelped when she flung a scoop of water toward me on my way to the back door.

"Remember I'll still be here when you get back in the pool, Ellie."

Laughing, I ran into the house and picked up the receiver on the fifth ring. "Hello," I said, breathlessly.

"Daphne?"

"No, this is Eleanor. Is this Gordon?" We hadn't seen him or heard from him in almost a year. He'd been living in Switzerland, alone. He and Quinn Tucker had ended their relationship three years before. Despite Daphne's best efforts to have him visit or for us to go see him, he'd always begged off. This didn't sound like an overseas call. "Are you calling from the States?"

"Yes. I moved back three weeks ago."

I almost asked him why he hadn't contacted us until now but thought better of it.

"Do you and Daphne have plans tonight?"

"No. We're dining in."

"Do you think she'd mind if I came over?"

"Heavens no, Gordon. We've missed you terribly. You can't believe how many times your name has come up these past months."

"How about seven?"

"Seven would be perfect. I'll let Daph know. She'll be tickled pink."

"See you then, Eleanor."

I hung up the phone with a niggling feeling of unease as I stepped outside to tell Daphne about Gordon.

That evening, Daphne finished primping in front of the bedroom mirror.

"Daph, you'd think you were getting ready for a date," I teased her. I'd dressed casually in a pair of jeans and cotton button-down shirt. She was wearing black trousers and a blue silk blouse.

She finished putting on her silver and diamond earrings. She would turn sixty-three next month and didn't look a day over forty. She'd started wearing her hair shorter a few years before. It was greyer now, but she refused to colour her hair or have any work done to her face, unlike many of the other actresses in this town. I loved her even more for it.

"I can't help it, Ellie." Daphne smoothed out her blouse. "We haven't seen him in so long, and I've missed him."

The doorbell rang. "Let's go greet our friend," I said. We descended the stairs together.

She swung the door open.

The man standing before us could not possibly be Gordon Scott. The once strapping leading man who'd been in such good health ten months ago was now gaunt and drawn. His blue eyes were glassy and four or five dark brown blemishes dotted his face.

I heard Daphne's sharp inhalation of breath beside me. My stomach fell with the knowledge of what I was seeing.

Oh, Gordon, no.

"Daphne, Eleanor, it's been too long."

Daphne embraced him in a long hug. He looked at me over her shoulder and winked. I hugged him next. I fought back tears when I felt his bony shoulders through his denim shirt.

"Come in and sit down," Daphne said, leading us into the living room. She kept her face turned away from him, but I saw her tears. We'd seen so many of our friends with this same gaunt appearance who'd left this world much too soon. I dreaded what Gordon was about to reveal.

With her back to us at the bar, she asked if we wanted drinks.

"Whatever bourbon you have is fine." Gordon sat down in the leather chair.

She brought him a tumbler of Jack Daniels and Coke. "Ellie?"

"No thank you," I said quietly. I noticed that she poured herself a gin and tonic with about double the gin she normally drank.

She sat beside me and placed a shaking hand on my knee. "Gordon, we've missed you."

"And I've missed both of you."

He swallowed his drink in two big gulps. He stared at the ice as he swirled it around in his glass. Then he raised his head, and I knew. I didn't want to hear what was coming next. I wanted to get up and run away and refuse to listen to his news.

"I have something to tell you. I'm sorry I've kept it from you for this long. I've gone to Switzerland for treatment, but we all know there's nothing they can do for this damn thing."

Don't say it. I wanted to scream the words. Instead, I clasped Daphne's hand in mine and squeezed with all my might.

"I've been diagnosed with AIDS."

Daphne uttered a choked cry. Before I knew it, she was in my arms. I held her against my chest.

"I'm so sorry," I said as tears filled my eyes.

"I wanted to tell you first. I've scheduled a press conference for Friday, but I didn't want you to be blindsided. And I'd like you to be there at the press conference."

Daphne sat up and took a tissue from the box on the table. "Of course, Gordon."

"How long have you known?" I asked.

"Since last May. Some friends told me about a clinic in Switzerland treating patients with experimental drugs. I thought, hell, I've got nothing to lose. Twenty thousand dollars later, nothing's changed." He pointed at the lesions on his face.

With the move, I noticed the same lesions on his hand.

"And yet our President still hasn't acknowledged AIDS even exists," Daphne said bitterly.

Gordon set his glass on the coffee table. "That's one of the reasons I want to do the press conference Friday. It might make a difference, if even a small one."

Daphne walked to him, pulled him to his feet, and embraced him. "I'll be there, Gordon. Tell me when and where."

Friday, 8 June 1984. I stood with a small group of our friends and watched Gordon and Daphne behind a bank of microphones.

Gordon addressed the reporters. "I was diagnosed with AIDS last May. You may ask why I'm coming forward, since I've not worked in film for the past several years. But I feel putting a face on the disease"—he smiled sadly—"even if it's an old actor's face like mine, will hopefully awaken this country to take action."

Reporters began shouting.

He stopped them. "And in answer to what I'm sure will be one of your first questions, yes, I am gay."

That brought a flurry of questions, one of them directed at Daphne.

"Ms. DeMonet, were you aware Gordon was gay when you married him in 1954?"

I worried this could lead down a very different path of questions.

Gordon cut him off. "I've asked Daphne to join me because we've remained friends these past thirty years." He turned to her. "Best friends, I'd say, wouldn't you, Daphne?"

"Yes."

"Let's not sidestep the issue," Gordon continued. "It's about this disease and what we can do to stem the tide."

"But—"

Daphne moved to the microphones. "Gordon's right. Our focus today is to raise awareness and to encourage our national leaders to step up and do something to find a cure. And in that vein, I'd like to announce that I'm pledging five hundred thousand dollars to start a fund for AIDS research."

Talk rippled through the reporters. The rest of the press conference dealt with how others could contribute.

"Thank you all for coming this afternoon," Gordon said.

Daphne put her arm around his waist and rested her head on his shoulder. The cameras clicked around me and snapped shots of what was once one of the most photographed couples in Hollywood. I feared these would be the last pictures taken of them together.

* * *

"What a horrible disease," Chelsea said. "It's good they have medications now that can treat it early, but back then, they didn't have anything."

Bailey flipped some pages. "There's a gap before she writes again in November. Do you want me to finish out the diary?"

"Yeah. This is another place where I know how it ends and don't want to listen."

"We can stop and pick it up later if you want."

"No. Go ahead."

Bailey smoothed down the page. "Saturday, 17 November 1984. I've not written these past five months. It's been difficult finding the effort to write anything due to the overwhelming sadness I feel at the prospect of losing a good friend…"

* * *

We visited Gordon twice at his home this week and feared that each time might be the last. They admitted him to the UCLA Medical Center last month, but he rallied enough to ask to go home for what he called his final days.

I took each step to his door with a sense of dread. Watching him deteriorate with each passing day was one of the most difficult things I'd ever endured. I felt helpless. More helpless than I'd ever felt in my life. Like Daphne, I could do nothing but be an observer to his impending death.

We entered his room where he lay in a hospital bed. He was all but a skeleton now, his skin pulled tight against his bones. A nurse sat in the corner.

"Is he able to talk?" Daphne asked her.

"Daph," he said in a voice wracked with weakness. He held out his hand to her. The nurse moved a chair close to the bed, and Daphne sat down.

"Hello, darling." She raised his hand to her mouth and kissed it. "How is my ex-husband today?"

He laughed, which became a coughing jag for several seconds.

"Oh, Gordon. I didn't mean to make you—"

"Stop," he rasped. "Your humour has helped me so much. Don't apologise, please." He coughed a couple more times. Daphne picked up the glass of water on his bedside table and held the straw down for him to sip. He managed to smile. "Do you remember all of the crazy parties we had back in the day? Weren't those grand?"

"How could I forget? We threw the best damn parties in town."

"I miss them. I miss the carefree feeling I had dancing with you." His eyes fluttered shut.

She brushed her fingers through his thinning grey hair. "Picture us dancing again to our song, 'Unforgettable.' Can you hear it?"

"Yes," he whispered, never opening his eyes.

Daphne hummed the song, tears trickling down her cheeks. "Do you see us, darling?"

I heard Nat King Cole's melodic voice as if he were in the same room with us. I forced my gaze away. If I kept watching, I would start sobbing. When I turned around, Daphne was leaning over the bed and kissing his forehead.

"He's sleeping again," she said.

Although I could barely see through my veil of tears, I walked to his bed, bent over, and placed my lips to his cheek. "Rest now, Gordon."

We left his room and his home, not voicing our fears. But I felt in my heart it would be the last time we'd see him alive.

Sunday, 18 November 1984. We shared a fitful night of sleep. The phone rang once in the early evening. We'd stared at each other, each of us dreading to pick it up. I finally answered and blew out a breath of relief when I heard the voice of one of our friends who was inquiring about Gordon.

I was pouring myself a cup of tea when the ringing phone nearly made me drop the tea kettle. I tried to will the phone to stop ringing. Daphne appeared at the doorway of the kitchen. She turned her back to me as she picked up the receiver.

"Hello?" She listened for several seconds before gripping the edge of the counter. "When? All right. Thank you." Daphne replaced the receiver on its cradle and said in a whisper, "He's gone." Her shoulders shook with sobs. "Oh God, Ellie, our Gordon's gone."

I cried as I took her in my arms. She buried her face into my neck. I stroked her hair and told her I loved her. It might not be enough, but it was all I could offer.

* * *

Chelsea sniffled. "I wanted it to change. I wanted him to live, but I knew it wasn't going to happen."

Bailey showed her the last pages of the diary. "I thought there'd be an entry about his funeral, but there isn't."

"Eleanor may have that in the diaries at her home, but I think it was too painful to write about. At least if I'm reading her right, that's what I'd say."

"She does have an entry about Daphne testifying in front of Congress in 1986 to get more funding for AIDS research. It's not a long entry. It's almost as if even that brought back painful memories."

Bailey shut the book and replaced it in the plastic bag. "I think it's time to call her and let her know we're ready."

"Let's get in the water first and at least try to enjoy the rest of the day. What do you think?" Chelsea looked at Bailey, hopefully.

"Yeah, let's try to have some fun."

Chapter 25

"I'd say the two of you got some sun."

Eleanor welcomed them into her home the next day. After not seeing her for several weeks, Bailey noticed she seemed even more drained than on their last visit. Bailey glanced at Chelsea who was looking at Eleanor with concern.

"It's still nice enough to sit out on the patio," Eleanor said. "I asked Niles to bring our usual."

They followed her outside and sat down.

"How've you been?" Eleanor asked as she poured tea into her cup.

"Good," Bailey answered.

Chelsea reached for Bailey's hand. Eleanor saw the move.

"How are the two of you?" She narrowed her eyes. "Wait. That glow isn't just from getting sun. I've seen it before from Daphne." She wagged her finger at them. "I'd say you two are sharing a bed again."

Chelsea felt a flush working its way up her neck. "Nothing slips past you, does it?"

"Not when it comes to matters of love. Good for you." Eleanor stirred sugar into her tea. "Is Ms. Addison pleased with what you've given her so far, Bailey?"

"Very. I sent her my most recent notes last night. She's traveling the next few days to interview a few leads."

"Oh? Some of Daphne's friends? There aren't many left, you know."

"I believe it's some of the younger supporting cast members from her movies."

"Ah."

Bailey took a drink of her coffee and watched Eleanor over the rim of the cup. "How have *you* been, Eleanor? You seem tired. Have you been getting enough rest?"

Eleanor dismissively waved her hand. "You sound like my

physician. She hasn't been pleased with my lack of sleep either."

"Have you felt ill?"

"My heart's just getting old, Bailey. It happens to the best of us. I must say, though, that the lack of rest is due to missing my mate."

Bailey understood that feeling completely. She remembered how lost she was without Chelsea. She couldn't imagine experiencing the helpless feeling that you wouldn't ever see your partner again—at least not in this lifetime.

"But enough about me. Chelsea? Everything okay with you? Have you made progress in reading the diary and finding what you need?"

"I've been fine, thank you. I've written notes after each reading of the diary and studied them last night. A lot there will help me as I go forward with the book."

"Good. I assume you left off with Gordon's death?"

"And your short entry about Daphne testifying before Congress," Bailey said. "We had a difficult time reading about his death."

"Seeing him deteriorate each day was sheer torture. And so quickly, too. Although they still don't have a cure, they can treat the disease sooner now with medication. Back then, there was nothing to stop the inevitable." Eleanor seemed lost in thought and didn't offer more for several seconds. Then she gathered herself with visible effort. "Well, I think it's time we continue."

"Before we start," Chelsea said, "we noticed there were months that went by without much written."

"Sometimes I got caught up in my life and didn't take the time. But I did try to write when something seemed profound. Do you know what I mean? You realize it's an important moment in your life as it's happening. Many times, we let these events pass us by until much later when we recognize how much of an impact they had on our lives. But for me, I just knew at the time." Eleanor took a sip of tea. "Who's reading this morning?"

Chelsea snagged a couple of shortbread cookies and bit into one with a sly grin.

"I'd say that means you're reading today, Bailey. Chelsea seems to be preoccupied. Or at least her mouth is." Eleanor slid the diary across the table to Bailey. "We're jumping ahead to 1990. This is when Daphne has her second stroke, much worse than the first."

Bailey opened the diary to the marked spot. "Wednesday, 12

September 1990. Daphne and I went into the city today to do some early Christmas shopping. Daphne was rarely recognised but occasionally garnered some curious stares from those closer to our age…"

* * *

It always delighted her if someone did come up to snap a photo or ask for an autograph, but she never went out of her way to be recognised. We kept to ourselves these days, with occasional visits from our gay friends in the industry. We were shopping today for some of them.

After three hours of nonstop walking, I was ready to head home. Seeing Daphne's weary expression, I decided it was time to call Perkins. The dear man was seventy-five now, but still as sharp as a tack and as steady behind the wheel as a twenty-five-year-old.

We slid into the backseat, each of us laying our heads on the headrest.

"Remind me again why I thought this was a good idea," Daphne grumbled.

"I believe your exact words were 'We'll get a jump on those mad, scrambling throngs that descend on the malls next month.'"

"If I ever say that again, ignore me, will you?"

"Daph, if there's one thing I can't do, it's ignore you."

She smiled. "I guess I am rather formidable."

I snorted. "That's a bit of an understatement."

Perkins turned into the drive and dropped us off at the door. I walked into the foyer and left the packages there. "Set yours here, too. I'll take them upstairs later. Right now, I'd like nothing better than a cup of tea."

"I never did break you of that habit, did I?" Daphne walked past, pulling off her sweater.

I continued into the kitchen while she stepped over to the bar.

"I think this deserves more than tea for my nerves," she said. "Those teenagers in that last mall drove me crazy."

I poured water into the kettle and yelled from down the hall. "But you have to admit that young woman who recognised you from her film studies class was rather adorable."

A loud crash came from the living room. I dropped the kettle into the sink and hurried down the hallway. Daphne lay by the bar. The bottle of gin was tilted on its side and liquid dribbled down to the carpet.

"Oh my God! Daphne!"

I rushed to her and dropped to my knees. The right side of her mouth drooped slightly, and she seemed surprised to see me.

"Daphne?"

She tried to focus on my face, but I could tell she was having a difficult time. I feared she'd suffered a stroke. I suddenly remembered a recent article I'd read. It listed three possible symptoms of a stroke.

Daphne moved to sit up. I helped her and then asked her to raise her arms. She struggled to raise one, but the right arm tilted to the side.

"Can you smile for me, sweetheart."

She was able to twitch the left side of her mouth up slightly.

"Can you say, 'I love you'?"

She tried and failed.

"Don't move. I'm calling 9-1-1."

I ran to the phone and alerted the service that Daphne had probably suffered a stroke. They told me to make her comfortable and not to move her any further. Within minutes of hanging up, I heard the sirens outside the house. I let the medics in and stood aside as they loaded Daphne onto the gurney.

One of the paramedics, a very masculine woman, asked Daphne if she knew her own name. She struggled to say her first name. The woman glanced up at me as they took her out to the ambulance. "Has she suffered a stroke before?"

I vividly recalled 1975 and the last time I'd found Daphne passed out on the floor. "I think she might have had a mild one about fifteen years ago, but it was never properly diagnosed."

They lifted her into the ambulance.

"Can I go with you?" I knew I couldn't reach Perkins in time to drive me to the hospital as quickly as I wanted. Driving in England had been easy for me, but I never attempted it once I arrived in the States.

"Are you family?"

"Well—"

"Because if you're family, you can ride." The medic gave me a pointed look.

I didn't hesitate. "Yes, she's my sister."

"Good," the medic said with a slight smile. "Get in."

On the way to the hospital, the medic asked me questions about Daphne's medical history, which I answered to the best of my ability. When we arrived, they hustled her through the ER doors. I wanted to follow, but they told me to remain in the waiting area.

I sat down in one of the plastic chairs, trying my best not to break down in front of strangers. An hour later, the ER doors swung open. A young doctor glanced up from his file.

"Sister of Daphne DeMonet?"

I jumped to my feet and hurried over.

"Yes. I'm… I'm Eleanor DeMonet. Is Daphne okay?"

"I'm Doctor Sturgeon. Follow me." He led me to one of the curtained-off rooms but stopped before we entered.

"We think your sister suffered a stroke. We need to run some blood tests and do a CT scan to be certain, but based on her slurred speech and her slight weakness on her right side, I'm fairly certain that's what happened. You told the EMT you thought she'd suffered a mild stroke…" He flipped through his papers. "Fifteen years ago?"

"Yes. The doctor at that time decided it was low blood sugar and didn't run any further tests other than to check for that." I didn't hide my disgust when giving him this news.

"That's not unusual. Sometimes milder strokes can go undetected. They've taken her back for her CT scan. Once we get that result, we'll know how to proceed. If there's a blockage, we'll treat her with an anticoagulant, which will help break up the clot."

"How long?"

"We should have her CT done within the hour. After that, we'll know what we're dealing with. Why don't you go to the waiting area? I'll call you back when we're done."

A little over an hour passed when Doctor Sturgeon led me to the lit X-rays showing Daphne's brain images.

"She has a small blockage here." He pointed at what to me looked like a glob on the film. "We're already treating her with Coumadin."

"What is the prognosis, Doctor?"

"Very good. You did the right thing in calling 9-1-1 and getting her to the hospital as quickly as possible. A lot of people don't react so fast. A little bit of rehab should restore her speech and weakness on the right side. We have an excellent facility that's achieved outstanding results for its stroke patients."

"Can I see her now?"

"Of course." He led me down the hall to her room. "This is a temporary room until we can get her upstairs." He opened the door. "Ms. DeMonet?"

Daphne was pale, her skin colour almost matching that of the bleached-white sheets. She saw me enter the room and her face lit up. Thank God. She recognised me.

"El... El..." She frowned.

"Ms. DeMonet, as I told you, you've suffered a mild stroke. Your speech should come back to you after some work here."

Daphne used her left hand to point to her drooping mouth and gestured to her right side.

"That should all come back, too. Your sister's fast action in calling the paramedics helped."

Her gaze shifted to me, and she looked confused.

"I was able to accompany you to the hospital since I'm family."

It seemed to click for her then, and the frown disappeared from her forehead. The left side of her mouth quirked up. Seeing that twinkle in her eyes lifted my spirits immensely.

"We've started you on an anticoagulant to help dissolve the small blockage in your brain. It should hopefully do the trick."

A nurse breezed in, checked the IV, and left.

Doctor Sturgeon pointed at the IV line. "We're giving it to you intravenously for a much quicker result. As I told your sister, we'll get you a room in the rehabilitation portion of our hospital. I don't anticipate you being there long at all. You should be able to go home and continue any further rehab through outpatient services."

"Thank you, Doctor," I told him.

He stopped at the door on his way out. "I love your films, Ms. DeMonet. Especially *A Sheltered Heart*."

She tried to smile. "Th... thnk," she slurred, then gave him a feeble wave.

"Someone should be in soon to take you up."

After the doctor left, I moved to Daphne's side and took her left hand in mine. I pushed her hair back from her forehead. "How are you doing?"

"Sc... scare." She shook her head.

"It's okay. You're in the right place. This is one of the best hospitals in the country."

"Stah." She gripped my hand tight.

"I'm not sure I can stay, love, but I'll ask."

Her beseeching expression was all I needed to see. I called for the nurse. As soon as she re-entered the room, I made the request.

"As long as Ms. DeMonet agrees."

Daphne nodded.

"She still needs her rest. Can you be quiet tonight?" the nurse asked me.

"As long as I can stay, I'll be quiet as a mouse."

"Let me see what I can do." Her gaze dropped to our joined hands, and a knowing look zipped across her face.

The nurse left the room and returned with the okay. They came for Daphne about thirty minutes later and wheeled her into a private room. Another nurse entered and checked her vitals. "We'll hunt down a recliner," she told me.

After she left, I went to Daphne's side. "I guess it helps sometimes to be a famous movie star."

Daphne did her best to roll her eyes.

I leaned over and kissed her forehead. "Don't think I didn't see that."

* * *

"She still had her sense of humor even after the stroke," Bailey said. "How long was she in rehabilitation?"

"Two weeks. As the doctor said, it was a mild stroke. And her health habits had always been good since she stopped smoking not too long after we met. The doctors thought she might be at risk because of her mother's stroke and death at seventy-six. We continued to be careful with her diet, but they told us that sometimes people are susceptible to these things. There was only so much we could do."

"Were you at the hospital while she rehabbed?" Chelsea asked.

"Every day and most nights. I know I teased Daphne about the famous movie star thing, but it really did make a difference. And most had deduced that we weren't sisters by the time they released her to go home. A very helpful nurse told her we needed to file the legal paperwork to allow me power of attorney. That way, my say in her medical care would never be an issue again. We'd never even thought about it. Not too long after we arrived home, we visited her attorney and worked out everything between us regarding wills and such. It's funny how something like this shock can jumpstart you into action." Eleanor stood and stretched. "Why don't we go out to the garden for the next reading?"

They followed her to a set of benches in the middle of the garden.

Chelsea admired the variety of flowers Eleanor had planted. "It's so beautiful, and I love the way you've mixed the colors."

"I've added to it over the years."

Violets, daffodils, petunias, irises, and a multitude of other flowers surrounded them in a colorful cocoon.

"Bailey, why don't you pass the book to Chelsea and let her read the next passages from 1996. This is after Daphne's third stroke. Unfortunately, they kept getting worse. Where you'll begin is when she comes home from the rehab hospital. She's regained her speech but still has weakness on the right side."

Chelsea smoothed down the page when it flapped in the breeze. "Tuesday, 12 March 1996. Daphne returned home last week after a three-week stay in the hospital. She still has work to do in getting her gait back to normal. I'd ordered the necessary equipment delivered to our home so she can finish her rehab work here. I set up the room to mirror the facility at the hospital…"

* * *

"You're a goddamn slave driver, Steve," Daphne snapped. Sweat dripped from her brow as she struggled to hold herself upright on the parallel bars.

Steve, the physical therapist, stood in front of her and urged her on, but didn't assist her in any way.

"Quite colourful language you have there, Ms. DeMonet," he said. Steve was tall, blond, all muscle, and very, very gay. I could tell he'd now be a dear friend. I'd already grown close to him in the limited time he'd been here. I admired him for many reasons— because of his line of work, but especially because he didn't put up with anything Daphne dished out. This stroke had left her ill-tempered, which can be normal for a stroke victim. The level of frustration is high when a person can no longer do what they did before.

"I'll show you colourful language," Daphne gritted out between clenched teeth. "You ain't heard nothing yet." She strained again to move her right leg forward.

I wanted to help her, but I knew it wasn't the thing to do. This wasn't about me. It was about regaining her independence and something she told me she felt she'd lost… her dignity.

"Come on. A few more feet," Steve said.

Daphne grunted and shifted her right leg forward with great effort to reach the end of the bars.

"Fantastic!"

She glared at him. "Just give me my goddamn walker."

He moved the walker in front of her.

She leaned onto the handles. "I think that's enough for this afternoon. I'm through being tortured."

"But look at the progress you made today, Ms. DeMonet."

I gave her a towel to wipe her brow.

"Steve, I think you can call me Daphne. You've seen me at my worst at the hospital. It's time to get on a first-name basis."

"All right, Daphne. Same time tomorrow?"

"Unfortunately, yes."

He gathered his things and left for the door. "Don't forget to keep doing those exercises I showed you."

"Yeah, yeah, yeah."

"See you around two, Eleanor?"

"That's fine. We'll be here."

After he left, Daphne struggled over to a chair and flopped down with a huff. She gave me a sharp look. "What's with this 'we' stuff? I'm the one doing all of the work."

I sat in the matching chair beside her and reached for her hand. "It's time you and I had a little talk." She tried to pull out of my grasp, but I held on tight. "Don't turn away from me, Daphne."

She wouldn't look at me. "Why do I think I'm not going to like this?"

"Because you'd be right. I do understand you're frustrated. But you need to focus on the positive and how far you've progressed these past three weeks. And the fact that they anticipate a full recovery."

"'Anticipate' being the key word."

I ignored her comment. "You also need to remember I'm here for you and always will be."

"Maybe I don't want you to be," she said softly.

My heart skipped a beat. "What do you mean?"

Daphne raised her head. "Maybe it'd be better if you weren't here to see this, Ellie. Maybe go to our home in Bloomington and get away for a while."

I found my voice. "That's a lot of maybes."

Her lower lip quivered. "I don't want to be a burden to you, Ellie. Ever."

I knelt in front of her. "Oh, sweetheart, I'd never think of you as a burden. You're my heartbeat. Don't you know that after all these years? I'm not going anywhere. Not unless you're with me."

Tears spilled over and trickled down her cheeks. I wiped them away with my thumbs. "I love you and will never stop loving you, no matter our age, no matter our physical condition. You're stuck with me, love."

She nodded slightly as she bit her lip.

I embraced her. "Why don't we go into our bedroom for a while, hmm?" She stiffened in my arms. When I withdrew, I sensed her fear. "It's okay."

"I don't think—"

I stood up and helped her to her feet. "Shh."

I followed her as she scooted along with her walker to the bedroom we'd set up on this floor. Before Daphne came home, Steve and a friend swapped the furniture from the den with the bedroom furniture upstairs.

She moved in halting steps to the edge of the bed and sat down. I took the walker and set it close by, but enough out of the way that I could stand before her. Our love life had remained passionate over the years. But this last stroke had made her hesitant to show even the slightest bit of affection. I wanted that to change today.

I began unbuttoning her blouse.

She gripped my wrist with her left hand. "Ellie, I—"

I leaned forward and pressed my lips to hers. At first, she didn't respond, but soon she relaxed. As our kiss intensified, I continued unbuttoning her blouse. I slid it from her shoulders and unfastened her bra. To me, she was still the gorgeous twenty-nine-year-old I'd fallen in love with more than forty-five years ago. I finished undressing her and discarded my own clothing. She made little resistance as I pushed her back onto the bed.

I took my time kissing her until Daphne's kisses became more ardent and she pushed her tongue into my mouth. Caressing her breasts, I looked into dark eyes full of desire.

"Okay?" I asked softly.

"Yes," she whispered.

I reached to the bedside table for the lubricant, poured some into my hand, and then slipped into her. "Still okay?"

This time she didn't answer with her voice but with the movement of her hips. I felt her wetness coating my fingers. I took my time exploring her, remembering all of the places she loved before stroking her clitoris. Knowing it wouldn't take much, I kept my touch light as I encircled her nipple with my mouth. She moved a few more times with her hips and then tensed, grabbed hold of my head, and pushed me into her breast even more.

"Oh, Ellie," she said in a hoarse voice.

I waited until her spasms slowed before slipping out of her. I kissed her, gentle and slow, lingering for a long time, relishing the fact that I still knew her body. Still knew what she wanted and needed.

She caressed my face with her fingertips. "What about you? I feel so inadequate that I can't make love to you."

I smiled gently. "Daphne, you just did. Every time I make love to you, I feel your touch and your passion. It's always been like that for me. Always."

She pulled me to her for another kiss. "How did you know?"

"I think I knew you were feeling disconnected from me since this last stroke, and from what you just shared, I think I was right. We both needed this—not only you."

I laid my head on her shoulder and continued my light caresses of her breast. I brushed my fingers over her nipple and made it harden again.

Daphne squirmed. "You keep doing that, darling, and I won't need any lubricant," she said in the low, raspy voice she reserved for the bedroom—and for me.

*   *   *

Chelsea looked up from the diary and met Bailey's eyes. "It's good to know that forty years from now, this could be us."

Eleanor chuckled. "It was a department we never fell short in. At that particular point in time, though, she needed to be reminded how much I still desired her." Her expression clouded. "In the six years after that date, we remained sexually active. But in the fall of 2002, she experienced a devastating stroke, and she was never the same. This one left her completely paralyzed on the right side. Her mind remained sharp, but she had trouble speaking. With the help of a speech therapist, it improved somewhat. She still slurred her words and remained self-conscious about it, even with me."

"Wasn't it in 2003 that the Movieland Film Industry honored her with their Lifetime Achievement Award?" Chelsea asked.

"Yes, it was. *That* was fun to get her to go along with."

"The scene at the awards show was very touching," Bailey said. "They still flash back to it in highlights from past telecasts."

Eleanor gestured to the diary. "Go to the next bookmark. I've also noted two passages after that one. Why don't you read all three?"

Chelsea opened the book to the first marked page.

"Saturday, 8 March 2003. Daphne and I sat in the solarium. We relished the warmth from the sun pouring through the surrounding glass. We were playing our typical game for a Saturday night. Five hundred rummy…"

* * *

"That's the second time you've thrown down an ace. You know I'm collecting them," I gently scolded her.

Daphne glared at me over her cards in a mock scowl.

I snickered. "That's one of the faces you'd make at Frank Teller when you disagreed with him over his direction."

"Pick up the damn card, Ellie," she said out of the side of her mouth.

Her speech was as good as it was going to get, according to her therapists, but I had no problem understanding every word. She rarely wanted to venture out these days, though, and allowed only certain visitors to the house. She was still a very proud woman.

The phone rang in the kitchen.

"Damn. Meant to bring out the portable before we sat down. Don't look at my cards," I said over my shoulder as I stepped back inside.

"Bitch."

I laughed. "I heard that," I yelled before picking up the portable right before it clicked to voicemail. "Hello?"

"Ms. DeMonet?" a deep male voice asked.

"No. This is Eleanor."

There was a slight hesitation before he continued. "This is Sam Trevor from the Movieland Film Industry. May I speak to Ms. DeMonet?"

I glanced at her and marvelled again how beautiful she still was. The sunlight cut a swath across her face and lit her grey hair with a soft glow. I was lost in staring at her and didn't realise he'd spoken again.

"Hello?"

"I'm sorry. Ms. DeMonet's unable to come to the phone." I wasn't sure how much I wanted to share with him regardless of whom he said he represented.

"I understand Ms. DeMonet suffered a stroke in the fall. I wasn't certain how debilitating it was, but I'm calling to inform her that she has been chosen as this year's recipient of the Lifetime Achievement Award."

"Oh, my. That's quite an honour, isn't it?"

"Yes, it is. Do you know if there's any chance she might be able to attend the ceremony in two weeks?"

I watched as she gazed out of the solarium windows, seemingly lost in thought. I so wanted her to be there for the award, but I wasn't sure how she'd respond.

"Let me speak with her, Mr. Trevor. Do you have a number where I can reach you?" I scribbled down the number. "Thank you. I'll get back to you as soon as possible."

I gathered myself before walking back into the solarium.

"Who?"

Daphne's questions and speech often became short and to the point, especially if she was tired.

"That was Sam Trevor from the Movieland Film Industry. He called to tell you they've chosen you for this year's Lifetime Achievement Award. They'd like you to be there in two weeks to accept."

"No," she said with a voice that brooked no room for discussion.

But I could be just as stubborn. I pushed my chair beside her and took her hand. "Daph, this is such a wonderful honour. Why don't—"

"Not dead yet." She frowned.

"Oh, who said anything about your being dead? They want to recognise your work. At least think about it, won't you?"

"Not like this." She motioned at her body with her left hand.

It would take a lot more convincing.

Wednesday, 12 March 2003. Sam Trevor was a persistent young man. That much was certain. I hung up the phone and turned again to Daphne as I had the past three times he'd called. She was already shaking her head.

"Sweetheart, think about it. He's told me they're honouring you not only for your film work, but also for your humanitarian work with the Gordon Scott Memorial AIDS Foundation. He knows how much money you've raised for AIDS research. Standing beside Gordon that day brought awareness to the disease not seen at that time. If not for your film work, at least consider attending to shine light on the Foundation."

Daphne narrowed her eyes at me. "Not fair."

At last. A chink in her armour. "It's not like it isn't true."

"One condition."

"Anything."

Pointing at me with her good hand, she said in a voice as strong as I'd heard her speak in some time, "If you go, too."

"I don't think—"

"That or nothing."

I sighed, knowing when I was beat.

Sunday, 23 March 2003. I kept nervously smoothing out my sequined blue gown and wondered again why I'd agreed to do this. We were backstage at the Easton Theater as we waited for them to call us out.

"Ellie."

I looked up from my task.

"Beautiful," Daphne said with a lopsided smile.

"No, you're beautiful, Ms. DeMonet." And she was, in her black gown and diamond jewellery. I'd called a designer friend of ours, and he gleefully brought over stacks of gowns for us to go through. We'd settled on the Versace she was wearing.

I heard the crowd cheering out front. The stage director motioned to us. "It's time."

I wheeled Daphne to the spot he'd shown us and watched as he counted backward from three with his fingers. Before he got to one, he retreated farther out of camera sight and pointed at us.

The curtain rose, and we walked out into blinding white light. From what I could see through the glare of the spotlight, everyone was on their feet. The sound was deafening.

We continued to our next marked spot, and clips from her movies began to play on the big screen. They had asked me how I wanted to proceed. Usually, this portion of the ceremony occurred while the honouree remained backstage. But without Daphne's knowledge, I'd told them to wait until we got out onto the stage. I wanted her to see it all. She'd earned it.

We looked up at the screen and watched as the snippets of her life in film played out before us. When scenes from *The Brave Few* appeared, she grabbed my hand that rested on her shoulder. They showed the pub scene with Gordon and then, to my surprise, played our scene together in the nightclub. The crowd reacted with laughter just as they'd done all those years ago, when Daphne delivered her line, "You look like a woman who knows exactly what someone needs."

From there, the clips moved through more highlights with a lengthy clip from *A Sheltered Heart* that drew even louder applause. Finally, the tribute ended with Daphne passionately speaking before

Congress in 1986 to call for more funding to fight AIDS.

With that, the screen faded to black and slid slowly up into the rafters as the applause continued.

A microphone rose up from the floor. Sam Trevor walked out to stand in front of it with the gold statuette clutched in his hands. The applause died down enough for him to speak.

"Daphne DeMonet, your career spanned many decades, and your films reached audiences worldwide. You won the Best Actress Award in 1963 and were nominated twice more, once for Best Supporting Actress in 1968 and for Best Actress again in 1970. But tonight, we're honouring you not only for your body of work in film, but also for your humanitarian endeavours in the battle against AIDS. Ms. DeMonet, may I present you with the 2003 Movieland Film Industry's Lifetime Achievement Award."

He took care to place the statuette in her left hand as I'd instructed him to do. She looked up at me in expectation. I swallowed my fear and stepped up to the microphone.

"Daphne thanks you, Mr. Trevor, and the Movieland Film Industry for this prestigious honour. Hollywood welcomed Daphne with open arms almost sixty years ago. She made many friends, and one who remained close in her heart was Gordon Scott. She'd like to remind everyone tonight that, although treatment for AIDS has improved over the last twenty years, we still haven't found a cure. She plans to fight on until that day is here. Thank you again for your kindness."

The crowd rose once more to their feet and applauded for several more minutes. Daphne caught my eye and motioned with her chin. Thinking she wanted to say something to me, I leaned down and put my face next to hers. She surprised me with a soft kiss to my cheek.

Overcome with emotion, I wanted to tell her I loved her. But I was incapable of speaking around the lump in my throat. She winked at me then, her eyes shining in the spotlight, letting me know in her own subtle way that I needn't say a word.

* * *

"We'll stop there," Eleanor said as she stood up. "We're almost at the end of our journey, my young friends." Her expression was sad, and again, Chelsea had the overwhelming desire to rewrite history to keep Daphne alive.

"We'll let you rest, Eleanor," Bailey said. "Is tomorrow okay to return?"

"How about ten?"

They agreed and she retreated into the house.

Bailey ran her fingers through her hair. "Damn it."

"I know what you mean. I was thinking the same thing."

They were quiet as they walked to the front and got into the Jeep.

"Check out the time." Bailey pointed to the dashboard clock.

"Wow, it's almost noon. Do you want to go to the Hoosier Hang Out for burgers and talk about the reading?"

"Yeah. When I get back to the house, I need to enter what we heard today into my file and send Joanne an e-mail. She'll want to know we're nearing the end."

Chelsea stared out the window and grappled with her sorrow. More than just the end of the readings and the interview—it would be the end of Daphne's story.

Chapter 26

"You think tomorrow's the last day?" Joanne asked.

"Where Eleanor had us stop reading and what she told us before we left, I'd say we'll hear about Daphne's death tomorrow." Bailey attached three pages of notes to her e-mail and hit Send. "You should get an e-mail on your end in a couple of minutes." She leaned back in the chair. "It'll be tough reading this last part."

"You knew it was coming," Joanne said with a note of exasperation. "I mean, that was the whole purpose in your going there. To talk about this woman's partner who'd recently died."

"Christ, Joanne, can you be any colder?" Bailey didn't try to hide her anger.

"I'm sorry. I didn't get as many interviews in Los Angeles as I thought I would. Talking to someone over the phone to tell them you're flying in to interview them and actually getting them to open up are evidently two different things. I knew Hollywood could be secretive, but I thought I had a shot. She quit working years ago."

"Daphne DeMonet was well respected and very much loved. The people within the industry didn't care who she slept with. She was a damn fine actress, and what she did with her AIDS foundation spoke volumes about who she was as an individual."

"You really admire her, don't you?"

"So much that I thought of asking you to keep Eleanor out of the book. At least not all the details that she's given us." Bailey waited for the explosion on the other end of the line and wasn't disappointed.

"Come on. I sent you there to do a job, and Eleanor Burnett agreed. She knew what she's having you read will end up in a book about her lover. She's not naïve, and as you pointed out to me, she's not senile. Do you think she would have shared all this with you if she didn't intend on having me go forward with the book? Or Chelsea, too, for that matter?"

Bailey slid her index finger up and down the side of her bottled water. "No, I guess not. It's just that…"

"It's just that what?"

"This has been like listening to a fairytale, Joanne. Chelsea feels the same way. There aren't too many marriages, let alone same-sex relationships, that last this long."

"And I will do my best to convey their love in my book, Bailey." Joanne's tone had softened. "I'll not tarnish her memory. You know me better than that."

"Yeah, I do."

"Listen, I'll let you go. Give me a call when you're done there. When do you plan on coming home?"

Bailey suddenly realized she hadn't shared her news of moving back to Bloomington. She told Joanne about their plans.

"I guess you two really are back together. Will you live there with Chelsea or buy another house together?"

"She rents this house. We're not sure yet what we're doing, but we're in no hurry. That we're back together is what matters."

"I'm happy for you, Bailey."

"Thanks, Joanne. I'll call you when we're done."

Bailey hung up and clicked on her notes to read what she'd sent. One thing was clear to her. Daphne DeMonet's and Eleanor Burnett's longtime relationship made one hell of a story.

* * *

Bailey rubbed her fingertips against Chelsea's bare shoulder. "How's it coming along for you?"

"Hmm?" Chelsea felt so languid after their lovemaking, she wasn't even sure what Bailey was talking about.

"The book. How's all that coming together?"

"Oh, that. It's going okay. I got a lot done at the office this afternoon while you were working." Chelsea leaned back on the pillow. "I think my approach to this biography has changed from what I saw it being at the beginning."

"How so?"

"Yes, it'll be about Daphne DeMonet's Hollywood career. But more than that, it's the love story between Daphne and Eleanor. That's the core of the biography right there. I'm not sure if…"

"I think I know what you're going to say. It's what we talked about before. You're afraid it's an invasion of privacy even though Eleanor freely opened up to us as much as she has. I had this same conversation with Joanne earlier."

"What did she say?"

"That she'd do her best to convey the strength of their relationship in the biography."

"Joanne's a damn fine biographer, Bailey. You need to keep that in mind. She's very good in writing about the private aspects of her subjects' lives."

"You're right." Bailey continued with her soft stroking. "You think you'll be okay tomorrow?"

"Not really. It's like the end of a great movie, you know? One that's been happy, that's had you laughing and crying. But you still know the closing scene is the death of one of the leading actresses."

Bailey kissed her. "I feel the same way. Let's get some rest. It's going to be an emotional day tomorrow."

* * *

Bailey got out of the Jeep and walked around the back to meet Chelsea as she stepped down. "Ready?"

"As much as I can be."

Bailey pressed her thumb against the doorbell and listened again to the theme music from *A Sheltered Heart*. Eleanor opened the door. She looked lovely in a peach cotton shirt tucked into a pair of navy blue slacks.

"Let's sit out on the patio, shall we? It's where we started our journey. I think it should be where we finish it."

They followed her to the patio and took their customary seats. Niles appeared, as he always did, at the exact moment Bailey was about to pour the coffee. After he poured Eleanor's tea, she dismissed him with a smile.

"You can have the rest of the day off, Niles. I'll be fine with my friends. After we read, I'll take a nap."

He looked concerned. "Are you sure, madam? I can stay."

"No. You rarely have a day to yourself. I'll be fine."

He left them alone.

"Sometimes I think that man fusses over me more than Daphne did. But I love him for it." Eleanor gave the diary to Bailey. "You should read today because I have a feeling our Doctor Parker might get a little too emotional. Am I right, Chelsea?"

"I won't deny it."

Bailey wasn't sure she'd get through it, either.

"I'll let you know what leads up to the final entries. It's May of this year, and Daphne's health has deteriorated even more since

2003. The doctors told me it was only a matter of time before she suffered another massive stroke. One that she probably wouldn't recover from. We moved back to Bloomington permanently in 2004. I made sure Daphne still received the best of care. Bloomington Hospital has a certified acute stroke center, so I knew she'd be in good hands." Eleanor motioned to the diary. "Let's read."

Bailey opened to the marked passage. "Friday, 20 May 2011. It had stormed all afternoon, casting a pall over my already dark mood. I had a sense of foreboding, and it grew stronger with each thunderclap…"

* * *

We were in the solarium. Remarkably, except for omitting the swimming pool, the builders had exactly duplicated our California home. I fed Daphne Jell-O as she sat in her wheelchair and looked out into our backyard. She couldn't eat solid food anymore, and her weight had dropped drastically these past several months. I tried to pretend she wasn't wasting away, but I knew better.

She shook her head when I offered her the last bite.

"Sure?" I asked, holding out the spoon.

She nodded and continued gazing at the rain trickling down the glass. The thunder and lightning had let up, but the rain hadn't finished its assault. The weather reminded me of England. I felt a twinge of sadness as I sometimes did when thinking of home. But I looked at Daphne and knew I was right where I wanted and needed to be.

I touched her arm and noticed how cool it was.

"You're freezing. Let me get your sweater, and we'll move into the living room. How does that sound?"

Daphne didn't acknowledge my question, but I left for the sweater anyway. I picked it up off the back of the sofa.

"I remember when I bought you this," I called out as I approached the solarium. I fingered the soft wool. "It was that quaint shop in Studland Bay, remember? The one run by that adorable elderly man and his daughter. Listen to me. 'Elderly.' I'd say I've reached that age, wouldn't you?"

I stopped short in the entryway. Daphne lay on the floor.

"No!" I ran to her and turned her onto her back. "Daphne?" She was unresponsive. I hit the button on the device around my neck that would summon the paramedics. As I waited for the arrival of the ambulance, I held her in my arms, petted her soft hair, and begged her to hold on. "Not yet. I'm not ready, God. Please not yet."

Within minutes, the paramedics arrived and put her in the ambulance. Niles was there and got the car to drive us to the hospital. We followed the ambulance to Bloomington Hospital, pulling directly behind them in the roundabout in front of the ER.

"You go ahead," Niles said. "I'll park and meet you inside."

I hurried into the entrance, but a hospital attendant stopped me when I tried to follow Daphne into the examining area.

"You need to wait here," she said. "You are?"

Without hesitation, I said, "I'm her partner, Eleanor Burnett."

"Do you have health care power of attorney?"

"Yes, as well as general power of attorney."

"Please take a seat. We need to get her medical information."

I sat down with my pocketbook clutched to my chest and tried to stop the piercing ache in my heart as I answered the questions. She clicked the keyboard with quiet proficiency.

"I see Ms. DeMonet's in our system."

"She's been a patient in your stroke rehabilitation facility."

She typed a few more keystrokes and told me to wait out front until they called me back. I eased into a vinyl chair, and Niles soon joined me. He remained quiet as if he knew I was in no shape to talk. The wall clock ticked by minute by minute until over an hour passed. I was about to approach the desk, but the same young woman called me to the door.

"You can come back now, Ms. Burnett."

On unsteady feet I followed her through the double doors to a separate room.

"Doctor Kalardi will be in soon."

I said a silent prayer for Daphne. For us.

The door swung open. A tall, dark-haired man entered the room. "Ms. Burnett? You're Ms. DeMonet's partner?"

"Yes, Doctor."

"I'm Doctor Kalardi." He sat down on the chair beside me and met my eyes with an earnest gaze. "I'm sorry to tell you your partner has suffered a massive stroke and has slipped into a coma."

In a daze, I watched his lips move and tried to make sense of what he was saying.

"Unfortunately, there's not much we can do except make her comfortable. We've admitted her to ICU."

"Is there any hope at all?"

His sympathetic expression told me all I needed to know.

"I'm sorry, Ms. Burnett."

"How long..." I cleared my throat. "How long does she have?"

"We can't be certain, but with a stroke of this magnitude, based on the brain images we've done, it could be a matter of days or hours. Or she could linger. You have medical power of attorney, correct?"

"Yes."

"Does she have a living will?"

"No."

"Then it may be up to you how long she's on life support."

His words hit me hard. That was such a huge responsibility.

"Can I see her?"

"I'll take you there."

He led me to an elevator, which we rode up to the third floor in silence. We walked past a circular nurse's station. He acknowledged the staff as we passed them. We entered Daphne's room. Her bed sat next to the windows on the far wall.

I staggered when I saw her ashen face. Doctor Kalardi held my elbow and steadied me. Her thin arms lay at her sides with IVs inserted in both hands. A bevy of hissing and beeping machines surrounded her. But they offered me no solace.

Doctor Kalardi picked up a chair and carried it to the head of the bed.

"I'll leave you alone, Ms. Burnett. Is there anyone with you?"

"Niles Crawford is in the waiting area downstairs."

"Do you need me to ask him to join you?"

"If you'll just let him know I'll be here for quite a while, I'd appreciate it."

"You also need to get some rest."

Only concern etched his young face, so I withheld my angry retort. "Doctor, based on what you've shared, I don't think Daphne will make it. I am *not* leaving her side."

He gave me a slight, respectful smile. "I'll let Mr. Crawford know."

After he left, I took Daphne's left hand in mine. I lifted her hand and kissed each knuckle. "I love you."

The machines emitted incessant sounds as they provided what she needed to cling to what little life she had left. Eventually, I drifted off, still holding her hand.

I startled awake when someone touched my shoulder.

"Ms. Burnett?" Doctor Kalardi stood beside me with a clipboard.

"Yes?"

"Could you come with me please?" he asked in a hushed voice.

I was reluctant to leave Daphne but had a feeling I knew what he wanted. He took me farther down the hall to a separate room with a table.

"You've told me you have medical power of attorney over Ms. DeMonet's affairs. I know this is under dire circumstances, and, again, I apologise. But as I told you, the prognosis for Ms. DeMonet's recovery is grim. I need to ask if you wish to sign what we call a DNR—a Do Not Resuscitate order."

My fears as to his intent were well-founded. "That means they will make no efforts to revive her should the machines fail to sustain her?"

"Yes, ma'am."

"Are you telling me this is what is best for her?"

"No, ma'am. I'm asking you if, based on Ms. DeMonet's prognosis, you would wish to sign a DNR."

I thought of Daphne's drawn face. We'd never signed living wills, almost as if we were afraid by addressing the matter, we'd hasten our own deaths. But I knew without a doubt she wouldn't want to linger if there was no hope. Still, the decision was heart-wrenching.

"I'll..." I had to catch my breath as I struggled to say the words. "I'll sign the form."

He produced the document and pointed to a line at the bottom. "I truly am sorry."

"Thank you."

He led me back to the room and left as quietly as he'd arrived, almost as if he'd been an apparition.

Sunday, 22 May 2011. I'd gone home briefly yesterday to shower and change clothes. Niles drove me right back to the hospital. Daphne's room was dark except for the panel of lights above her bed. I watched her chest rise and fall with each shallow breath.

I drifted back to sleep, but at just after two-thirty in the morning, I awakened with a start and shook off my stupor.

I focused again on Daphne's face as I shifted down the bedrail to sit beside her. I gently touched her face. "I love you, Daphne," I choked out as tears slid down my cheeks.

Suddenly, her eyes flew open and focused on mine. Gone was the dull, watery stare from the past few months. Instead, her gaze was clear—as clear as the first time I'd met her. These were the eyes of a young woman flirting shamelessly with a frightened twenty-one-year-old.

I clutched her hand in mine. "Daphne?"

She tried to smile as she squeezed my fingers weakly with her own. Then the lucidity slipped away as fast as it appeared, and her eyes closed. Her hand became limp in mine, and a long breath passed her lips.

Daphne was gone. I didn't need the strident beeping of the heart monitor to tell me what I'd seen and felt. Her spirit had left her. Left me.

I stepped aside as the nursing staff hustled into the room and unhooked everything.

The nurse who'd been so kind to me while I sat vigil touched my shoulder. "We'll let you have a few moments alone with her."

I moved again to Daphne's side and brushed my fingers through her hair for what I knew would be the last time. I leaned forward and pressed my lips to hers.

"Good bye, love," I whispered. "You're at peace now."

With one more caress of her cheek, I straightened and left the room.

* * *

Chelsea pulled a tissue from her purse and handed one to Bailey. Eleanor made no move to wipe away her own tears.

"Do you want me to go to the next marked page?" Bailey asked after a slight delay.

"Give it to me please," Eleanor said. Bailey handed her the diary. Eleanor took out a pair of reading glasses from a glass case and slipped them on.

"Wednesday, 25 May 2011. Yesterday, they cremated Daphne. I'd done as she'd asked, but I planned to keep my promise, too…"

* * *

I'd find someone to take our ashes back to England and Studland Bay. I wasn't worried. As I'd told her when we stayed at the Gentry House, God would send me someone.

Her ashes sat in an oak box on top of the mantel. I understood the logic. But the confines of the box couldn't contain who Daphne was to me and who she was to so many others.

I approached our old stereo. After taking a vinyl record out of its sleeve, I placed it on the turntable. I set the stylus on the first song, turned up the sound, and swayed to "Can't Help Falling in Love," lost in the music. I could still feel Daphne's body against mine as when we danced among our friends that night in 1963.

Tears slipped down my face. She'd been my best friend, my lover, my soul mate. But she really wasn't gone. She was immortal, living on through the reels of film that had been her livelihood. And she lived on in my heart. I imagined her hand sweeping down to my hips and up my back, pulling me tighter.

I smiled for the first time in days, surrounded by Daphne's love.

Our love.

* * *

"The End," Eleanor said softly and closed the diary. "That is my last entry."

They sat quietly as a breeze blew in and the wind chimes rang out their melodic song. Chelsea heard the whispering again through the tree branches and a hushed "Ellie" in the dying breath of the wind. This time, she didn't need Eleanor's acknowledgment to know what she'd heard was real.

"What you need to take from our readings is what a remarkable woman Daphne was for her day," Eleanor said. "She didn't accept the yearly salary doled out by the studio and chose instead to negotiate her own price for each film. It made her the highest paid actress in her time. Yes, she was demanding on sets, but when each filming finished, what you saw was the best possible performance she could deliver, no matter how long it took to get it on celluloid."

Eleanor paused briefly, as if remembering everything Daphne meant to her. She pinned them with a sharp, blue-eyed stare. "I sense both of you are hesitant in sharing our story, that you're somehow intruding on our privacy." She awaited their response. "By your silence, I'm assuming I'm right. Well, I'm telling you don't be. Bailey, take this crystal clear portrait of Daphne back to Joanne Addison and tell her to do her damndest to give her the respect she deserves. And, Chelsea, pay homage to the actress, the humanitarian, but especially to my life mate. When you write, think of Bailey and what she means to you. You'll then capture what I want you to capture in writing about my Daphne."

Eleanor slowly rose to her feet and winced as pain flickered across her face.

Bailey stood quickly and placed her hand under her elbow. "Eleanor?"

"I'm fine, my dear. Quite." She straightened and warmed Bailey's heart with an affectionate smile. "My young friends, I've enjoyed our time together. You've brought me much joy going through these readings with you. But the most joy I've gotten is seeing the two of you reunite. Daphne would be proud she had a part in it." Eleanor pointed to the path. "Let me walk with you."

They headed around to the front and stood by the Jeep. Bailey was reluctant for the day to end. She wished she could think of more questions to extend their time together, but she knew she had what she needed for Joanne's book.

"Don't cry, Chelsea," Eleanor said. "This is a happy parting."

"Sorry." Chelsea blinked. "It's just that—"

"No more tears. Bailey, take care of this young woman. Together, you have a long, joyful life ahead of you." Eleanor shook her finger. "Don't mess it up."

Bailey chuckled. "Don't worry. We won't."

"Good. Now, give me a hug."

They each embraced her and got into the Jeep.

"We can come back to visit, can't we?" Chelsea asked.

"You're always welcome." Eleanor squeezed her arm. "Be safe."

Bailey pulled away and watched Eleanor in the rearview mirror. She waved. Eleanor raised her hand and folded her arms in front of her chest. She stood there until Bailey could no longer see her around the bend in the drive.

"We'll visit again soon," Chelsea said as she patted Bailey's leg.

Bailey didn't answer.

Chapter 27

The next week, Chelsea and Bailey flew into Denver to meet with Tara and follow through with the sale of the house. They'd reached an agreement to sell her most of the furniture, too, with arrangements made as to when Bailey would return to box up what she needed and drive it to Bloomington.

On the return flight to Indiana, Bailey laid her head back.

"You okay?" Chelsea asked.

"A little tired."

"This is what you wanted, right? Selling the house?" Chelsea's voice was tentative.

Bailey noticed the lines of worry on Chelsea's brow. "Remember what Eleanor said? Wherever Daphne was is home? That's how I feel about you."

Chelsea's expression softened. "It's so good to hear you say that."

"You'd better get used to it, Chels, because I plan to be with you for the rest of our lives."

* * *

The following Wednesday, Bailey looked over her final notes, made a few small changes, and sent the file on to Joanne. She stared at the computer screen after she sent the e-mail, lost in thought. She picked up her cell phone. She intended to call Eleanor to inform her she'd finished her work and to ask when Chelsea and she could come for a visit. Just as she flipped the phone open, it rang. The caller ID showed Eleanor's number.

"Hello?"

"Ms. Hampton?"

Bailey recognized Niles's voice immediately.

"Yes."

"This is Niles. I found your number in Ms. Burnett's papers.

I'm sorry I'm not telling you this in person." There was a slight pause. Bailey pictured the stately gentleman trying to compose himself. "Ms. Burnett passed away in her sleep Monday night."

Bailey, struggling to speak calmly, said, "I'm so sorry, Niles."

"As you know, Ms. Burnett requested she be cremated, which will take place later this week. There will not be a service."

"No, I didn't think so." Bailey blinked back tears.

"Within Ms. Burnett's paperwork was an envelope addressed to you and to Doctor Parker."

"An envelope?"

"Would you like me to mail this to you, or do you wish to pick it up?"

"I can pick it up this afternoon, if it's okay."

"That will be fine. I'll be here, of course, so anytime will do."

"We'll be there by three." Bailey ended the call. She debated about calling Chelsea and telling her the news, but thought better of it. She'd go to her office.

On the drive to campus, Bailey recalled the conversations she had with Eleanor, the ones shared between just the two of them, and she remembered the night she'd played cards with Eleanor over a couple of beers.

She was going to miss the fiery Brit.

* * *

Chelsea finished typing her last thoughts about Eleanor and Daphne. She read over what she'd written. She never thought she'd take to the old woman as much as she did. Movement in her periphery drew her attention to the doorway.

"Bailey, what are you doing here? Not that I'm not glad to see you, but you said you had to work on your notes this morning." Something was wrong. Bailey was never good at masking her feelings, and something was definitely wrong. "What is it?"

"It's Eleanor."

"No." Chelsea felt like a little kid, wanting to cover her ears to avoid hearing bad news.

"I'm sorry, Chels. She passed away Monday night in her sleep. I got off the phone with Niles about thirty minutes ago. I came right here to tell you."

Chelsea buried her face in her hands. "No, no, no."

Bailey's arms slipped around her shoulders. She let Chelsea cry for as long as she needed.

Chelsea grabbed a tissue from the box on her desk and blotted the moisture on her eyes and cheeks. "She got to me, you know? She irritated the hell out of me when we first met, but then she got under my skin, and I couldn't help but love her. And then she goes off and leaves us. Damn it."

"There's other news. I hope you're not doing anything this afternoon."

"I don't have anything on my schedule. Why?"

"Niles said she left an envelope addressed to us. He said he could mail it, but I told him we'd swing by before three."

"I wonder what it is."

"Only one way to find out."

*   *   *

Chelsea rang the doorbell. Standing there knowing they'd never see Eleanor again felt odd.

Niles opened the door. Normally impeccable, he appeared disheveled and lost. "Doctor Parker, Ms. Hampton, thank you for stopping in on such short notice."

Chelsea wanted to hug him but thought better of it.

"Come inside, and I'll get the envelope."

They walked into the living room and stood beside the mantel to await his return. Chelsea looked up at the painting of Daphne and Eleanor. She sensed a peaceful outcome with the hope they were now reunited.

Niles returned with the envelope and led them back to the front door. They stepped outside, but before they got too far away, Niles's voice stopped them.

"She was very fond of both of you. She talked about you often."

"We were very fond of her, too, Niles," Chelsea said. "Thank you for all you did for her. I'm sure you'll miss her."

He cleared his throat. "Very much." He straightened and tugged down his vest.

"Please let us know if there's anything we can do for you," Bailey said before she got into the Jeep.

He nodded at her from the doorway.

Chelsea listened to the crunch of the gravel under the tires as they took the long drive out to the state road. Perhaps it would be the last time they'd visit here.

Bailey pulled to a stop at the end of the driveway. "Where do you want to go to read the letter?"

"The lake?" Chelsea could think of no better place to be alone with her sorrow while listening to anything Eleanor had written them.

"I was thinking the same thing."

* * *

Bailey and Chelsea held hands as they walked down the incline to their spot.

"Do you mind sitting in the grass without a blanket?" she asked Chelsea. "I didn't think about bringing one."

"Not at all."

After they got comfortable, Bailey offered the envelope to Chelsea, but Chelsea shook her head. Bailey studied Eleanor's distinct black script at length before pushing her thumb along the enclosure. She pulled out the thick stationery and smoothed it down.

Dearest Bailey and Chelsea,

If you're reading this, I am no longer present in this world and am at peace now with my Daphne. I wanted to tell you what I had done for you while I was still alive but thought better of it. I never wanted any discomfort to taint our many visits, for to me, those were precious minutes of my days spent sharing the love of my life with two highly receptive friends. Because that is what you came to mean to me. You were much more to me than interviewers, well before we finished our journey. You were a reason for me to go on living, if only to tell Daphne's story. Our story.

As to what I've done for you, I consider myself rather cunning. No, perhaps shrewd is a better word. Yes. Shrewd. Rather than write a will, Daphne set up a revocable living trust with herself as the grantor and naming me as the successor trustee. Hence, all of her property and assets passed on seamlessly to me upon her death. Of course, I would have given everything up in a heartbeat if it had meant the return of Daphne, but sometimes life isn't fair.

Because I have a revocable living trust, rather than a will, what I set into motion will go much more quickly than waiting for a will to drag its heels through probate court.

So, without further ado, you are the beneficiaries of five million dollars—

Bailey tried to focus on the words that now blurred together. "Holy shit. Holy fucking shit."

"Oh my God, is that what it says? Let me have that." Chelsea snatched the letter from Bailey and continued reading.

and our home and property here in Bloomington.

Chelsea raised her head. "Holy shit," she said, echoing Bailey's words. "She left us her home, too."

Bailey was suddenly lightheaded. "Keep reading. I don't think I can."

Chelsea went back to the letter:

Now that I have your attention, let me continue. The only thing I request of you is to go to the funeral home and collect my remains, then take our ashes back to my home soil and spread them in Studland Bay. Perhaps this is asking a lot, but something tells me you can now afford a trip to England.

Bailey laughed, hearing Eleanor's teasing voice.

You needn't worry about Niles. I've bequeathed him the cottage in Banbury, plus a retirement fund that will allow him to live very comfortably. Daphne earned her money through film work and wise investments. The remainder of her fortune, approximately ten million dollars, will be divided between the Gordon Scott Memorial AIDS Foundation and the Daphne DeMonet Hospice for AIDS Patients in Los Angeles.

I am also leaving my precious diaries to you. I realise you probably have what you need for your work, but please keep these books as a remembrance of our time shared together. And as a reminder to never again let anything come between you.

You may think of me as too generous in the money I've left you, but there are no children or grandchildren to leave any assets. My brothers died some years ago. Daphne had no living relatives, or at least none with whom she wished to share her wealth.

What do you do with five million dollars and a home and property worth one million dollars? You live, you laugh, you grow old together. You love each other with every fibre of your being.

And on some evenings, when you're feeling especially nostalgic, you drop an old LP on the turntable, dance to "Can't Help Falling in Love," and accept that, like the lyrics say, some things really are meant to be, such as the love you two share.

Godspeed and bon voyage on your life's journey.
—Eleanor.

Chelsea turned to the next page. "There's an attorney's business card stapled to a note in Eleanor's handwriting."

Doctor Parker, I took the liberty of looking up your address. You and Bailey should receive a letter from my attorney within two weeks to sign the proper paperwork. When you go to his office, he will give you my diaries that I mailed to him.

With shaking hands, Chelsea folded everything and put it back into the envelope.

They sat in stunned silence. For how long, Bailey hadn't a clue. She finally spoke. "I guess we have a house now. And then, of course, there's the five million dollars."

"Holy shit, Bailey," Chelsea said.

"Yup."

* * *

They stood in the security line at O'Hare. Chelsea set the oak box containing Eleanor's remains on the conveyor belt next to the box containing Daphne's. She tried not to fidget as she had in Indianapolis. She wasn't doing anything wrong, but with all of the added security precautions, she felt like she was.

She and Bailey had already shown the security personnel the paperwork from the funeral home verifying the contents of the two boxes. After the boxes were X-rayed, there was one last inspection for explosive residue, and it was on to London.

"I don't know about you," Bailey said as she picked up Daphne's box, "but I'm ready to catch some *Z*'s on that plane."

"I'm with you on that. We're all set with a rental car at the airport?"

"Yes, and we're all set at the Gentry House."

"Great. Studland Bay here we come."

* * *

"I think this might be the same room," Chelsea said with a note of awe in her voice.

Bailey couldn't suppress a grin. "I wanted to surprise you. When I called, I asked for this room. The manager knew what I wanted after describing it to him." Bailey noticed the yellow paint, cherrywood furniture, and bay window. "I don't think they've changed it, based on Eleanor's description from her diary."

Chelsea fell backwards onto the king-size bed. "I'm exhausted."

Bailey flopped down next to her. She stared up at the beamed ceiling. "Me, too."

Chelsea shifted on her side. "How about we tackle what we came for in the morning? Maybe around the same time that Daphne and Eleanor met out at the rocks?"

"Feels right, huh?"

"Yeah, it does."

The next morning, Chelsea stepped out of the bathroom with her hair pulled back in a ponytail. Like Bailey, she'd dressed in jeans and a sweatshirt. It had been nippy last night, and they'd anticipated the same temperatures this morning, if not cooler.

"Ready?" Bailey asked.

"I think so."

They each picked up their boxes and proceeded outside and down the hill to the outcropping of rocks Eleanor had described in her diary.

"I can see why they loved it so much here." Chelsea gazed at the white cliffs and the sea below them. The sun had risen two hours before, splashing the cliffs in a blaze of orange.

"Me, too. The view is pretty amazing." Bailey opened her box and took out the plastic bag containing Daphne's ashes.

Chelsea did the same with Eleanor's.

"The wind's blowing behind us, so I think if we toss them up in the air together, they should float out to sea," Bailey said. "Do you want to say something before we do it?"

Chelsea furrowed her brow, then it smoothed out and she smiled. "How about, here's to two wonderful women who loved and lost and loved again."

"Perfect. I think Eleanor would like, here's to two kick-ass ladies who did it their way." They opened their bags. With a nod to each other, they tossed the ashes into the air.

They watched the ashes rise on the wind. Bailey stood behind Chelsea, her arms wrapped around her as she rested her chin on Chelsea's shoulder. At first, it appeared that Daphne's ashes would go one way and Eleanor's the other, but as if by magic, the breeze shifted and swirled them together.

Laughter floated down. Bailey heard Eleanor's distinct laugh and then heard what must have been Daphne's joining in.

Chelsea stiffened in her arms. "Please tell me you hear that."

"Oh, yeah, I hear it all right."

A gust of wind carried the ashes far below until they were no longer visible against the blue of the water. Bailey and Chelsea stood there a long time, each lost in thought, surrounded by the call of the seagulls.

Chelsea sighed. "At last they're together again." She turned around and the sunlight sparkled in her green eyes as she looked up at Bailey. "I'm kind of hungry. You ready for breakfast? The hotel restaurant's open."

"I don't know." Bailey gave her a soft kiss. "What was it Daphne said?"

"We could go to our room and order room service?" Chelsea pressed against Bailey. "Why, Ms. Hampton, are you suggesting what I think you're suggesting?" she asked with a British accent.

"Why yes, Doctor Parker, I am." Bailey slipped her arm around Chelsea's waist, and they began their journey back to the hotel. As they reached the crest of the hill, the faintest hint of familiar laughter once again tickled Bailey's ears. She smiled and pulled Chelsea tighter.

Thank you, Eleanor. Thank you indeed.

THE END

Author Chris Paynter   Photo Credit: Phyllis Manfredi

About the Author

Chris was born in a British hospital and happily lived a nomadic childhood as an Air Force brat, before settling in Indiana after her father's retirement. She graduated from Indiana University with a Bachelor's degree in journalism and a minor in history. After graduation, she worked as a general assignment reporter and a sports reporter. In her current position as an editorial specialist, she supports third-year law students in publishing a quarterly law journal. She continues to work on her novels, including *From Third to Home*, the final book in the *Playing for First* series, and her next stand alone romance. Chris and her wife live in Indianapolis with their beagle, Buddy the Wonder Dog.

Visit her website at www.ckpaynter.com. You can also find her on Facebook.

Coming Soon from Blue Feather Books:

Appointment with a Smile, by Kieran York

For artist Danielle O'Hara, even though romance is nonexistent and her art career has nearly stagnated, she's reasonably content with her circumstances. Then, when she's nearly sixty years old, the greatest adventure of her life begins.

Danielle leaves her Colorado home to attend her first major solo art exhibit in London. While roaming through a street market, Danielle catches sight of her first and only true love, Molly, who had left Colorado and their relationship thirty years earlier.

Danielle never accepted Molly's explanation that the reason their relationship had dissolved was Danielle's compulsion to paint. Although the art world has provided Danielle only minimal recognition, an undying belief in herself has kept her moving forward.

Her encounter with Molly forces Danielle to revisit the past and to confront an uncertain future. In addition to finding Molly again after three decades, she meets Bethany Cortland, a beguiling, confident woman, who is all that Danielle desires in a woman—everything, that is, except that she's not Molly.

The London journey takes Danielle on a trip to the interior of her heart, a place where previously, only her art had been allowed. Now, against her will, she discovers that love and professional success have their own agendas and timetables.

A Kiss Before Dawn, by Laurie Salzler

Country girl Chris Martel has struggled all her life to form strong, lasting relationships. For Chris, love, compassion, and trust are critical. In their absence, Chris has turned to her dog and her horse for the emotional fulfillment she craves. Then along comes Mary Jo Cavanaugh.

Fresh out of veterinary school, Mary Jo inadvertently antagonizes Chris with her overconfident assumptions about how to care for animals. She comes to learn that Chris's practical experience provides both a wealth of knowledge and a friendship unlike any she's ever known.

The carefully built walls around Chris's heart begin to crumble as she acknowledges the unfamiliar feelings evoked by being with Mary Jo. Just as she believes she's found the happiness that had always eluded her, someone from Chris's past comes back into her life, intent on winning Chris's affections, no matter what the cost.

Can the love between Chris and Mary Jo survive so that they can share *A Kiss Before Dawn*?

Coming soon, only from

Make sure to check out these other exciting Blue Feather Books titles:

www.bluefeatherbooks.com

CPSIA information can be obtained at www.ICGtesting.com
Printed in the USA
LVOW071842050212

267134LV00002B/4/P

9 781935 627883